NO PRISONERS

NO PRISONERS

A Novel

Thomas Lynch

Godine

ALSO BY THOMAS LYNCH

Fiction
Apparition & Late Fictions (2010)

Poetry
Skating with Heather Grace (1987)
Grimalkin & Other Poems (1994)
Still Life in Milford (1998)
Walking Papers (2010)
The Sin-Eater: A Breviary (2012)
Bone Rosary: New & Selected Poems (2021)

Nonfiction
The Undertaking: Life Studies from the Dismal Trade (1997)
Bodies in Motion and at Rest: On Metaphor and Mortality (2000)
Booking Passage: We Irish and Americans (2005)
The Good Funeral (2011, with Thomas G. Long)
Whence and Whither: A Miscellany (2019)
The Depositions: New & Selected Essays (2020)

Drama
Lacrimae Rerum: A Play in One Act (2013)

Published in 2025 by
GODINE
Boston, Massachusetts
www.godine.com

Copyright 2025 © by Thomas Lynch

ALL RIGHTS RESERVED.
No part of this book may be used or reproduced in any manner
whatsoever without written permission from the publisher, except in
the case of brief quotations embodied in critical articles and reviews.
For more information, please visit our website.

LIBRARY OF CONGRESS CATALOGING-IN-PUBLICATION DATA

Names: Lynch, Thomas, 1948- author
Title: No prisoners : a novel / Thomas Lynch.
Description: Boston, Massachusetts : David R. Godine, 2025.
Identifiers: LCCN 2024060161 (print) | LCCN 2024060162 (ebook) | ISBN
9781567927054 hardcover | ISBN 9781567927061 epub
Subjects: LCGFT: Fiction | Novels
Classification: LCC PS3562.Y437 N6 2025 (print) | LCC PS3562.Y437 (ebook)
| DDC 813/.54--dc23/eng/20250331
LC record available at https://lccn.loc.gov/2024060161
LC ebook record available at https://lccn.loc.gov/2024060162

FIRST PRINTING, 2025
Printed in the United States

This book is for

CORRINE D'AGOSTINO AND SUZANNE RUMSEY

fellow pilgrims, thanks be.

NO PRISONERS

Odds are the poor man was trying to please her,
because her pleasure would have pleasured him,
adding, as it would have, to his image of
himself as a latter-day Man of Steel,
able as always to leap tall buildings
and off of whose chest the bullets would bounce,
his five bypasses notwithstanding,
nor withstanding how his heart had grown
flimsy with hard loving and bereavement.
Or maybe it was the Marine Lance Corporal
in the snapshot of himself in the South Pacific
he kept in the corner of the bathroom mirror:
bare-chested in khakis and boondockers
with Billy Swinford Smith from Paris, Kentucky,
posing as always for the girls back home;
the ready and willing eighteen-year-old
who went from right tackle with St. Francis DeSales
to light machine-gunner with the Corps
and came home skinny and malarial later
to marry the redheaded girl of his dreams
who had written him daily through the war,
beginning her letters with My Darling Edward
and closing with All My Love Always, Rose.

We found those letters, years later, in a drawer
and tried to imagine them both young again,
dancing to Dorsey and Glenn Miller tunes
under the stars at the Walled Lake Pavilion
before they had any idea of us.
"Six sons," he'd laugh, "enough for Pallbearers!
And girls enough to keep us in old age."
So when our mother took to her bed with cancer,
it was, of course, the girls who tended her
while my brothers and I sat with him downstairs,
being brave for each other. When she died
he knelt by her bedside sobbing, "Rosie,
my darling, what will I do without you?"
And grieved his grief like Joe DiMaggio
who never missed a game and took a rose
to place in the vase at her graveside daily
then came home to sit in his chair and weep,
those first nights without her thereby replacing
as the worst in his life a night in '44
on Walt's Ridge in Cape Gloucester, New Britain,
when he and elements of the First Marines
survived five Bonzai charges. The Japanese
foot soldiers kept screaming, kept coming, blind
into the cross fire of light machine guns
that he and Billy and Donald Crescent Coe
kept up all night, aiming just below the voices.
In the morning he crawled out of his hole
to poke his bayonet among the dead
for any signs of life and souvenirs.
Whatever he found, he took no prisoners
and always said he wondered after that
how many men he'd killed, how he'd survived.

He'd try to make some sense of all of it,
but if he did, he never told us what it was.
And now he is dying of heartache and desire.
Six months into his mourning he became
an object of pursuit among the single set
of widows and divorcées hereabouts;
the hero of a joke his cronies tell
that always ends But what a way to go!
Last night, mistaking breathlessness for afterglow,
a woman nearly finished him with love
and barely made it to the hospital
where they thumped his chest and ordered oxygen.
The First Marines are off to war again.
He watches CNN in ICU
while leathernecks dig trenches in the sand.
The president says No More Vietnams.
The doctors tell him Easy Does It, Ed—
six weeks, six months, who knows. It's up to you.
Avoid excitement, stimulation, sex
with any but familiar partners.
He tells them War is Hell. It takes no prisoners.
A man must have something worth dying for.
The Persian skies are bright with bombs and fire.
My father's sleep is watched by monitors
that beep and blink—his sore heart beating, still.
I wonder if he dreams of soldiers killed
in action—Japanese, Iraqis, old Marines
who died for flags and causes, but in the end,
among their souvenirs, we only find
old snapshots of their wives and women-friends.

CONTENTS

Prologue.. 15

Chapter One: Passe-Partout....................... 19

Chapter Two: Moorings........................... 63

Chapter Three: Prepuce 103

Chapter Four: Old Dogs 125

Chapter Five: Hypatia 155

Chapter Six: New Year's Eves 183

Chapter Seven: China Marine.....................211

Chapter Eight: Letting Go 249

Acknowledgments 265

PROLOGUE

Call me Doyle Shields," read the first line of the memoir he'd promised his dead wife, Sally, he would write and that, alas, he would never finish. He thought a good start might bode well for the project—help to establish some trust and humanize himself so that the reader might chance another page in a story about lifelong pursuit and surpassing gestures, settling accounts and darker purposes. And he thought it ought to end with something evocative: "The savage sea hawks sailed with sheathed beaks." Especially if he could get the reader to hear the word *sheathed* with two full syllables, so *sheath-ed beaks* instead of *sheath'd*. It would add a bit of olden day elegance, he thought.

A revised version began with "The best of times, the worst of times—the times of our life," and Doyle thought the irony of the plural *our* and the singular *life* might indicate just how much the two of them had become, in the several decades of their consortium, one, much as the chubby priest who'd done the nuptials always claimed would happen in a good marriage.

Another, more Joycean, version finished on the word *yes* and included a line that had always stuck with him from a story Joyce titled "A Painful Case" in which Mr. Duffy, the protagonist, was said to have "an odd autobiographical habit which led him to compose in his mind from time to time a

16 • NO PRISONERS

short sentence about himself containing a subject in the third person and a predicate in the past tense." This rang immediately true to Doyle, as did the detail about the little distance from his body Mr. Duffy was said to live at.

But Doyle always returned to the opening that echoed the terrible account of *Moby Dick:* the damaged Ahab, the albino sperm whale, and the sole survivor, Ishmael, with whom Doyle had come to identify, not least for his affinity to coffins, and who could be trusted with the narration of nearly everything.

It seemed a suitable paradigm for his own adventures—how wanting to tell their story had become an exercise in self-examination and disclosure, even if it proved impossible to complete.

Sally had always called him the love of her life, and when her cancer was diagnosed and her end drew nigh, she got him to promise that the story of their long romance would be told. They'd made monogamy look really good, Sally and Doyle had, and she wanted to tell her grandchildren and great-grandchildren that it might work for them as well, though she would not live long enough to see them into their own romances.

"But you have a story in you, Doyle," she would insist to him. "Our story, ours alone, a story of love and grief, sweetness, sadness, the sames and differences. Promise me you will get it told."

Of course, Doyle just wanted to allay her grief at missing the future they'd hoped to share, and would have promised her anything, anything, though he was helpless to undo her disease, her dying, and her eventual death. The grim routines of coming and going could not be much altered, he reminded himself; we are not in charge of people, places, or events.

And she'd been the love of his life too, since he first beheld her in the fifth grade of St. Francis DeSales in Detroit. Her red hair and pretty aspects and her smiling at him smote his heart. And when he went off to the boot camp a few years later, he asked her to write to him every day, and she promised she would, and he wrote her back. She saw him for the wounded man he was when he got home from the war in January of '46. And not wounded in body as much as spirit, not wounded by combat but in a bar fight, and by the existential fear and moral trespass the US Marine Corps had required of him. Sally had known the boy he'd been at twelve, standing in line for their first communion, that first taste of godliness, and knew the older boy that left with the marines in '42, proud of his sharpshooting in '43. And when the US Marines sent the damaged goods of Doyle Shields back to Detroit, having barely survived an evil he betook in January of '44 at a place called Walt's Ridge, it was Sally who'd shared with him the curative dose of mighty nature, its succor and comforts and bodily bliss that restored him to good form and fettle because whatever he'd done or endured through that evil, she approved of him.

After Sally died, and he seemed vanquished by it, desolate of soul and lost in the dark, it was the glimpse of Sally's godly love in the way Johanna came to him, herself damaged by evil, and sought to mend herself by mending him that restored him to a kind of hope. And here was the glimpse of God he finally got, in the midst of his deep bereavement, when Johanna came and pressed herself against him, and ministered to him in his desolation, that though he'd lost his faith in almost everything and kept shaking a fist in the face of a God he no longer believed in, nonetheless, the truth that Johanna made manifest in her goodness to him was that to love one another was god enough, sufficient for the everyday gift of being.

Though he had made a study of the sacraments and theories of atonement, of vicarious redemption and moral influence, though he'd been both the doomed and favorite son, the burnt offering and the ram found in the thicket, he could no longer believe the origin stories the nuns and priests had taught him. He had supped from the fruits of the tree of knowledge—some of them good and some of them evil—and had fallen in love with the better than nothing, the not that bad, and the good enough, having come finally in his elder years to believe in neither an almighty Father God or Mother Nature, or in any of the options these binaries offered. Rather, he sensed the grace there was in the love that was made between each other, the press of precious bodies against one another, and that the best and worst of times for him had been the pursuit of the moby dick of desire, the great whale of want and longing for intimate knowledge of another.

He'd shared this with Sally for forty-three years and survived his widowhood by seeing in creatures like his kindly assistant, Hypatia, the beauty of being in an imperfect world, and when he'd given up on true love and its blessings, and had resigned himself to being a sort of bystander to the feasts and beatitudes of life shared with another of his species, Johanna had restored to him a taste for that goodness that he'd lost hope in after Sally died. She had come to him free of pretense but clear in purpose. She'd offered herself to him unambiguously and without conditions, as if such goodness were bred in the bone, part of human nature and inheritance, seeking to align our natures with one another: a gift of being so intense it made him regret that he'd ever have to die. It filled him with perpetual thanks and made him believe, however provisionally, in a life of the spirit. Such mysteries and miracles left Doyle mostly speechless except to proclaim, at the crescendo of bliss, occasioned by Johanna's most provocative kindnesses to him, "O God, O God!" And Whomever God Is on any particular day, unfailingly answers, in God's perpetual whisper, "Be patient, dear Doyle. Wait and see."

Chapter One

PASSE-PARTOUT

25 February 2015

He loved to call himself my cunnilinguist."
Johanna sighed deeply as the casket slowly lowered on broad green straps down into the open ground. She tightened the arm she'd looped through Hypatia's arm. The chill of late February kept them close.

The younger woman looked at Johanna, a little astonished at the sudden declaration, then looked back at the wooden box descending into the earth.

"He said it gave him a sense of higher purpose."

"Higher purpose?" Hypatia whispered. "Do tell."

"Something worthy of life and time," Johanna said. "He always wondered how he might make a difference."

The two women stood at the graveside in the gray midwinter, waiting for what might be happening next. The noise of heavy equipment rumbled over the hillside.

The men at either end of the grave leaned in and, taking hold of the green straps that had lowered the casket, worked them out from under the box, rolled them back onto the lowering device, and, moving in unison, lifted the device away from the open grave and began to remove the faux greens that lined the burial site.

"And he called me his fellatilist."

"His stamp collector?" Hypatia asked, looking puzzled.

The older woman grinned. "Oh no, dear, his fellatio-ist, his *cocksucker*."

They both laughed demurely, trying to maintain some decorum among the dead, their solemnities and stones.

"My pooh-bah of perpetual pleasure, God be good to him." Johanna sighed.

How these pronouncements got into the graveside colloquy was a mystery to the two of them, who otherwise stood quietly watching, with the occasional catch in their breath or sob, as the duties and details of the burial were enacted before them. Their brief giggles were a kind of tonic, lightening the funeral's sad hold upon them.

"Sex and the dead," Doyle Shields was famous for telling anyone in earshot, quoting the poet Yeats, writing to a former lover, Olivia Shakespear, "are the only topics worthy of the serious mind. Or was it a scholarly mind?" he'd ask himself aloud; either way, according to Doyle, sex and the dead were the only deserving topics for contemplation.

The two women agreed, and their deceased friend had died in lifelong pursuit of the key to the meaning and matter of things.

The years of his widowhood, as he worked his way through his dead wife's extensive and eclectic library, had given Doyle's anecdotage a professorial tone, almost esoteric, as if tweed coats and pipe tobacco informed his pronouncements. It reminded Johanna of her dead father, the old priest, who had the same aspect to his final years, a homiletic aspect—as if whatever he said were sumptuously annotated and researched in a liberal arts course outline. She wondered if that hadn't drawn her to Doyle at the start.

"Sex and the dead, indeed," Johanna said. "Oral sex and winter burials. One thing seems to lead to the other." There was a summary aspect to her talk now.

"Everything leads to everything else," said Hypatia. "Ours is only to connect the dots."

"Sounds like something Doyle told you."

The younger woman grinned and nodded. "Taught me. He was always concerned about my education."

Johanna was hoping that Hypatia might, now that Doyle was dead, finally disclose whether there'd ever been anything beyond talk between them—the old man and his young assistant, the years of their long association, conversations, and travel—anything beyond their professional connection. Johanna had never been entirely certain. Hypatia never said.

The young marines who'd done the graveside honors came over to say their pro forma goodbyes to the two women, then piled in the van they'd come in and drove away. They had fired their rounds, played taps, and folded and presented the flag, along with the spent shell casings from the rifle volleys. They might have guessed Johanna to be the widow and Hypatia the daughter of the dearly departed, given their apparent ages and the deference with which others paid their final respects. They'd presented the flag and shell casings and the president's proxy sympathies with their spit-and-polish precision and stoic good looks.

"You can see how Sally might have been right and truly smitten with a young marine in his dress blues, home from the war and eager to love her," Johanna said.

Men were made to fill holes, Patty remembered Doyle saying, the double entendre a favorite device, referencing no one in particular. Sex and the dead ever on his mind.

There'd been the meaningful hugs and small talk as the others departed. As his longtime assistant and his last spousal equivalent, Hypatia and Johanna were, if not next of kin, his nearest and dearest, his saddest survivors.

It hadn't been much of a turnout. Doyle had outlived most of his contemporaries. A graveside service in Northern Michigan in the middle of winter was hardly a draw. Johanna had paid the sexton for an extra night of thawing the grave so he could open it, what with the frost and snow. The small company, family distant and extended, local AAs among whom Doyle had achieved the status of old-timer and guru, with his forty-nine years of sobriety, and mortuary sorts for whom Doyle Shields still embalmed on occasion or oversaw a difficult case with a newly minted embalmer. Even some of Sally's old friends were there. They'd all assembled for the solemnities and once done, returned to their cars and their own lives and times, leaving Johanna and Patty there together, as coequal claimants to nextness of kin, to see the job to its predictable denouement: the vault lid lowered onto the base, their flowers tossed into the grave as a sort of release, surrender, the earth returned to the open grave, the orderly landscape restored, the sense that they'd done everything that could be done, had gone the distance with their dead man, Doyle. It all began to feel like a consolation.

The weather had cooperated, if not balmy, still, not as cruel as February could be. A mild, windless, damp, and dreary morning: 2-25-2015.

Doyle would have approved the vague numerology—another effort to assign meaning to meaningless things: life, time, history, happenstance—the way the twos and fives echoed themselves, two, two five, two oh fifteen.

"'Behold,' he'd whisper, 'the gift of tongues, those flickering uraeuses of flame,' he'd say, 'that hovered over heads on Pentecost.'" That this sign of the holy spirit gave the apostles languages had been for Doyle a further sign of the holiness of words in all their deployments.

"God knows, he had a way with words and holy writ," Patty replied. "He savored them. Like foodies, with the right wine and matching cheese."

It felt good to giggle together. It restored a kind of balance to the goings-on, between the heaviness to hand and the light-hearted repartee.

"Though he'd quit drink and dairy years ago," Johanna said.

"But he fed the old dog Taleggio with its meds," Patty reminded her. "He said it reminded him of Venice. He so loved Venice, the rot and beauty."

"And as proud as he was of his apostasy, he was scripturally literate, religiously erudite, and deft in his deployment of pericopes and gospel texts."

"If I speak with the tongues of men and of angels," he would often intone, from Paul's epistle to the Corinthians. Its numbers pleased him too, 1 Corinthians 13, one one three. "And have not love," here he would pause, look deeply into the eyes of anyone listening, and deliver the coup de grace. "I am as sounding brass and tinkling cymbals."

It was, the two women agreed, the nuns at St. Francis De-Sales that schooled him in the glorious and sorrowful mysteries, the spiritual and corporal works of mercy, the cardinal sins and contrary virtues, and the perpetual examination of his conscience. He knew the liturgies, the lectionaries and ejaculations, indulgences and dispensations.

24 • NO PRISONERS

In apparent thanksgiving for which, Doyle Shields would visit the mother house in Monroe to check in on the aging women of his parochial youth, and in compensation for their educating him, he would travel to the town from wherever he was, whenever he got word of one of the blessed virgins succumbing to the press of age and time, prepare their perpetually covered bodies for burial in the company of two living nuns, who would chaperone his embalming of their dead elder sister. Whatever secrets their poor, immaculate, untouched bodies gave up in death, they were safe with their former student and first-rate embalmer, Doyle Shields, who was trade embalmer for the largest Catholic firm in southeastern Lower Michigan. When he moved up north in retirement, he told them to call whenever one of the sisters died. He'd consider it his lifelong mission. Though he no longer shared their religious fervors, he treasured the lexicons of faith and doubt their tutelage had nurtured in him.

His late wife, the much mourned and saintly Sally, had given him a doorstopper of a dictionary—a *Webster Universal,* which he'd open at random every day and find a word that was new to him to add to his vocabulary. Sally had found him the dictionary and the lectern he kept it on at the Salvation Army secondhand shop south of Cheboygan. They occupied a space, the book and the book stand, ready to read from like a daily breviary or Roman missal, by the door to the lakefront porch. His habit was to consult it before going out into the day and, once he'd settled on a word, to make the sign of the cross on the broad page with his thumb, like a priest blessing the text before proclaiming the gospel, and then to use the word a dozen times over the course of a morning, which would lodge it, he reckoned, securely in his permanent lexicon. He would construct sentences that he would preach to the squirrels and mergansers and chickadees, his coffee cup on the porch rail, the day that was in it brightening before him, sometimes pissing between the spindles as a kind of oblation, making of his morning water a kind of aspergillum and holy office, to which he might add, "In the beginning, it surely was the word!"

To this massive text, Sally had, through the four-plus decades of their marriage, gotten him a word-of-the-day calendar for Christmas every year. These words, too, he installed into his conversations each day, reminding him with every occasion of his longing for Sally, whether he was at work or she was away, or, as had been the case now for twenty-five years, he was widowed by her early demise.

"Another local *imbroglio*," he'd say between sips of his coffee, "the upcoming millage vote." Then he'd piss on the hostas that bordered the porch. Before too long *imbroglio* could be deployed in his everyday conversations.

A variation on the gift of tongues, he called it, a vocabulary, a living lexicon, a sense of words and their highest and best possible uses.

The day he came upon *sitzfleisch* in the dictionary was one of his best days ever, and he loved the two meanings listed for the word, to wit: 1. Buttocks, as in what one sits on, as in sitz bath, he thought, and 2. Staying power, endurance, perseverance at a task. The etymology, from the German for sitting and flesh, was a perfect compounding of simple words for a rich concept. Doyle loved how the roots of words made such easy good sense, often doubling back to connect with some commonsensical facts. The way *human*, for example, was connected to humus, wherefore humic, meaning the first few levels of soil whence our gardens, our growing, our human being as creatures of the dirt, the earth, the dust-to-dustness that makes us all one and the same but different.

What is an open grave, he often thought rhetorically, but an invitation to return home to the humic density of mother earth whence we came.

"You have great sitzfleisch," he had said to Patty once, as she bent to remove a tray of peanut butter cookies from the oven one Monday. When she asked if he was saying something inappropriate about her having a great ass, he told her, "It's staying power—all these years, putting up with my blather." Patty had learned to dodge the pissing matches Doyle enjoyed getting into with her. He had sensed early on her natural contentiousness, and he never tired of triggering her argumentations.

He'd hired her soon after Sally had died, after he'd destroyed another small oatmeal pan by putting the water on to boil and then forgetting about it, lost in some curiosity aroused by Sally's many books, which had become, along with the roseate memories he nursed, the principal inheritance of his marriage to her. He'd gotten rid of most of her clothes and jewelry. Most of it was secondhand before Sally got it at the resale or Salvation Army. He'd given away her little collections of Belleek china and Pewabic pottery. But her books had become, in a sense, part of the household, in bookcases built-in and stand-alone—every room of the house held portions of her personal library. She'd always been a bookish woman, and reading the books that she had read gave Doyle a sense of her presence in the early days of his widowhood. In time, he'd become a bookish person too. Unlike Sally, who seemed to have a serviceable knowledge of any topic but would never profess or pronounce or hold forth unless she were asked specifically to give an account, reading had made Doyle all the more boorish, with mindless and unsolicited opinions and an inextinguishable flow of banter and blather.

The blather was hushed now, perpetually. And Hypatia, though nearly twice the age she'd been when Doyle had hired her, still had a comely buttocks and steadfast staying powers. And mother earth had opened the ground and beckoned to her old man, Doyle, to return after his ninety-year sojourn in the land of Oz.

The two women, both in black, were the last ones standing at the graveside, hugging themselves against the mid-February chill and damp. Johanna in her seventies and Patty in her fifties, the two of them women of a certain age now, distanced by time from the younger versions of themselves that first began their association with the man in the box in the hole in the ground about to be filled in with the dirt piled there. The snow and the dirt and the opened ground created an odd amalgam of the elements. The bald trees moved very little in the windless morning. The casket had been lowered into the vault, which fit quite snuggly in the open grave; some carnations and gladioli had been tossed in on top, a shovel of dirt and that was that. The rest was left to the cemetery crew with their chain fall and backhoe, by which they made quick work of the burial—the inhumation.

"He'd say that he longed to worship at the tabernacle of my bliss." The older of the two women sighed heavily. "He seemed never to be impatient in his ministrations. He loved what he called 'the laying on of hands.' He never wearied of what he called my 'nether regions.'" This last thing she said in a low whisper, and looked around to be sure there was no one in earshot. "'A knight of the golden yoni' is what he called himself," she whispered.

He had a fascination with oral sex, how the nuns and priests had to condemn it as irresponsible pleasure and unnatural because it had nothing to do with making babies. He even joined the Yippee Yoni Sisterhood, an online group of women who'd adopted the Sanskrit term for female genitalia and spoke

28 • NO PRISONERS

mostly through podcasts and chat groups, in word salads, heavy on affirmations and authenticities, about their vaginas, orgasmic entitlements, and the means and methods of effective masturbation. The online catalog of vibrators and dildos, yoni oil, moisturizers and humectants, deodorants, lubricants, and other provisions took major credit cards and PayPal. "Invest in your pleasure, your power and your pussy," their homepage encouraged prospective new members, and only when they were tipped off anonymously that Doyle didn't have a yoni was he removed from their newsletter mailing list. Whereupon he had Patty join and paid the forty dollars per month subscription for her so that she could continue to monitor the Yippee Yoni Sisterhood as his proxy. She would share with Doyle on an irregular basis the links to the regular monthly Visiting Sisters Lecture Series on such topics as chronic stress and breathwork, healing women's trauma, love bean cacao, gua sha, and herbal medicine.

He was steadfastly opposed to the Catholic proposition that all sex must be married sex and all sexual episodes must be "open to life," which is to say, "genital to genital," climaxing with a male's ejaculate making its way like a thrown dart or thrusted spear, according to the sixteenth-century Latin roots of its etymology, toward the waiting egg in the one version approved by the catechism.

"What a shame," he always said, "the catechism's ignorance on sex," and insisted that the tendency, gender neutral near as he could figure, for climaxing humans to intone their pleas "oh God, oh God, oh God" was sign and wonder enough of the holy and sacramental nature of oral intercourse. Some mornings he would ease out of bed in the predawn dark and kneel on a pillow and pull Johanna's little body toward him and bury his face in her pudenda—a word he would sometimes remind her traced its meaning to the Latin for shameful—and then quite shamelessly welcome her into a blissful dawning of the day.

Possibly this was the knowledge of good and evil the church was most fearful of, that the supply of pleasure—godly, goodly, goosebump-inducing pleasure—was abundant between humans who were happy, joyous, and free to please one another sexually. The great scam perpetrated by Christians and capitalists was to make believe there was a shortage of such bliss and that a certain belief or purchase might offer access to such happy conduct between humans. Plead blind faith, buy this car, this house, or outfit, this bouquet of roses, say these prayers, when all two humans need to please one another is to be naked and adjacent and willing to play with each other.

"He put his money where his mouth was, to be sure," Patty replied. "He had me bid online on some woodcut by a Czech artist, Max Švabinský, of Adam going down on Eve. They wanted fifteen grand for an original woodcut. He offered ten, they countered at fourteen, he came back at thirteen but wouldn't budge beyond that. It never was an apple, after all, he told me, that got them evicted from the garden. It was the knowledge and praxis that pleasure could be had for the sake of pleasure, without the threat of pregnancy."

Johanna agreed that her lover had been more than a little obsessed with the prelapsarian Eden, original sin, and the conversation between God and Creation. And the notion that sex for the sake of pleasure alone was godly was contrary to the teaching of the church, which seemed to have pleased Doyle especially. "Why," he would always ask rhetorically, "ought we listen to a crowd of mommy's boys, ponces, and chastitutes on the ins and outs of sex, after all. They haven't a clue."

30 • NO PRISONERS

"Or maybe it was the notion of original sin, Adam and Eve, the whole tree of the knowledge of good and evil business," said Johanna. "He was endlessly curious about that story. He said that Sally thought that oral sex was the original sin."

Like many Catholic women of her generation, Sally Shields, née Duffy, had been taught that sex must have a procreative motive to be good and godly. Pleasure for pleasure's sake was meaningless, the nuns assured her in the sixth grade.

Sally was Doyle Shields's late and only wife. They'd been married for forty-some years before she got lung cancer and died when they were both sixty-five. He'd outlived her by twenty-some years with the assistance of these two women—Hypatia, hired in her mid-twenties, now a woman in her fifties, and Johanna, his lover and intimate, who'd taken up with Doyle in her fifties and traveled with him up till the end.

The undertaker had nodded at the sexton, who'd signaled the gravedigger in the backhoe to begin, and the men and the machinery began their slow approach while the women backed away from the grave's edge after tossing their roses in and the men moved the boards and faux turf surround to make room for the heavy equipment to backfill the hole.

The two women, both shivering a little in the damp and chill, stood there, arm in arm, at a safe distance from the excavations, having each placed their token shovel load of dirt in the grave on top of the box that held the dead body of Doyle Shields, the fresh corpse.

They rolled their eyes, turned from the grave, now full to overflowing with the backfill, and walked toward the black sedan at the curb that would take them back to their own cars at the funeral home.

There was an air of completion now, if not the promised closure, because they'd seen their dead man to the very end, had gone the distance with him, had gotten him where he needed to go and thereby got where they needed to be, to the edge of a new life they would live without him, without his kindnesses and conceits, his brilliance and blather, his gentlemanly ways and lurid imagination.

Johanna and Hypatia were feeling self-congratulatory, as people do when they've seen the difficult duty done, the grave filled, the dust settling—that they'd finished the job, gone the distance with the old man, seen him into his final resting place, such as it was, next to his dead wife, Sally, dead all these years.

"She was only sixty-five, so young," said Johanna, who was seventy-five now and feeling, though they had never married, suddenly widowed.

"He was young, too, to be left alone, still full of life when he hired me," said Patty. She confided in Johanna that she had not known, when he first hired her, exactly what his expectations were. He seemed so sad and angry, so alone. She'd been his companion and conversationalist, his sounding board and witness. Eventually she came to believe that he just didn't want to die without someone to report his passing. Of all the things Doyle talked about related to his long years in the embalming trade, none were more disturbing than his recollections of the long dead who were found in advanced states of decomposition and putrefaction. The maggoty cadavers of the dead but undiscovered or unremarked bespoke nothing so much as a disconnection from the traffic of fellow humanity, from children and grandchildren, siblings and service people, all the regular interactions humans have with others of their kind, who might grow wary of the lights left on or left off, the newspapers on the stoop, the mail filling the mailbox, the odor. He remembered the case of a family murdered in their vacation home near the Straits of Mackinac one late June but not discovered till the following month, when the odor of six rotting bodies caught the attention of a hiker who happened too near the residence in the woods. He'd been called by the funeral director in charge to transport the bodies from Petoskey, where the autopsies had been done in an open-air pavilion at the county fairgrounds with the cigar smoking pathologists gagging at the state of the remains, to the funeral home in southeastern Lower Michigan, where it fell to Doyle to get them treated topically and arterially enough to re-pouch them and seal them into their Batesville Monoseal caskets and eventually send them to church and cemetery without giving offense, without mortifications.

The floaters found after the ice melted off of lakes and the thermal inversion filled the drowned bodies with sufficient gases to get them to surface, the victims of murder and frantic burials, the hikers who climbed too high beyond the scrutiny of search parties and helicopters and got snowed in to their wintery entombments and were not found until a springtime thaw in a future they were never part of, the elders who died in bed or at tables or in easy chairs but were not found for days or months raised in Doyle the fear that such a death might be his own. Every morning, coming down the stairs to make his coffee and begin his day, he held on to banister and stair rail, paid especial attention to his footfall and balance lest he trip and fall and fracture something. As much as anything, he'd hired Hypatia because his long-held belief that he'd pre-decease his Sally had proved to be mistaken, and the fear that he would die alone and undetected persisted and increased as he aged. That he'd scheduled her to work a few hours every Monday, Wednesday, and Friday, and he paid her per diem to travel with him—to the Lesser Antilles in the winter, to Europe some summers, even once to Australia and Papua New Guinea for a reunion of his old outfit in the First Marine Division—gave Doyle the sense that his corpse would be tended to soon after his death and that the best could be made of a bad situation by the attentions of a competent embalmer. The anxiety about the preparation of his remains belied the irony of Doyle's long-held and contrary opinions about death and mortality, to wit, that the dead don't care—a thing he would tell himself when something in the embalming distorted the features of the dead—and that it is better to be seen than viewed, which is what he perpetually responded when someone would say on meeting him in casual or formal circumstances that it was good to see him. "Better to be seen than viewed," he'd wryly respond, "is what we say in my line of work." At the end of the day, to the old embalmer, both Patty and Johanna agreed, the appearance of the corpse did, in fact, matter, however provisionally or esoterically.

Once age and diabetes had taken his erection into what he called the parish of the past tense, Doyle Shields discovered the pleasure of pleasuring a woman with his mouth and fingers and would spend hours on his knees beside the bed, hands under Johanna's buttocks, face in her pudenda, slowly stimulating her private parts.

"I've never known a lover so fond of my vagina," the older woman said, "so willing to go down on me, so determined to slowly open the orgasmic window as wide as possible. The only way to make him cease his licking was to tap his bald head and whisper, 'Enough, enough,' which, of course, required a separate act of will, because whether or not you were on the way, you know, whether you could see the orgasm in the distance, on the horizon so to speak, the journey was always going in the right direction and was so pleasant."

"He told me once he was a qualified masseuse," the younger woman said. "It was the closest he ever came to making a pass. I was his employee, and he remained scrupulous about the professional boundaries. I might've tried a time or two to test those waters, but he never wavered. Of course, the forty years between us was a great encumbrance."

The two women got to the limousine, a black Cadillac at the curb, and made their ways back to the funeral home, where their separate cars and separate lives were rearticulated.

"Let's not be strangers, Johanna," the younger woman said, as the pair parted ways in the parking lot. "We've more in common than we know."

Johanna got into her late model Audi, Patty into her old Toyota. They waved, going off in different directions. The daylight was fading from the sky.

Johanna had been Doyle's correspondent and eventual lover since their first encounter more than twenty years ago. She'd heard him on a local radio program, on the subject of widowhood and learning to live alone. He sounded normal and approachable, and so she sent a note in care of the station, asking them to forward same. In it she gave some of her particulars, her residence in the radio's broadcast region, her work with a local nonprofit, how she'd grown up in the area, the daughter of a teacher and a churchman, her own lonely status as a twice-divorced woman, the mother of a teenager, her appreciation for the remarks he'd made about living alone and without partnership. In receipt of same, Doyle had sent back thanks for her kind words and attached a personal ad he'd composed but never published that read:

NOT THAT BAD A GUY
SEEKING ARRANGEMENT

Semiretired gentleman (left) with more money than time, some years beyond his "use by" date, seeks spousal equivalent, full- or part-time, to accompany him into his age and decrepitude. Retired undertaker, nonsmoker, nondrinker, avid reader and unpublished author, old and bald and fat and married for life, farts, snores, grunts, but otherwise is nice enough, long widowed but still smitten with his departed wife, will pay for the company of a nonsmoking woman of substance, a bookish human of a certain age, for companioning, colloquy, snappy repartee, light housekeeping, shared cooking, fine dining, and occasional travel. Separate quarters provided on-site, rent and utility free: a room, bed and bath of her own with fireplace, view of the lake, serviceable library, desk and closet space and accessories, all meals, and generous stipend in trade for at will employment, full- or part-time, short- or long-term as the situation merits. No intimate or sexual favors required, but menu of services and fees for same remains negotiable. Send résumé, references, and photo to Hypatia Casey (right), PO Box 13, East Jordan, MI.

Above the text of the ad was a photo of Doyle and Hypatia taken by the barista at Bajo el Sol on St. John in the Lesser Antilles. They both looked tanned and happy at the end of a

36 • NO PRISONERS

fortnight's winter vacation. And the many years between them diminished by the sunny demeanors and juxtaposition.

A couple days later Doyle found, in his email inbox, this response:

To: Not that bad a guy seeking arrangement
From: Woman of a certain age

Working single parent and lonely heart (right) with not much money or time, some years beyond her "best before" date, offering to accompany not that bad a guy "into his age and decrepitude." Church employee/laywoman with a unique skill set, theology student, nonsmoker, drinker in moderation, terrible sweet tooth, on the short side of tall, twice married and divorced, also farts, doesn't snore, and otherwise is "nice enough." Possesses a reasonably well-developed sense of humor, substantial in her curiosities about the world and those who inhabit it. Enjoys reading over copious cups of tea, conversation over good food and drink. Runs, cycles and swims for strength of body and mind and to manage a life-long eating disorder. Also enjoys walks in quiet places and travel, seeks both companionship and from time to time a "room of one's own." A good cook, housekeeper, and inexpert gardener. Not much interested in a generous stipend in trade for employment, nor spousal equivalency, but open to negotiating a friendship to mutual satisfaction that is short- or long-term "as the situation merits." Sex? Yes, though while the mind is willing and wanting, unsure if the body is able. Nevertheless, intimate touch is longed for. Full résumé and references available upon request, including from resident teenager (left). Please pass to Hypatia Casey of East Jordan, MI, as necessary.

Johanna's photo was with her teenage son, both smiling over pieces of pumpkin pie, festooned with whipped cream and a maraschino cherry. She was wearing a light-blue sweater, unbuttoned enough to show her very fine bosom and embonpoint. The photo, Doyle later found out, was taken by her former spouse, the father of the teenager, who, though divorced from the boy's mother, still shared parenting duties with joint custody and, apparently, holiday dinners.

That night Johanna thought about the years of loving Doyle Shields, how he was loving to her, but would not marry. She was too restless to sleep, so she called Patty and asked if she wanted to come by for tea or a drink.

"You're the only one who knew him as long as I knew him: hell, longer. The only one with whom I can share the stories. The only one with Doyle stories of her own."

"I wasn't prepared for how much I miss him, Johanna, like a parent, even an old flame or mentor. We were attached in so many ways. He knew my heart."

"He always said he was your Splenda Daddy, Patty; he got all of the expenses and no real sugar."

"No sugar, indeed," Patty sighed. "Alas, he was a gentleman. Though God knows I tested his resolve a couple times."

He had hired Hypatia after the first years of widowhood, to travel with him and to dine with him, to converse and contend with and eventually to get his groceries and prescriptions, do up some evening meals. He felt justified by what he regarded as a disabling loneliness. She was in her mid-twenties and he was in his mid-sixties when he hired her. During the dinner over which he conducted her job interview, he'd asked if she'd be offended by his making clumsy passes at her. She'd told him matter-of-factly there'd be "no context in which any inappropriate contact would take place." And, though they spent long weeks and months together in distant and romantic places, and though Hypatia was beautiful and Doyle lonely, there never had been a declaration or intimation of sexual interest on either side. The forty years between them seemed like the Great Wall. They both had behaved, though with some few exceptions, accordingly.

Doyle had known Hypatia's parents and grandparents, and when he'd mentioned to her aunt and uncle that he was looking for an assistant, they both said he should hire their niece, Hypatia.

"She's smart and reliable and could use some direction," her aunt told Doyle, and she set up a time for an interview. It was, in hindsight, the elusive win-win situation so seldom accomplished, good for Doyle and good for Hypatia.

Johanna and Doyle first met in person, after months of correspondence, quite by chance, at an AA meeting in the Topinabee Berean Bible Church basement. She'd gotten pulled over one evening after a couple glasses of wine and a chin-wag at a girlfriend's divorce party at the Breakers. She was court-ordered, as an alternative to an arrest on her record, three recovery meetings a week for six months. The county sheriff had been stopping patrons of the Breakers for years and making them blow into the Breathalyzer as a way of collecting taxes for the chronically underfunded police department. The judge in Cheboygan was always cooperative with what was, for her and her staff, a make-work project producing the extra revenues, what with fines and court costs and related expenses. Johanna was not nearly under the influence, but figured she'd play by the rules, and maybe the society of others a few times a week would do her no harm. So she found her way to the Topinabee meeting of Alcoholics Anonymous to dip a toe in the water of compliance.

It met on Tuesdays at 7:30 p.m. in the basement hall of the church, and the last Tuesday of every month they scheduled a potluck dinner and an open talk by someone with more than a few twenty-four hours of sobriety.

She liked what Doyle, a veteran of the group, had said about his tendency to shake a fist in the face of a God he no longer believed in, asking *why me?* and *show me* and *give me*, or some variation on his strident apostasy. And there was something about his voice and delivery she thought familiar, as if they'd met in another life.

"The only thing this fellowship requires you to believe," Doyle could be counted on to say about the spiritual aspect of Alcoholics Anonymous, "is *if* there's a god, you're not it. No tithe, no dress code, no bishops or bell choir—just show up, shut up, listen up, share your experience, strength, and hope, and get with the program. Put a buck in the basket if you've got it."

It was at the end of the meeting that Johanna introduced herself to Doyle. "The judge thinks I may be an alcoholic," she told him, which she didn't really believe but had discerned was the ante everyone tossed into the pot before sharing any portion of their story. She told Doyle how much she liked his black bean buffalo chili, a pot of which had disappeared along with the cheese and onion and oyster crackers he brought along to add to the bean and onion and bell pepper rich chili. "A nice little kick, but not too hot," she said when he nodded and smiled.

"You sound the same in person as on the radio," she said, and it was then Doyle began to connect the dots of their acquaintance to their written consortium.

She was fifty-something, slim and shapely, and he was late sixties when she heard him share his story at a closed meeting of Alcoholics Anonymous. He seemed articulate and well maintained. Johanna was lonesome for touch and talk.

"Have we met before?" Doyle asked her.

"I don't know," Johanna answered, "but there's an aspect of déjà vu to all of this. Possibly in another life?"

"Or maybe destiny?" Doyle countered, smiling.

"Or divine intervention? Possibly God?" Johanna countered.

The years between them mattered less and less the older they both got. In the time since, they'd become travel companions and moved in and out of each other's homes for residencies of various durations, with the usual divisions of labor. She'd do his laundry, he'd take out her recycled garbage, promising to put the paper in one bin, the plastic in another, and everything else in yet another dumpster. Their kindnesses to one another never lapsed. Both seemed eager to please and relate and deepen their intimacies. Theirs had been an easygoing romance, more glowing embers than fireworks, free of drama and agreeably normal, quietly mundane. They'd been good to and for one another. Each took pleasure in pleasuring the other.

Johanna knew that she would eventually have to share the details of Doyle's end with Patty, how it was that he came to inhabit a former tense, how he came to be what he always called "the dead guy," as in "you've gotta have a dead guy for a proper funeral." "Someone's got to agree," he'd say, "to quit breathing, forever." Doyle had joined the crowd who'd agreed to quit breathing forever. Johanna was with him when he stepped over. She knew that Patty wanted to know.

It is important to get the story straight, he had told them both and told them further to make it sound like he had died doing something meaningful. "Not whacking off in a chair or dreaming of naked adventures in bed," he told them. "Whatever happens, get the corpse downstairs and to the desk and make it look like I died whilst writing something, something memorable." It had amazed them both how, in the years since Sally had passed, he'd taken to reading her old books, and the reading soon led to the writing of things, and Doyle had self-published a book of mediocre poems and a book of opinion pieces he'd submitted to the now-defunct weekly paper that almost never made room for such ruminations. Nonetheless, he had come to identify himself as a sort of down-market homespun man of letters, a minor poet because, as Patty had frequently reminded him, poetry was a minor art practiced by too many people and too few truly worthy writers.

"It's a little like suicide," Doyle had remarked. "More women try it, more men succeed. An odd word—succeed— when attached to self-destruction or self-disclosure in verse. Either way, a mug's game, after which we look fairly ridiculous."

"After suicide or poetry?" Patty had once asked the old man.

"Either," he told her. "Both."

Since his daughter Fiona's death by suicide, he was not as cavalier in conversation about self-destruction. The spiritual life, he reminded himself, from one of the texts in the fellowship, is not a theory; we have to live it.

At the image of Fiona his imagination served up, alone on a bridge at the other end of the continent, having run out of reasons to live at all, only brief years after his beloved Sally had died, Doyle's eyes grew rheumy with the pool of melancholy that ebbed and flowed within him. Sometimes it was a hymn or song on the radio, a paragraph in some book he might come across, a made-for-TV movie, or a game show where some unlikely contestant with a backstory of struggle emerged triumphant. Some sudden clarity on a passage from scripture or an old bromide that rang newly true in a different context, maybe the snippet of a poem or something on one of those changeable signs in front of a church or something he remembered from a dream. He was always haunted by his cloud of witnesses, happily, it must be said, but their appearance during sleep or in the faces of his grandchildren unfailingly tipped the tide pool of tears inside him toward overflowing. It did not require Mahler adagios or pietàs or warm fuzzies from the Hallmark Channel to get his eyes to moisten. He rarely shook or sobbed or seized up, but the edges of his eyes, like levies leaking from the slow accretion of loss, let tears work their slow way down his face for no apparent reason.

There were all sorts of diapers and over-the-counter drugs for dripping pissers, wipes for the toilet rim and tile floor, but nothing for what he called the *lacrimae rerum*—the tears of things—the low-grade, ever-present well of damage and its sad tributaries and sluices, the flowing of which sent him rummaging through the catalog of sadnesses, large and small, he had assembled, his personal parade of terrors, horrors, losses over the long years of his life, the mean time of which he never felt going. These reviews, which he could neither predict nor divert his attention from, might wake him from a sound sleep, interrupt an otherwise blissful morning or evening or enterprise.

Possibly, he told himself, it was the open-heart surgery he'd had in his eighties to replace a valve. They stabbed his sternum and spread his rib cage wide open to expose the heart they were going to work on, and once the work was done, they stapled and stitched him back together, sent him home with the drain tubes still in him and sent a visiting nurse by for a couple weeks to be sure everything was mending as they'd planned. And of course, it was, mending. And he was grateful for it, for the fact that he could breathe again. But apart from the new lease on breathing it gave him, the most noticeable side effect of the surgery seemed to be the *lacrimae rerum*, the eventual sadness of it all, the beauty of being, the ceasing to be.

"That should be good for ten or fifteen years," the surgeon told him. "Next time you'll be old enough, we'll go through the groin, just like the heart cath, nothing to it," to which Doyle responded, "Unless they can do it over the phone next time, you'll never have another shot at me." The doctor only smiled and nodded his head.

At the graveside in Northern Michigan, it suddenly astonished Johanna that less than a week had passed from the morning offices on the deck of the villa in the Lesser Antilles that Doyle had rented for the month of February—a wicked little month, he always called it and, further to the conversation, explained how it shortened the Michigan winter to get the hell out of the worst of it in February and how he'd gotten into the habit, after Sally had died, of spending his Februarys on St. John, the smallest of the United States Virgin Islands, where one could depend on the weather to be kind and the sea to be warm and the beaches not entirely overrun.

He always rented the same villa, Elysium, on a dead-end road halfway up a hill on the south side, overlooking Fish Bay and the salt marsh it created as the sea washed inland. He loved sipping his first coffee in the morning on the veranda, looking out over the Caribbean and the yachts at their moorings, and over the salt marsh for egrets and scarlet ibises making their brief reconnaissance flights over the wetlands. Elysium had two stories, a swimming pool, and two bedrooms, and in the years between Sally's death and meeting Johanna, Doyle had invited Hypatia to come along because he feared traveling alone and dying at a distance from the grave next to Sally, which he knew his corpse would be finding its way back to, regardless of where he finally came to an end. And though it was not inexpensive, the month in the sun in the middle of winter had become an essential to Doyle's sense of well-being, and though he missed Sally there, where they'd been content and happy, he enjoyed traveling with Patty, their daily contentions, their colloquy in restaurants while others looked on, trying to figure out their arrangement and relationship. He felt gladdened to know Patty in her prime, her youth and beauty, which he endeavored, though not always successfully, to avoid ogling. He admired her bookishness, contrarian nature, unabashed confidence, high energy, constant curiosity, and spiritual depth and had come to regard her as a force of nature. Still, decorum dictated that his affection for her was parental, paternal, protective in nature.

And he loved Johanna fiercely, as the younger but more age-appropriate travel companion and gift to his advancing years that she was. They had become intimate in all the ways he'd been with Sally. And while he ruled out the prospect of marriage, Johanna had become, in all ways, a spousal equivalent.

"Life changes too fast," Johanna now recalled her Doyle often saying. How else to explain how a few days could bring such changes, from the bougainvillea and tropical perfumes and breezes, the hummingbirds and night songs between them, to this cold opened ground and poor Doyle's lifeless body in the box going into it?

Passe-Partout • 45

Ten days ago she'd gotten him to Francis Bay on the north side of the island. It was calm and there was no swell to the sea, so Doyle had gone in up to his shoulders and floated like an old manatee while Johanna swam her distances, then walked the long beach back and forth, and Doyle sat among the sea grape and frangipani and noni fruit trees for the shade, listening to the conversations of other beachgoers and the gently lapping tide. White yachts, schooners, and sloops tethered to buoys in the curling bay. Nearby, a man with a thick New Jersey accent was teaching a young man how to juggle, mentioning figure eights and internal cascades and showers. It was from this that Doyle came up with his latest and last-known theory, which he detailed to Johanna that night over dinner at a beachfront eatery in Cruz Bay, that what you needed to start a movement was a specialized lexicon, a far-fetched narrative, and a personality cult built around an unlikely figure with an appetite for spectacle.

"Jesus of Nazareth, the Juggler from Jersey, Joan of Arc— folks love the drama and the stage, the table and the blade," he told her, "church and the circus, the scaffold and pulpit, the political rally and public execution. You want to move people, give 'em a show."

Like much of what Doyle declared of late, it was hard to make a connection between it and any context in which it was related to the real world. Notions just floated through the old man's consciousness, like fallen leaves on a flowing stream, some to be ignored and some to be pronounced upon. Johanna was never sure but knew it was her job to affect the attentive listener to the old man, who like other old men, was mostly in need of an audience, paid, captive, or incidental.

He'd argued not long before that the only reason to keep Texas in the United States after they had elected so many

46 • NO PRISONERS

nitwits was the compensating fact that Lyle Lovett came from Texas and still made music there, including writing what Doyle believed to be the best rhyme in contemporary music when he sang, "Honey, put down that flyswatter and pour me some ice water."

Another of his steadfast theories asserted that the way to end war was to replace the drafting of men to do violence to other men, strangers from strange lands, all in their sexual prime, was to draft women in their sexual prime to do sexual kindness to strangers, say thirtyish, two years of civic duty to have sex with mostly the old men who start wars but do not fight them. If war was a way for old men to act out their sexual aggressions, their fear of sexual decline or loss of prowess, why not disabuse them of such concerns by sending a perfectly agreeable woman by to satisfy him and herself and leave him feeling peaceable and grateful rather than violent and aggrieved?

Johanna had come to believe, and Hypatia agreed with her, that these pronouncements were often done just to get a rise and response out of whichever woman was listening at the time. They further concurred that Doyle had gotten worse since Sally died since their impression was that she would not have suffered fools, however much she loved one, and would not tolerate any misogyny in her husband's decrees. Since her death, he had taken to writing letters to the editor at first the local papers and then the national outlets, even once getting an op-ed in the paper of record titled, "A Man's Right to Choose," in which he argued for the opening of community clinics within the premises of Planned Parenthood where not only could women undo, as part of their reproductive options, an unwanted pregnancy, but a man, an impregnator, could likewise renounce any paternity or attendant rights or responsibilities associated with same, unilaterally, as one of his reproductive choices. If reproductive choice is good, Doyle argued, and agreed it was, then it is good for both goose and gander, Jack and Jenny, and ought to be regarded as a human issue rather than solely a women's issue.

The objections to such a prospect were loud and legion in the letters that followed publication of his opinion piece. "If a man doesn't want to be a parent, he should keep his trousers on," was the general refrain, to which Doyle only answered, "So ought she." This further infuriated the readership, who, nonetheless, found Doyle's insuperable logic, well, insuperable.

Johanna would tell Patty how she had followed him into the shower, worried now, as she'd been for a few years, that he might slip or fall or get lightheaded in the heat and steam. How even the advanced age they'd both achieved, he at ninety and she at seventy-five, had not diminished the calm delight and abiding pleasure of their shared naked, sodden bodies together, the play of their intimacy. "We are as we are," she would whisper to him whenever his disappointments were made manifest, his dozing off during foreplay, the failure of his manly parts to rise to their occasions. He loved the shining of her wet skin. Nonetheless, their tender embraces seemed as fine in their much latter years as they'd seemed at the start. They'd never been teenagers together, but they had made each other feel young and alive and in love, which seemed like a gift outright between them.

And Doyle still loved to kneel, sitting back on his haunches in the shower, and press his face into Johanna's nether regions and tell her that she tasted like panna cotta or crème anglaise or tapioca. She would press his bald head into her groin and sometimes arch a leg over his shoulder, holding onto the handrails she'd had installed to steady them at their sodden and slippery laving and lovemaking. And as limp as his poor penis had become from age and medications and diabetes, the feel of it in her mouth when she would return the favor was familiar and endearing. That it still pleasured him she could discern from its harmless and occasional throb and from the chitchat and heavy breathing that were part of his joy. "Oh, Johanna," he would say, "you are so very kind." Once in a great while he would seem to climax, then slump to the seat in the shower stall with his face gazing helplessly heavenward. "Sweet Jesus," he would say, though he'd lost all faith, or "God is love, insuperably."

Only this time, that is, the last time, he slumped to his knees, trying to hold onto her hips to steady himself, and rather than gazing helplessly heavenward, his chin lay on his chest and his eyes were downcast and a faintly purple blush moved up his neck and face as if a rubber band had constricted circulation. Doyle had become the hero of a joke he used to tell that always ended with "but what a way to go."

The old marine was taking his leave the way he had always hoped he would, to wit, getting head from one of the women of his dreams. She called 911, though she knew he was dead. Two West Indians, a man and woman, removed him from the shower, while Johanna, wrapped in towels, sobbed quietly behind them. One of them couldn't help saying, "Well, at least he's clean." He meant this to be a sort of consolation, but it fell flatly on the ceramic tiled floor between them. Nonetheless, in death Doyle Shields was, indisputably, very clean.

"It's not the story he wanted us to tell," said Johanna to Patty. "It has a punch line and a good laugh attached, but I think he longed to have made some difference, something of lasting merit, a chance at permanence." Doyle had always told them that the story matters, especially the story about the end, last words, free advice from the dearly departed, things like that.

This brought to Johanna's mind a thought she felt duty bound to share with Patty, about the correspondence he had told her about between himself and Sally in the late months of 1945, when it was clear that he'd soon be coming home alive and that their plans to marry would come to pass. He wanted to take up the matter of oral sex, specifically the hope he made known to Sally that they'd both avail themselves of all the various fleshy pleasures that young and able men and women might share between them. He was aware of the course of nunnish instruction Sally had had that instructed Catholic girls on the responsibilities of sexual intercourse, notably that only such conduct that could lead to reproduction was permitted to good Catholics, so that the sort of pleasure for the sake of pleasure practices of fellatio and cunnilingus were specifically "unnatural" in so far as they did not, in and of themselves, allow for pregnancy. Doyle had tried to convince Sally that the nuns were simply mistaken about this, and that not only as foreplay but as destination, both the pleasure given and received by oral sex was sufficient to imbue the conduct with meaning and purpose and the same dignity as intercourse. Whether Sally believed this or not and behaved accordingly remained between Doyle and his departed spouse. It did, however, help to shape the sexual agenda between Doyle and Johanna. Furthermore, Doyle shared his sense that the Christian concept of original sin, the sin of Adam and Eve in the garden involving forbidden fruit from the tree of knowledge, had little to do with apples or obedience but rather that Eve's proffering of her nether regions for Adam's attentions, and the approval she would no doubt make known to him in the course of their consortium, was the original knowledge of good and evil the nuns and priests most feared an education in. Indeed, some nights, spread open for Doyle to delight in, Johanna would gaze at the moonlight in the bedroom's eastern window and think of Eve alone in the garden with her Adam lapping at her vagina and imagine the entire magisterium of the church being brought low by such boundless, generous pleasure, its abundance and ease and eventual crescendo into a hymn of approval.

The sound of his name in Johanna's moaning approach to orgasm, "Oh, Doy-al"—each syllable catching an emphasis of breathlessness and intake was in fact a sort of music to his ears. Nothing pleased him more, nor did repetition diminish the beauty of it.

In his lifelong search for meaning, an exercise mostly in disappointment, Doyle had arrived at a negotiated truce with Whomever Is in Charge Here, the power greater than himself, or Maker of Everything and Everyone, to wit, it would be enough to be the man who pleasured Johanna Ramsey, and did so every chance he got, bringing her to a place on the continuum of bliss where she got some little glimpse of the face of gods, those in nature and beyond that had in common the known properties of love. It was enough, as Doyle now figured it, to have been worthy of such happy work and delightful duties that had, certainly, pleasured him and added purpose to his being.

After everything, he knew it amounted to nothing—the long arc of his being, nine-tenths of a century and counting—the works and days of his hands, a paternity of sons and a daughter, a forty-three-year marriage and lifelong love of the same woman, a life of capable service to his fellow nothings, the heart, swollen with its own inconsequence, battered and broken, and half-heartedly pounding forth; he knew it would all add up to nothing by every calculus of history and memory and time. He'd been both one of a kind, with the emphasis on the singular, and one of a kind, with the emphasis on the general.

And that is when the notion of a surpassing gesture came to him: an act so incomparably bold and bespoke as to fix him ineluctably into the firmament of meaningful lives, possibly only as a moment and twinkling, but there nonetheless, visible to the naked eye, in the pitch blackness of the proper dark, the light and spark of his having been. Doyle Shields could think of nothing but a surpassing and excellent gesture by which his being and person could be summarized for all and always; something to gather the passion of his heart and principles of his mind and persistence of his body into one surpassing gesture of his being, a being apart from the garden variety, lackluster, serviceably quotidian specimen of humanity he knew himself to be.

Life, he was fond of saying, takes no prisoners. It comes and goes and goes on with or without our participation or approval. It runs over us like litter on the long road of life. Time swallows everything in its fathomless maw, and all we can hope for is something forever assigned to us—the job well done, the first or last or best of something, the sui generis heroic or ignoble conduct.

He understood the suicide bomber and the manic candidate for public office, the saintly recluse and the star of the show— each making their individual effort to separate themselves from the herd of humanity, if only momentarily, to stand surely and certainly apart. And he noted the difference between the hollow lives of celebrities and the substantial lives of heroes. He contemplated the desolation, no longer foreign to his own experience, of the ones who douse themselves in gasoline and put a match to their bodies, self-immolation seeming the next step for someone burning inside with the dumpster fire of a wasted existence, making of their deaths a statement that their lives had failed to make, to wit: I am, I was, I mattered, some. In his youth it had seemed like everyone was making an effort to fit in, whereas the hunger of his age was to find a way to stand out from the crowd, the community, the rest of his fellows.

There had been times in his youth, of course, when he counted on moments of great fear or suffering or danger he'd been part of and survived to fix him into the local or global record. But time, the slow accretion of it, day after day, week after week, year after inexorable yearly dosage of it, had disabused him of any sense of his own confluence with memorable or meaningful history.

He'd grown up a nothing, a native of nowhere special, and after a predictable matriculation he marched off to war with the United States Marines at the service of a president who actually made a difference, was somebody, shaped the world. Now, as he approximated the relative worth of his being, he came up empty-handed. Neither the good job as right tackle for St. Francis DeSales High School at Fenkell and Meyers in Detroit, nor the valiant service in the South Pacific as fodder for the Second World War, nor the long and faithful marriage to the love of his life, nor the serviceable parenting to his children and grandchildren and now great-grandchildren made much of a difference in the larger scheme of things. No ledger entries under Doyle Shields would change one iota the bottom line of the comprehensive history of things. Only a surpassing gesture, a one-off, unmistakably premeditated act of courage or outrage or seismic change would change a thing. At some time in his middle eighties, he set to contemplating his final options.

If his life in its longevity lacked much meaning or memorable outcomes, he might only have his one and only death left to ante up.

He thought about Sally, dead now for twenty-five years, a shade in an occasional dream, a phantom of his memory, the photos in the family album now distributed among her children.

She was to him an ache like any other, beyond reach or repair, ever pressing the sore place where her absence was more keenly felt in the evening and the dark of night, the winters, the silences when he listened for silence and could not hear hers. He had never sought closure and thought the concept idiotic and anyone who promoted it as a goal of this or that conduct or therapy an ignoramus to be avoided at all costs. He did not hold it against his sons or his daughter, who seemed to think he should move along, make a peace with his bereavement, invest his heart in some other partnership, and regain what they called a zest for living. He did not hold their rosy prospects against them, neither did he try to go along, basking in the blackness of his blighted self.

His quarter-century-old bereavement had changed Doyle in ways he might never have experienced had he not been widowed at sixty-five. In other aspects he was steadfastly the same. Soon after Sally's death, he'd hired Patty Casey as an assistant—to travel and talk with, dine with on occasion, discuss books and events, and to get to know the world through the eyes of another, much younger generation. And then, quite by accident or happenstance, he had met a woman, fifteen years his junior but still "age appropriate" compared to Hypatia. He hadn't planned to pursue a romance with Johanna or anyone else; rather, she'd heard him one day on the local radio station, where he was being interviewed on the subject of widowhood and living alone. A correspondence followed, each disclosing to the other some facts of their lives: how they came to be "single," their hopes for the future, the remnants of family and responsibility. Over the course of months they'd become almost intimates. There were phone calls, cards for holidays and birthdays, season's greetings.

Doyle drew the line when Johanna invited him to her church, the local Episcopal one on the south end of town. He didn't want to get any gossip going among the churchy sorts. It was enough that her late husband, the Methodist pastor, had died in ambiguous circumstances and that there were rumors of a relationship between Johanna and—and here Doyle's memory was less than precise—either the former priest at the Episcopal parish or the parish deacon, the former a woman, the latter a man; what's more, Doyle's agnosticism had only hardened in the years since Sally had died.

When Doyle and Johanna began to sleep together, it had an organic feel to it, a seamlessness Doyle trusted. She came by with a casserole, he'd bought a pecan pie for dessert, there was wine for her and conversation into the late night about former spouses and children. He thought she better not chance the drive—the weather, the wine, the late hour—and offered the room at the top of the stairs with its fresh sheets and its own bath. She'd asked if he'd mind if she slept with him. He said he wouldn't mind. They walked upstairs like old marrieds, Doyle admiring the shape of Johanna's bottom as she made her way.

And while, at their ages neither was eager to chance having sex, both seemed, in the quiet and the dark, eager to chance their sexiness, their willingness to touch and to be touched, to kiss like lovers, to caress and fondle, to hold and embrace and to press themselves against one another. There had been, if memory served, some mutual weeping, not with sobs or wailing, rather joyous but tearful because it had been far too long for both Johanna and Doyle since either of them had been touched and held with such tender desire, such intimacy, so that such tears as were shed between them were tears of restoration, as if the long embargo had been broken and a new version of reality was coming forth into being. After their embraces they rolled to their separate shoulders and slept deeply, dreaming of blank slates, somethingness and nothingness, grace and peace. It was daylight before either of them shifted or awakened.

He remembered the homily spoken over the corpse of a retired pastor, a reflection on the gospel account in Matthew for the third Sunday in Advent some years, of John the Baptist, imprisoned by Herod Antipas, having heard of Jesus's miracles in Capernaum and the environs, wanting to see if Jesus is in fact the one they've all been waiting for, for whom John, soon to be beheaded, has been a lifelong harbinger. And poor John is wondering if his life was relevant or wasted on prophecy and preparing the way for the Messiah. Doyle still wondered, these many years since, if his willingness to die for his country, his combat in the sodden jungles of New Britain and on Okinawa and his clean-up duties in China after the war, had made any discernable difference in the history of the species. It had not, though it stole many sleepless nights and sickly days from him, between the nightmares and malaria; it hadn't made any difference at all. Some lived, some died, some won, some lost, so what, what else is new? The same could be said about his long romance with Sally, his years as a trade embalmer, a father, a fellow pilgrim, another recovering alcoholic. What difference might it possibly have made in the lives of others or their deaths? Not one jot, Doyle reckoned, not one tittle. Which brought him back to the slow years of his anecdotage, when he'd become the cunnilinguist to a younger woman, the man in charge, more or less by default, of pleasuring her. As well him as any other, he thought, as well her. Otherwise, little difference in the history of the world.

Still, he had come to believe that pleasing her was reason enough to be alive, that her pleasure, such as he had come to know it, pleasured him so utterly that he reckoned it was love itself, the rare and abundant gift that humans give themselves that seems like God in the scriptural sense that Doyle still could quote from, that God is love and who abides in love abides in God and God in him and thus, if God is love and love is God, which seemed formulaic, mathematical, then Doyle had achieved, in his pleasuring of Johanna, a godliness that needn't be improved upon. Age and infirmity, his lapsed erection and the indignities of time, had not subtracted from his hunger for Johanna's private parts nor from the intimate contacts he enacted between his and hers and the pleasure her apparent pleasures gave him. If not manifestly heroic, it nonetheless had meaning sufficient to Doyle's lifelong pursuit of meaning and purpose. It meant something to Johanna that Doyle loved her and something to Doyle that she loved him too.

Furthermore, he had, over the years, managed to attribute to his skills as an embalmer a kind of meaning and purpose for his being in the world. He'd managed to return the dead to the living in a form they could get a handle on. He'd closed their eyes and mouths, folded their hands in an aspect of repose, stitched them back together from the mayhems and murders that took them away. He had lessened the terrors of age and its emaciations, tended to bloating and belly gases, cleansed the corpses in his care of the more horrific manifestations of nature and mortality. He'd laid the dead out in manageable vignettes of peace and repose to make their presence at their own funerals passably agreeable, which gave the living a sense that they were doing right by their dead, which mitigated, Doyle always supposed, some of the burdens that grief heaped upon humans.

The history of Doyle's honorable if not unnecessarily heroic, and often downright petrified, service in the US Marines, which began in 1942, the November after Pearl Harbor, and ended in 1946, the January after Hiroshima and Nagasaki, had not been published beyond his own dark and retreating memories, and though he'd violated several of his own moral codes in combat and its attendant horrors, he had, it could no less be said, signed up, showed up, pitched in, and done his part when his nation was in peril and the world was at war. And though he'd leapt at the chance to be reassigned to the Headquarters Company, where he would type intelligence memos for those in charge, only returning to combat after the K-3-5 got shot up and shit showed on Peleliu, it was not cowardice so much as the moral trespass he'd experienced obeying orders to dispatch wounded Japanese troops, who might instead have been taken prisoner, treated for their wounds, and survived the war as he would. He had quit his courtship of Sally at eighteen, postponed his plans for their future together, and changed the carefree trajectory of his life early in December of 1941, and after graduating in the class of '42 at St. Francis DeSales with a letter in football and lackluster grades, and after reading accounts of the Old Breed at Guadalcanal, he signed up that November, took the train to San Diego, the boat to Melbourne, Australia, and Papua New Guinea, then landed on Cape Gloucester, New Britain, on New Year's Day of 1944, whereupon he and fellow gyrenes in K Company, Third Battalion, Fifth Regiment of the First Marine Division spent the night of January 9 and the early morning hours of January 10, 1944, repelling and surviving five Banzai charges of Japanese foot soldiers on Aogiri Ridge, which became Walt's Ridge ever after to honor Colonel Lew Walt, their commanding officer, who ordered them on the morning of January 10 to "take no prisoners," which meant Doyle and his outfit killed dozens of Japanese soldiers who hadn't been killed the night before. They walked among the dead and wounded bodies of young Japanese and sunk bayonets deep into the chests of those who showed any signs of life. These were the faces he would see in dreams for years after the war was over, after nights of carousing and trading stories with men like himself who'd been ordered to do things they were not proud of, in the war they never really understood, but who were still glad to be alive. Neither the action he saw at Walt's Ridge, nor the action he saw on Okinawa, nor the intelligence work and typing he'd done during his turn with the Headquarters Company made, he had to consider now, one jot of difference in the outcome of the war or the history of the world. Though the most compelling time of his life, a watershed of horror by which he'd been forever haunted, it literally made no difference. Nor could he attribute to his husbandry or paternity any purpose beyond the normal pride and expectations. He'd done his part like every other mammal. His offspring would not be curing cancer or bringing peace to the world by their agency or endeavors. They would repeat, in their own time, the inconsequential preoccupations, utterly dispensable in their enactments, of every generation: They came into being, they'd loved and bred, or not, but lived out their lives, then ceased to be.

What had vexed Doyle more than anything in his life had been the heretofore unsuccessful pursuit and enactment of the surpassing gesture he thought would make sense of his being and ceasing to be—something unlikely to be replicated or forgotten, something he would maybe be remembered for. He thought with unabashed regret of the failure he'd been, deep in his dotage, going at ninety, in Tulsa, on the stage of the opera house, with the daughter of the senior senator singing her aria, "I want to live!" in front of the hometown crowd and her proud father four rows deep on the main floor of the auditorium, the very same senator who had a couple months before put the kibosh on the Clay Hunt Veterans Suicide Prevention Act. Named for a fellow marine who'd killed himself some years before, the bill sought to address the twenty-two suicides every day among veterans of Iraq and Afghanistan. The price tag was a paltry $22 million, and one senator, Dr. No was his nickname, blocked the vote. Doyle thought maybe seeing what it looks like when a marine kills himself might shake up the senator and get him to do the right thing.

He'd gotten the grenade from an old pal whose son worked at the armory at Camp Grayling, convinced Hypatia to drive him west, had his dress blues all dry-cleaned and pressed, and spit shined his plain-toed black oxfords. He'd prebooked a ticket for the matinee performance, and at the right moment had gotten up on stage, near to the shocked mezzo-soprano, turned to stare the senator in the eye, pulled the pin, and shouted, "This is what veterans' suicide looks like," but he couldn't let go because he'd caught a glimpse of Hypatia at the back of the room, mouth agape, shouting, "No, Doyle, no!" He suddenly understood the trouble she'd be in for driving him from Michigan to this rendezvous for his surpassing gesture, this spectacle of a suicide grenade man with pin in his right hand and ordnance in his left. He tightened his grip on the grenade lest it detonate in front of all these people. He couldn't let go and let his surpassing gesture come to pass. Rather, he leapt from the stage and ran to the side exit door and out into the sunlight, followed by Hypatia who'd double-parked the car at the curb. They drove a little frantically around Tulsa, while she screamed at him for even thinking of doing what it seemed he had been ready to do, until he told her to take him to the base of the Prayer Tower at Oral Roberts University, which could be seen from the opera house, and when they got there, still holding the grenade in his left hand and the pin in his right, he ran to the base of the Prayer Tower, fell on the grenade, released the clip, and waited to be blown to smithereens. Despite his planning, that never happened.

Hypatia drove him back to Michigan, stopping only for gas and to pee. They were back in twenty-four hours or less. Doyle wept most of the way, and when he wasn't weeping, he slept.

While he slept, someplace in the middle of Illinois, Hypatia phoned Johanna to tell her what had happened. Johanna wasn't shocked, had been aware of Doyle's deepening depression, the sense he shared with her that he'd been alive long enough and there was little hope of living long enough more to do anything unforgettable or especially worthy of his having been alive for going ninety-one years. Johanna told Patty she'd heard for years about Doyle's pursuit of a meaningful death because life, as he saw it in his advancing age, seemed so meaningless. He thought something violent most likely to make the newspapers—the way the crucifixion worked for Christ.

"Talk about your surpassing gesture," Doyle would always say. "A suicide by cop turned into a personality cult and world religion!" Johanna would roll her eyes but could never come up with a counternarrative for the Nazarene and his followers. Rather, she regarded Doyle as she thought Mary Magdalene must have regarded Jesus—with love and desire and a sort of longing to engage with his manifest goodness. How else to explain the episode, the surpassing gesture, for which the Magdalene has been remembered since, where she anoints Jesus with the costliest oil, as if to prepare him for burial, and cleanses his feet with her tears, which she wipes away with her long beautiful hair. She imagined Mary about the age she was herself when she first met Doyle and they began their romance. And she imagined Mary Magdalene loving Jesus and longing for love between them, though she knew that he wasn't long for this world. Nor would romance between them be ever possible, given the difference in their ages, not to mention his deity. They remained inseparable; she was there on Calvary with him, there for his burial, there on the first Easter, the first one to behold the risen man, the one who delivered the news to the cowering apostles.

Johanna saw herself in the image she'd found on the internet of Raphael's *The Deposition*, painted early in the sixteenth century. A strawberry blond woman, looking distressed, is holding the hand of the corpse of Jesus as it is moved by Joseph of Arimathea and Nicodemus toward the tomb. And reviewing the day that had been in it, Johanna took some bit of consolation from the certain knowledge that she had been with her Doyle till the end, had gotten him where he needed to go, and had gone the entire distance with him.

She prayed now to be happily haunted by him.

Chapter Two

MOORINGS

16 October 1990

The older he got the harder it was to put the boat away. Harder still to get the old dog, Bill, into the boat. Bill the Bernese was not fond of water or moving vessels. More than anything it declared the year inexorably bending toward its dark denouement. The subtraction of light seemed a cruelty. Taking the old Chris-Craft in seemed like surrender. Especially if the day was fine, he found it difficult. All the more so if the extended forecast did not foreclose the possibility of reprieves, however fleeting, the odd day of mild weather, higher temps, a little sun. At sixty-six, he would tell himself, there was still some time for him, just as there was still some warmth in October, even November; Indian summer, he told himself, and looked at the gold in the trees and thought how glorious they would look in the autumnal light. Surely he could wait it out, though Jamesie from the marina had already called to see if Doyle didn't think it time to bring it in, and he'd be happy to send Sheila over to bring the old Chris-Craft up the river if it was too miserable, what with the chill and threat of rain, for a man Doyle's age to make the journey. Ever since Sally died,

64 • NO PRISONERS

nearly a year ago now, folks treated Doyle like a hobbled man, which in many ways, of course, he was.

The boat was old; Doyle was older still; both of them still in serviceable, if sometimes shaky, working order. It wasn't so much of a journey, Doyle would always tell Jamesie, and he'd been bringing the boat back to its winter storage longer than Jamesie had been on the planet, and he'd be bringing it back this year in his own good time, thank you.

"I'll have it there before the freeze. Always do," he insisted. "And thank you, thank you for checking," Doyle always added, because he didn't want to burn any more bridges by his crankiness than he already had. God knows he could imagine a favor he might need from Jamesie Parker, who was the service manager at the marina and in charge of the boats they stored for the winter, mostly float boats and runabouts for the local swells and their much indulged kids. The suburbanites and weekenders liked the big barges with cushy wraparound sofa seating and built-in coolers and sound systems and huge pontoons for the floating cocktail parties they had, loafing around the shoreline of the big lake in affected languor, counting their blessings, looking at their neighbors' store-bought landscapes, and whispering what gossip they had about each home's inhabitants.

One year all the talk was about how some mogul from downstate had sunk $20 million into the purchase of Red Pine Point and had a white clapboard mansion built there, taking full advantage of the lake frontage that gave a view to the northwest and a view to the south. Seems the old money at Mullett Lake Village had treated him like the pig-rich jackass he really was, so he crossed the lake and built a place they could all look at for the rest of their lives, that would make them all feel like pikers.

Then it was the wedding of the century when some well-heeled father of the bride had a ten-thousand-square-foot deck built out on the water and a bridge walk from the yard to accommodate a sit-down dinner under a tent for two hundred and a dance floor with a band in the gazebo and from another deck an hour-long pyrotechnics show to festoon the bride and her new catch. The huge installation appeared the week before the nuptials and was gone the week after.

There were deaths and divorces and bankruptcies and every few years an ax murder or drug bust or some other local mayhem to jawbone over.

Though there were bass boats and ski boats, duck boats and rowboats, canoes and kayaks, it was the resident fleet of pontoon boats that idled around the lakeshore laden with swells and wine and cheese and talk of the neighbors that reminded Doyle why he kept to himself.

Doyle wasn't a very good neighbor. Years back he had moved from the side of the lake he and Sally first settled on, west and a little north of the river mouth, with the grand view that gave that stretch of lakefront its name. The lake stretched thirteen miles to the north and maybe a mile or two across, with plenty of sandbars and sunken islands, deep trenches and tributaries. Doyle had moved to the other side of the river mouth to an old house that he refurbished, with enough frontage and forest on either side that he couldn't see his neighbors and could count on the fact that they couldn't see him. He liked to piss off the porch on the lakeside and out the back door when the sound of running water in the kitchen made it urgent that he do so.

He had an old twenty-foot mahogany. He'd bought it used from a fellow near Topinabee, whose bad knees and bum hip made getting in and out of it dangerous. In those days before you could replace such parts, a broken hip meant a trip to the nursing home with a pin or a couple screws in place and a regimen of rehab retraining one to take steps, or as turned out more often than not, an extended bedfast fall into pneumonia, which remained, in those days, the old man's friend. Doyle had paid three grand for the boat in 1960, when it was four years old, and kept it in good fettle for the price of its storage and upkeep—something that cost him maybe that much again every decade, what with the varnish and valve jobs, now and then a new prop. He identified readily with the old boat. It was a classic. The valve job, the odds and ends of upkeep that it required were no more than he needed himself. He'd never had it fully restored like the other vintage boats that were displayed every August up in Hessel at the Les Cheneaux Islands Boat Show, but Doyle always knew he had that option, to put some money into its refurbishment and sell it for the rare old thing it was, for sixty or eighty or a hundred thousand, whatever the traffic would bear, he thought. But as it was, his was a working boat with daily duties and obligations, not as well turned out as the new ones, maybe, but surviving on performance.

He tried to get it in the water by May 1 and back around the end of October, much like the season at the Grand Hotel. If they could still run ferries full of fudgies to Mackinac Island, he reasoned, he could keep his boat moored to the shore station next to his own dock.

And when he finally made the trip upriver, and left the boat at the marina, where they would winterize it and keep it in one of the huge pole barns until next spring, there was, the older he got, the ever-increasing sense that he was making a final journey, that life changes too quickly and winters were tough on old-timers, boats and old boys like him alike, and he could never be sure he'd be back in the spring. So there was this valedictory quality to the ride along the southern point of the lake, into the wide gaping mouth of the river through the reeds and wetlands, following the channel markers as slow as he could go in the no-wake sections to protect the habitat of loons and otters, mute swans and other waterfowl and wildlife that lived there.

The river flowed under the interstate that made the trip between downstate and up north a cakewalk now, then past the tidy riverside homes in Indian River and then to the old marina with its row of covered and uncovered slips for summer moorings. He'd leave his in the covered section, drop the keys in Jamesie's drop box, and get a ride home from Sheila, who cleaned the boats every spring for tips.

Then he'd call the kid who removed his shore stations and muscled his dock in its sections out of the water and set them at the edge of his property to winter out until the snow melted and the ice went off the lake and the boats began to reappear next spring. He had done these things himself or with the help of his three sons when he was a younger man, but now it was more than he could manage, so he paid for younger, stronger men to do these chores that marked the year's unrelenting progress toward its end. It was the end that was ever looming now—the last trip up the river, the last summer, the last autumn, the last turn of the key in the door and southbound journey to another house where there was no one waiting for him to come home. Nor anything much that had to be done.

He drove down every so often to get his mail, do a little banking, have dinner with the boys and their families around the holidays, see the old farts, maybe vote or pay taxes. Otherwise, he pretty much lived up north now, with his old dog, Bill—the third or fourth in a line of Bills that connected Doyle

68 • NO PRISONERS

to his life with Sally, who had always claimed it was the dog that would be the death of her.

It was squamous cell carcinoma of the lung that killed her, whether from the Pall Mall cigarettes she'd given up ten years before or the Kent filter tips Doyle never could quit, an old man's version of the Lucky Strikes he got hooked on in boot camp. Or maybe the asbestos wrap of the pipes in the basement, or some cruel twist of fate unknowable to mortals. Whatever it was, it wasn't Bill or himself, Doyle told himself. They were, if not quite innocent, not guilty in the end.

"What about no didn't you understand?" she'd asked him, years ago, when he turned up with the original Bill, an eleven-pound puppy, black and white and brown, mewling and pissing on everything. Soon enough it had grown up to weigh more than Sally.

"I thought you'd changed your mind. You told me I could call him Yeats," Doyle said, which was, indeed, what she had told him when he said, as he sometimes did in those days, "I think I'll get a dog."

He was accustomed to her response.

"Are you out of your fucking mind?" she'd say. "We finally have the place to ourselves, a little peace and quiet, we can come and go as we please, and you want to get a dog? Who's gonna feed it and clean it and take it for walks? Don't be silly! If it's not broken, don't fix it. No, we're not going to get a dog." Doyle loved it when Sally'd say *fucking* because he knew she knew it worked against his sense of her as a Goody Two-shoes. A good Catholic girl, schooled by nuns, devout in her observances, orthodox in her religious praxis.

Then one Sunday when he broached the topic again, "I think I'll get a dog," instead of her usual refusal, she told him maybe he could name it Wordsworth. It was the poem Doyle had written out for her on their anniversary, one of Wordsworth's, something to do with nuns and their narrow rooms, and put it on the fridge for her to read. He wrote it out a dozen times, trying to memorize it, planning to say it to her aloud, but the perfect moment never presented itself. Nonetheless, there it was on the fridge, better than any Hallmark card. He got it from a book he had given her early in their marriage. Sally loved poetry, and while Doyle had no use for it, he loved Sally.

Thus convinced that her heart had softened on the matter of a dog, he went out and found one and brought it home.

"What about no didn't you get, Doyle?" she asked him, but it was too late. She'd seen it and held it, and when Doyle said he would call it Wordsworth, as she had suggested, she said, "Bill will do. Or Bill W. He's a fucking dog."

So Bill it was.

Taking the slow ride upriver each autumn was, for Doyle Shields, an occasion to inventory all that he'd lost—Sally, who never actually got old and gray, and Fiona, their long-estranged daughter, a handful of lifelong friends, and soon enough, he supposed, the current Bill the dog, who was angling toward his eleventh year, dotage for a big dog, and now, it seemed, even the memory of them, harder and harder to hold on to, like the nimbleness required to get in the boat and lower it into the water by himself and drive it up the river. The fear of falling in the water, cracking his head or something essential on the frame of the boat hoist, the terrible outcomes. Everything was a challenge that had to be chanced and planned for. "God loves a chancer," Sally would say, having heard it from her father who'd heard it from his and lost almost everything in the Great Depression. Doyle wondered how long it would take before someone would wonder why they hadn't seen or heard from him. Was it time to hire someone to check in on him, pick up some groceries, bring in the mail? Was hiring an assistant too bougie? Someone to travel with and talk with, maybe? Or was he only kidding himself?

What would Doyle do if he couldn't climb out of the boat? Would there be someone there to give him a hand up and a foot hard planted on the narrow boardwalks between boats? Was there enough gas left in the tank for the last journey? Would he have to take a piss, or worse still, a shit? Did he have any toilet paper on board? What if the day, once he got up the river, was just too heartbreakingly beautiful, too fine a thing to even contemplate bringing the boat's access to such beauties to a close? What if he changed his mind and turned around between red markers and green markers—"green right going, red right return"—and made his way back out the river mouth, maybe bought a dozen crawlers at the Landings and went out and caught some walleye for dinner or a pike, or enough perch to sauté in the pan to feed himself and declare himself still a dangerous man and not think of putting the boat away for another week maybe, maybe two. Not until the Feast of All Saints, All Souls, wouldn't that do? God loves a chancer, he told himself.

He imagined this was like the decision the old terminal cases made—the ones who eschewed hospice and intensive care, assisted living or moving in with the kids and decided rather to end it all with a cocktail of odd drugs, a bottle of aspirin, or a carefully aimed bullet from their plentiful guns.

He could remember the body of one poor old sonofabitch he embalmed maybe fifty years before, who pressed the muzzle of his .45 on his chest and squeezed off a round that took out his lung and missed his heart by a good few inches so that he had to regain his composure and steady the gun just over his sternum and finally blew himself to death on the second try, no doubt wheezing and dying, Doyle thought, with some embarrassment at his insuperable fecklessness—that it would take two rounds to kill himself because he couldn't quite figure where his heart was in the end.

Doyle never had a suicidal thought. He'd felt homicidal often enough and had a hair-trigger temper, even now; still he advised his pals that if he was ever found dead of what seemed to be suicide, they should look for the sonsofbitches who killed him. It would take more than one, he was certain.

Doyle had his contingency plan, if it ever got impossible to get in the boat or out of it, or up the river, or if he shit himself more than once in a great while or couldn't quit pissing, he'd know what to do. He had his fail-safe methods sorted out. There'd be no gun play, nor half-baked attempts. To be a failure at suicide was more of an indignity than he could stomach.

The gaping maw of the river mouth opened to a wetlands where the loons and mergansers and mute swans tended their nests and broods and fed in the shallows on minnows and sucker chubs and other baitfish. Now and then Doyle spotted the wake of a larger pike or muskellunge cruising for a careless duckling. The reeds would shake with the violence of the underwater drama of the food chain. Likewise the raptors, osprey and eagle, various small hawks and falcons, circled overhead waiting for their chance. Doyle kept following the channel markers—red on his right and green on his left—and admired the steadfastness of cormorants perched on the posts between their own feeding flights. At the Landings he docked the old boat to fill the tank with gas for the winterage. The Landings always charged a penny or two cents less per gallon than the marina where he stored it.

The slow float up the river gave Doyle time to consider the differences he did not make in the history of the world during the year behind him.

72 • NO PRISONERS

"The trees are in their autumn beauty / The woodland paths are dry" kept haunting his slow going through the reeds and rushes as the river narrowed from the gaping maw of the river mouth to the canal it eventually became as he motored past the habitats of waterfowl and abandoned nests of mute swans that had invaded the wetlands of Michigan's northern waters. Doyle had heard it was the Methodists at Bay View, just north of Petoskey along the edge of Little Traverse Bay, early in the former century, who thought the great white birds of Yeats's poetry would add a dash of calm and class to Northern Michigan. However lovely they looked in their flotillas and flights, the mute swans were cranky aggressors, especially protective of their cygnets and cobs. "Under the October twilight the water / Mirrors a still sky." Poetry always conjured a sore memory of his darling Sally, who'd left him a library of poems, however brilliant, however haunting, scant compensation for her presence in his life, and boat and bed. Her death had left him the more so purposeless, bereft of motive and design. He'd gone about his mindless life and times, a creature of habits and repetitions, hoping to do something incomparably meaningful to someone or some group or cause worthy of his attention. The farther up the river he went, the keener his bereavement, the deeper his isolation, the sharper the loss of his life partner seemed to Doyle, like an old mute swan who'd lost his mate and for whom the calm autumn water seemed pointless. Doyle still came away empty-handed in his lifelong search for meaning. This pursuit he had associated with an "evaluation" he had to write as a schoolboy when Sr. Jean Terese instructed her third-grade students to sum up the year just finished one June.

Of course, for Sr. Jean Terese and for all her students, the purpose of life, why God made us, was to "know, love, and serve God in this world and to be happy with Him forever in the next." He still had, somewhere, his dark green copy of the Baltimore Catechism.

Doyle had traded in this God of his grade-school training for the higher power of the program that kept him sober. It was a lower bar to believe that if there was a god, it wasn't himself, and the only miracle required was to keep Doyle sober and orderly, reasonably happy and able, and living life on life's terms. Whether this was the God of the Universe and Creation and the Loaves and Fishes, the One that parted the sea to save the chosen people or flooded the world to get a do-over or cured the paralytics and lepers and put the ear back on the centurion hardly mattered to Doyle. He hadn't had a drink in years and didn't miss it, and he seemed, though of no real consequence, more grateful than aggrieved by life and its indignities. This higher power could be a cocker spaniel or Bill the Dog, any being that could hold its liquor and keep Doyle sober. But sobriety was not, Doyle reasoned, a purpose worth living for, though it made living with purpose possible. And sober or not, easing between the numbered buoys, red on his right and green on his left, watching the loons and mute swans looking for shelter, he could think of no way in which he'd changed the outcome of anything for anyone since making this trip the year before.

He had not run for public office or swayed the vote on the millage or governance of the local library, he'd not recycled his paper products or composted his kitchen wastes or joined the ushers at any local church or lent a hand on any one of their most worthy projects. He'd survived the winter, gotten the boat out of storage and into the lake and onto the shore station in good form. He'd driven it a couple times around the near end of the lake, even across the lake and up the Cheboygan River to dinner at the Hack-Ma-Tack when someone visited. He'd eaten, slept, read, and watched TV, filled the dog bowl with

74 • NO PRISONERS

kibble and another with fresh water daily, watered a couple plants that Sally had kept alive against all odds. He continued to read his way through Sally's own library, and reckoned how long it would take to read his way through all the books she'd left him. He'd maintained another season of sobriety by the grace of whomever was in charge of things, and by the two or three meetings of AA he attended every week in church basements in the area. But he'd made, by his own calculation, no difference in the world at large or in the life of anyone that really mattered to him, himself included. And about the time that autumn was giving up its ghosts and winter was making known its intentions to assert its cold purposes in the coming weeks, Doyle would carefully get into the old Chris-Craft, turn on the blower, and start it up and back it out of the shore station and make it to the river mouth and up the river to the marina where they would store it for the dark and bitter months of winter in Michigan.

Still, hard to know which day to do it. Hard to know when the good days were at an end or merely taking some time off. "Where there's life, there's hope," he could remember saying, though whom he'd first heard it from was lost to him now. Who could say when hope was gone? How many Novembers with temps in the sixties or even seventies, the sun beaming if only for a few hours every day, had Doyle kicked himself for putting the boat away? He could have held on and held out for another triumph, a big fish, some old gal he could woo into taking a boat ride, one of the boys visiting, someone to show the lake to. Or for the solitary pleasure of being the only boat on a big lake late in the season, driving the shoreline from Grandview to Topinabee, up past Long Point and the Village to the mouth of the river that made its way into the Straits of Mackinac and the

Great Lakes, and the ultimate connection to the waters of the world. Or over to Red Pine Point and along the east side of the lake. There was a handful of year rounders and off seasoners who, like himself, kept track of the dates—the first snow, on one side or another of Halloween, the first freeze on the lake, most often in December, and the thaw, as early as Saint Patrick's Day, as late as mid-May. There were still those who watched when a boat crossed in front of their places in the autumn calm to try and figure out the motives and methods afloat before them.

Of course, there were the mid-Novembers when the snow came early and heavy and rimmed the lake with white and slumped the limbs of the fir trees and blew into drifts and closed the roads and remained on the ground for six full months before letting the lake out of its cold embrace. There were Novembers when the glaze of ice would form at the shoreline and widen its grip on the lake all day under gray skies and falling temps.

The Feasts of All Saints and All Souls became, over time, the outside limit of his chancing fate, the latest he would wait it out. It was late October, a year ago, when Sally died, after all the misery that cancer could exact from them. That last morning she was fitful with seizures and delusions and finally quiet. She was buried on Halloween. Doyle remembered the odd juxtaposition of casseroles and bouquets coming in the back door, left over from the wake and funeral luncheon, and trick-or-treaters coming to the front door in the gloaming of that awful day—wee ghosts and goblins, princesses and pirates, with pillowcases to be filled with treats. Sally had managed before she died, to get one of the boys, Liam, to decorate the porch.

He could still see Liam passing out candy and wiping his tears.

And driving the boat up the river mouth, now, "green right going, red right return," Doyle Shields couldn't help thinking about his father, dead these thirty-some years, and his long-widowed mother, dead a few weeks before Sally, and Sally herself, a year in the grave. That was a bad old year, his mother and his wife and all the other losses, saints and souls, which, like cormorants perched on the stumps in the river, like pallbearers awaiting their calls to duty, inhabited his journey and his dreams and visions. He was right and happily haunted, he thought; maybe there's something to it after all. Would he see the winter through to spring? Would he survive the cold and snow and isolation? He could die of a dozen causes, not least among them loneliness, which he felt keenly in the changing of seasons, the chill in the air, the industry of migrant birds and resident species.

The boat made its way up the river without a wake, protecting the habitat of waterfowl and otters, muskrat and beaver, egret and green pike, black bass and bullhead. Doyle sighed and zipped his jacket up, tight under his chin. He felt the chill.

He remembered the morning years ago he first saw this part of Michigan. He was taking a body up to the UP for burial for Noah Potti, who did all the Finnish and Swedish funerals in Detroit. Noah wasn't a regular account, but called on Doyle whenever he had a bad case—a withering cancer or car accident—anything that required more restorative art than the tidy old Lutherans who died in their sleep that Noah happily embalmed himself.

This kid was the worst case that Noah had seen, he told Doyle, when he called: "Split his damn face down the middle with a thirty-ought-six, the poor bastard, over a girl, of all things. But his people insist on seeing him." He'd done it out at the Finnish Camp on Loon Lake in Wixom and lay in that June heat for a couple of days before anyone thought to check on him. He'd been drinking and threatening his fellow campers for days before laying himself out on the bed, taking the gun barrel into his mouth, and pulling the trigger with his toe.

"Then a couple days in this heat and humidity. No sign of maggots yet, but there were plenty of flies," Noah told him. "I've got some kerosene."

It was 1957, Doyle remembered, because it was the first new car he ever had, the 1957 Plymouth station wagon that he had bought with money he borrowed from his mother-in-law. His first "dead wagon." Perfect for the paterfamilias and jobber, it diversified his offerings, adding removals and road trips to his trade embalming. Plus, he could put Sally and the kids in it for family outings and Sunday masses. He'd march them into St. Columban's like boot camp, in order of age and rank, preteen and toddling versions of young marines. Connor, the first and tallest, then Fiona, then Finbarr, and Liam, the youngest.

Multitasking, they'd call it now, he thought, this two-birds-with-one-stone approach, how the car was good for business and family. In a pinch he could haul units for Batesville on weekends from their warehouse in Southfield all over town. Shields Specialty Services, he called the enterprise, and titled out the Plymouth in Sally's name because the insurance was less. He had some pamphlets printed up and passed them out among his regular accounts, and mailed out some others to funeral homes in the metro area. He ran an ad in the trade journal published by the state association and had some first-call sheets made up with his twenty-four-hour phone number on it. "When You Require the Best, Call Triple S," was the slogan that appeared at the bottom in italics. It came to him doing a double post one night for Al Desmond at the Highland Park place. In the fullness of time, he'd hire young embalmers straight out of the mortuary school—the best and brightest, he called them—guys like himself who wanted no part of dealing with widows and orphans and the newly bereaved, nor had they the connections to finance nor ambition to start up their own funeral homes. They didn't want to be indentured to brick and mortar. They traveled light with their embalming kits and were glad to pay Doyle his 15 percent for keeping them working all over town. They knew how to tend to the dead at a moment's notice and at all hours and preferred the stillness of the prep room and the corpse to the glad-handing and mindless blather required upstairs at the front door or the back office or the bank or Rotary. Doyle was a trade embalmer and jobber. He could repair most damage done to a body but had no appetite or patience for the care of the living. He was a frontline guy, but he wanted nothing to do with being in charge. His name on a pad of first-call sheets was OK, but he did not want to be the boss or have his name on a sign. He could get a body out of the county morgue, prepped and dressed and laid out before evening calling hours, but he didn't want to upsell caskets or burial vaults or urns. He didn't want to worry over payroll or vacation schedules or cash flow or property tax. He didn't want the bankers or lawyers or sales reps or headaches that came with a brick-and-mortar enterprise. He wanted to show up, pitch in, do his part, and get paid and on his way. For funeral directors, reputation was everything, their standing in the community, the "generations of compassionate care." For Doyle Shields, there was none of that. He didn't have to deal with the living. And the dead, he was fond of telling Sally, don't care. The worst that can happen has already happened. Whatever Doyle did was more good than harm. There were no complaints or unreasonable demands.

"I never heard a dead guy say, 'I'd rather the blue pinstripe suit or penny loafers or roses or mums or 'Amazing Grace.'

They are entirely mum on the subject of personal preference. They just don't care."

He drove Black and brown bodies back to home places in the Virginias and Carolinas for the House of Diggs, well-to-do WASPs back to graveyards in the east for the Hamilton Company, hillbillies back to Appalachia and Harlan County, Kentucky, for Frank Bird in Walled Lake. "Walltucky," they called it, they were so thick on the ground. They'd all come north for good-paying jobs at Wixom Assembly and Pontiac Motors. He'd drive Yoopers back to the Upper Peninsula, first generation Irish and Finnish and Swedes who'd come from that strange country north of the Straits of Mackinac where they worked the copper mines.

Noah had hired him to drive the poor client up to Copper Harbor for graveside services and burial. The Lutherans would have a funeral for him downstate, but he was to be taken back to the family plot up north for military honors and burial. Doyle was to read a psalm, say amen, and nod to the honor guard, who'd do taps and fold the flag and do three rifle volleys more or less in unison. The downstate pastor had written out Psalm 51 for Doyle to say to the assembled. It all seemed easy enough, and the pay was good. In addition to the mileage and per diem and his professional fee, he'd get the little stipend for the clergy stand-in at the graveside service. And he'd make a little vacation out of it, early in June as it was. He took his boys out of school and brought them along for the ride, telling Sally to tell the nun that they'd learn more on the road trip than they would in school. Connor was ten and Finbarr eight at the time. He hoped they'd keep him awake on the road, what with their endless questions and curiosities. Liam was too labor intensive and still wet the bed; besides, he told him, the front seat was only big enough for three of them. Fiona must have already made known her discomfort with corpses. Doyle couldn't remember her on any of those road trips. Her long estrangement from what she called her "family of origin" kept her a schoolgirl in her father's memory. She had come when they removed her mother's lung, but she made a point of getting out of there after the doctor came out to tell them they thought they got it all. She had mostly sent cards after that, for birthdays and Christmas and get-well-soons, but otherwise had managed to keep her distance. At Sally's funeral she did not sit with them or say anything, and she never turned up at the church after the burial for the luncheon the sodality had prepared. Some few months later, she drove out to California and leapt off the Golden Gate Bridge to her death. Doyle got her home, her body anyway, to let her go again.

The boat was approaching the point in the river where the freeway, I-75, crossed over it. Two overpasses, one northbound and one southbound, made the old inboard echo off the concrete walls as the traffic sped by overhead.

Fiona's suicide remained to Doyle a vexing mystery, a pool of sorrows that always beckoned him toward a swampland of dark ruminations, of what-ifs and if-onlies where Fiona was concerned, so he tried to think about the '57 Belvedere station wagon with its tinny dashboard and whitewall tires and fold-down back seats that made room for the casket, a cloth octagon that Noah had donated because he was doing the whole job for what the VA paid and what the church could collect for the poor man who had served his country honorably, worked hard for his family, then went astray, according to Pastor Allwardt, who reminded Doyle to read the psalm slowly, like poetry, he told him, and to enunciate and articulate it and let it sink in among those who were hearing it when they assembled at the grave.

"Have mercy upon me, O God, according to thy loving kindness: according unto the multitude of thy tender mercies blot out my transgressions."

Pastor Allwardt said it from memory, enunciating slowly, letting the words work out their syllables in a way that made Doyle think of the holy.

"I did the Gettysburg Address in school," Doyle had assured the pastor. "I came second in the declamation contest."

"A competent Turk," the pastor had said, to which Doyle tilted his head like a dog to a strange noise.

Noah had given Doyle enough cash for the road—meals and rooms, tolls and ferryboat fares across the straits and back. He gave him directions from Houghton, a check for the sexton and gravediggers, a tip for the military honor guard, a copy of the death certificate, and the burial-transit papers in case there were any questions en route. He had two days to get there. The service was set for Saturday afternoon in Houghton—family and a few friends and, of course, the military.

These were the days, in the middle fifties, before Eisenhower built the interstates, and six hundred miles over surface roads would require steady operations. And Doyle could remember pulling away from Potti's place, a certain pride at sitting behind the wheel of a brand new shiny black wagon beside two freckle-faced boys in matching blue button-down shirts and blue school trousers and blue school ties with a cooler of apples and tuna fish sandwiches on the floor of the front seat, the windows open and June bright and blue out before them as he made his way north on Telegraph Road, past Pontiac to Dixie Highway, picking up Saginaw Street just south of Flint, thence through Saginaw, Bay City, Midland, and Clare, where he picked up US-27 past Houghton Lake, past Grayling, through Hartwick Pines, past Otsego Lake, and into Gaylord, where they stopped for a chocolate malt, and pressed on through Vanderbilt and Wolverine to Indian River, where they rented a cabin for the night at Indian River Motel and Cabins on the Sturgeon River that ran, in due course, into Burt Lake, which connected by the Indian River to Mullett Lake, all part of an inland waterway between the big lakes named for John Mullett and William Burt, who had surveyed the area before the Civil War, a thing he read about in a paragraph on the back of the menu at Christopher's Restaurant, where he and the boys had dinner before getting back to the cabin and hitting the hay.

How, he sometimes asked himself, could the name of the restaurant they ate a lackluster meal at all those years ago remain accessible flotsam in the rivers of his mind, whereas much about his sons' boyhoods had become a blur. Why do we remember the meaningless and forget the profound? How he had backed the Belvedere wagon up to the curb outside the motel room door and checked all the locks lest anyone tamper with the casket or the corpse inside, but forgot to roll the open windows up, so that the nightlong rain had drenched the seats by morning.

"Have mercy upon me, O God, according to thy loving kindness . . ." He still had traces of the fifty-first psalm, which he had endeavored to memorize before he got to Houghton. And though he lacked the confidence to do it from memory, there's where most of its verses lodged, so that over the nearly sixty years since Pastor Allwardt had written it out for him, he had many times invoked a portion of it. The page of the pastor's impeccable script was framed and hanging over his bed. Some mornings he read it aloud.

"Against thee, thee only, have I sinned, and done this evil in thy sight . . ."

"Purge me with hyssop, and I shall be clean."

"Create in me a clean heart, O God; and renew a right spirit within me."

"Deliver me from blood guiltiness, O God."

Doyle could still picture himself astraddle the crapper in the riverside cabin in Indian River, reciting the psalm in hopes that he'd have it by heart in time.

It was a hand-drawn For Sale sign the following morning, just north of Indian River, south of Topinabee, that turned Doyle off the Straits Highway onto a dirt road that wound back to what another sign called Grandview Beach Rd. He liked the sound of Grandview—it reminded him of Mountain View or Montevista, which was the street on which he'd grown up in a brick bungalow in northwest Detroit. By the time he got to the end of the road, where he could see the lake and the road circled back, he could see that the road came by the name honestly.

"Are we gonna buy it?" Connor asked, when his father took out a pad of paper and wrote down the phone number. "I'll bet the lake is full of perch."

"Maybe someday, son," Doyle had told him. "Your mother would love it here, I'm sure."

On they went past Topinabee and Cheboygan, up the Straits Highway to the State Dock at Mackinaw City, where they waited in their cars with other pilgrims for the ferry to make the crossing. The town was packed out with workers building the bridge that would span the four-mile divide between Michigan's Lower and Upper Peninsulas. There were stories in the daily papers about the builders' progress. There was a sense, that decade after the war, that they all stood, there at the tip of the mitt, Doyle called it, on the brink of a future where no expanse or expense could keep them from their American Dream. They had won the war. They had bombed the Germans and the Japanese out of competition with the Motor City, and the arsenal of democracy that had turned out tanks and dozers, bombers and Corsairs, was cranking out new Chevys and Caddies and Lincolns and Fords that looked to Doyle like rocket ships—bright chrome and fins and multicolored. Even his dead wagon glistened in the bright sun, hot and humid, but luminous compared to the squat black cars before the war.

Out on the water they could see the glistening behemoth that worked the straits between Mackinaw City and St. Ignace, making its way with its cargo of cars and trucks and people. When it opened its great jaws and stuck out its tongue, dozens of cars and their drivers disgorged from the dark interior for their onward journeys south. Then the northbound pilgrims and their cars drove forward, parking bumper-to-bumper in rows. Connor and Finbarr had already sweated through their clothes with the excitement and anticipation of their first adventure over water. Doyle had taken them on the Boblo Island Ferry and rented boats for panfishing on Orchard Lake, but never before had they seen a ship like this, or water like this, or offshore islands.

Once parked, Doyle locked his car lest anyone tamper with his cargo, and took the boys up to the deck, where they counted seagulls diving for fish, and then the huge double-ender set off. It was a hazy blue day, but they could see the islands, Bois Blanc to the east, and Mackinac, with the white patch of what Doyle told his boys was the Grand Hotel.

"The morticians have their annual meetings there. Maybe I'll take you one of these years. You'd have to ride bikes or horses, though, no cars allowed."

Smaller boats were working the water between them. In the distance they saw the edge of the UP, to which none of them had ever been.

On the deck of *The Vacationland*, Doyle flashed back to the deck of the LST he had boarded on Christmas Day of '43 in Milne Bay to make for Cape Gloucester. The scent of brine and the taste of danger and the false bravado of the other teenagers and their lethal weaponry, it was, like *The Vacationland*, nearly four hundred feet long, seventy feet at the beam, its gaping jaws gobbled up hundreds of humans and vehicles and haulage in hold below, and he was nineteen and all the sea miles and land miles and preparing for combat from northwest Detroit to the Dampier Straits, to wait in reserve until New Year's Day, afloat offshore of Yellow Beach 2 to reinforce the Seventh Regiment and clear the Japanese from Borgen Bay. Destroyers were pummeling the beach with their big guns, while bombers worked the interior.

Why, he kept asking himself, did men have to go so far out of their way to savage one another in the waging of war? Could they not have agreed upon other tests and locales? The old-timers from Guadalcanal had filled the younger marines with stories of horrible suffering and privation.

"The Japs don't know what it means to surrender," he was told by his gunny sergeant. "Wounding one of them is only half the battle. They're coming after you until you are dead or they are. And take your atabrine. Malaria's no picnic." They were cautioned about crocodiles, falling trees, poisonous snakes, pythons and rats, spiders the size of pumpkin pies. It seemed to Doyle a more hospitable battleground could have been located nearer to home. He had to keep calculating the day and the time it was back home. The Feast of Stephen in New Guinea was Christmas back home. His parents and his sister gathered in the living room on Montevista, the tree bedecked with ornaments and tinsel and sparkling with colored lights, his father walking down the block to midnight mass at

St. Francis DeSales, then returning to put things under the tree and eat the cookies and milk they'd all left out for Santa.

Between Christmas and New Year's he had the week to cool his heels aboard the troop transport and worry about the future. He had never felt so utterly alone, and he wished he could talk to his father. He didn't know if he could kill a man. He feared that he would be killed himself, alone, a long way from home. He feared he might not rise to the occasion, that he might dishonor the corps or his own sense of duty. He wanted his father and mother to tuck him in, to swaddle him in the safety of home. He wanted to sleep soundly and not alone, like the picture on the cover of the magazine his mother sent him, safe and sound, his parents keeping watch, or the guardian angel they said was watching too.

The ship he was on was crossing dark blue water, far from home, about to take him to an unknown geography. He wanted to acquit himself honorably, in a way that would make his father proud. His father, who'd given up drinking and smoking in a deal he made with God to bring Doyle home to him safely.

He went to the bar and had a beer, and then another with a glass of whiskey, because he was shaking a little and Connor looked frightened.

It was Connor who came and got him.

"We're almost there, Dad," he said, meaning the docks at St. Ignace in the Upper Peninsula, and Doyle smoked another Lucky Strike and went down to their dead wagon with its corpse in the back and his boys up front. He could feel the little buzz off the shots and the beers he'd downed during the half-hour ferry crossing.

After lunch in St. Ignace, they headed for Ishpeming, and Doyle was giving out facts about the Ojibwe and Wyandot people and the battles they'd fought over control of the straits and the priest and explorer Fr. Marquette who was buried at St. Ignace, though he had died downstate at the mouth of a river they would name for him. But what Connor and Finbarr wanted to know about was the huge bridge under construction that seemed to connect one part of Michigan to the other. They had seen it waiting for the ferry to come and seen it from the deck of *The Vacationland*, spanning the five-mile stretch of the straits. It had huge towers and cables, and there were trucks and machinery all over it.

"It's supposed to open at the end of the year," Doyle told them. They were both staring at the massive bridge in the distance over the casket out the rear window of the Plymouth wagon as it motored westward along Route 2.

"Turn around, lads," he told them, when he'd run out of information about the so-called Mighty Mac with which to educate them. "Watch where we're going, never mind where we've been." But the road ahead seemed utterly vacant, bounded by forests, as the long blue edge of Lake Michigan on their left bottomed out a few hundred miles south in Chicago, where Doyle had shipped out from in November of '42 and shipped back home through in early '46.

Now, after a decade of domesticity, making babies with the redheaded girl of his dreams, who'd written him so faithfully throughout the war and accepted the ring he had his father purchase with money Doyle'd saved and sent home from the measly stipend—sixty-five dollars and change every month for risking the rest of his life—he thought of himself as on his way. He provided and protected and kept making progress. He'd married his better, went to school on the GI Bill, passed his exams, and got his embalmer's license. They'd gotten out of the apartment over Bill Vasu's old funeral parlors in Highland Park and bought a newly built brick bungalow in Birmingham. He had his marriage, a mortgage, his car, and his junior partners with the missus. He'd finished off the attic into two new bedrooms and a half bath, added a garage and family room to the little Cape Cod on Banbury Street, and was sending the kids to parochial school. Sally even had a girl in on Wednesdays to iron and change beds and do the laundry, and Doyle was pretty much his own boss, bringing home the bacon through honest, gainful labor of a sort that he'd been well prepared for by the US Marines.

Still, more than ever, he seemed haunted by the war, lost at sea in the South Pacific, and Doyle was only beginning to see how it had shaped and changed him.

Doyle let the boys nap as he drove northwest along US-2, which wound along the north shore of Lake Michigan. They got past Naubinway and turned north at M-77, the road taking them through Germfask and through Seney to where Sally's mother's father had opened a bar. He woke the boys to show them where the "lace curtain" side of the family had come from.

"The Graces were upper-crust people, to be sure, boys," Doyle told them. "Rely on your Nana to tell you so. And the Duffys with them, to the manor born."

"And the Shieldses?" Connor asked.

"Ah well, now, Connor, there's another crowd entirely. Shanty Irish, sure haven't we the shanty back home?"

They turned westbound north of Seney on M-28, driving through Shingleton to Munising, where Sally's father, P. V. Duffy, had come from. On they drove along the south shore of Lake Superior, Doyle telling them stories about their grandfather hunting and fishing and outsmarting bears in the deep woods and waterways of this strange country.

"How did he and Nana meet?" Connor asked, though he'd only been five when the old Yooper died, and Doyle reckoned could hardly remember him.

"They met downstate at Ann Arbor, where they both went to school. Oh, brainy people, I'll give them that. You get that cleverness through your mother's side. She was something of a music prodigy, your Nana, and Pop Duffy played clarinet in the marching band. Maybe she fell for a man in uniform." Doyle liked sinking a little barb into the belly of matters of fact.

They gassed up in Marquette, and Doyle went into the bar of the Northland Hotel next door and had a beer and bought the boys a vanilla phosphate, which they shared. It was just after four, and the day was good for five more hours of good light anyway. And they were within range of Houghton, just north of which the burial would be. So, inspecting the map before hitting the road, he told the boys they'd be making a little detour to Ishpeming to see an old buddy from the Corps.

Whether it was the long haul, the water crossing, or the endless patter of Doyle's tutelage, by the time they pulled into Ishpeming, the boys were sleeping. He got a room at the Chippewa Hotel off the main drag, got some grilled cheese sandwiches in them, and put them to bed with the TV on, then went down to the bar, where he asked the bartender whether Wayne Primo Ally still lived in town.

"Ol WPA? We don't see much of him anymore. He's living with his folks out at the lake, hunting and fishing and making trinkets for the tourists. Arrowheads and moccasins."

"Do they have a phone?"

The bartender was already dialing their number and stretched the phone to Doyle at the bar, and when a woman answered, Doyle asked for Wayne. Half an hour later the tall

Ojibwe came through the door in his undershirt and dungarees and sat next to Doyle, who was on to his second shot and beer.

Wayne Primo Ally was a member of the Bad River Band of the Lake Superior Tribe of Chippewa Indians. He spoke Ojibwe and lived on the Bad River Reservation on the southeast end of the Keweenaw Peninsula and looked a little like the statue of Old Ish, a Chippewa brave, in the square in the center of Ishpeming.

"What brings you to the UP, Corporal?"

"I've a burial in Houghton tomorrow. Just passing through. Thought I'd see if you're keeping body and soul together. Never had a chance to thank you, after . . ."

"Thank me? For what, Doyle. I coulda killed you."

"That Ka-Bar wound was my ticket out of China. I got points for a 'service-related wound' because I was on duty at the time. You were out of your skull."

"I know I was, Doyle. Goddamn drink—the marines taught me two things. Booze and murder. But I've given up. I'm on the wagon since '52. It was killing me. Or woulda killed a bunch of Yoopers by now."

The bartender had poured a cup of coffee and a glass of water and put them on the bar in front of Wayne. He put a shot and a beer in front of Doyle. Wayne offered Doyle a cigarette. They smoked and laughed and settled in as if it hadn't been twelve years since they'd seen each other. Doyle thought it odd that they could take up their talk as if nothing had put any distance between them.

"Do ya hear from any of the old crowd?"

"There's a few up at the rez who get together at the VFW hall in L'Anse. None from our outfit. Some Second Marines who were at Tarawa. A couple from Iwo. A good few from Okinawa. They drink and tell stories. They are all disabled in one way or another. I keep to myself. I can't drink with them. And the story they keep telling themselves is bullshit. There was no glory. No honor. Not for red men. We went to kill yellow men for white men, then came home to the same shit. They gave us drink and a few dollars, and we traded our lives and honor."

Doyle ordered another beer and a double shot of V. O. and winced after he'd downed the whiskey.

"Hard to know what to make of it now, Wayne. Just trying to put one foot in front of the other and stay on track. If I start down that other road, it's a long way back."

Some nights all he heard was "Maline! You die!" and the Japanese are roaring over the ridge down on the line that he is holding with Billy Swinford Smith and Donald Crescent Coe and Wayne Primo Ally is his assistant gunner and runners keep bringing boxes of ammo and by the time the night is over they've gone through eight boxes, a thousand rounds, and still the worst is yet to come.

Other nights, after he'd had enough to drink, sipping himself into a stupor of sedation, he could change the soundtrack to Jo Stafford singing "Haunted Heart," which he played over and over on the record player some nights after Sally and the kids had all gone to bed, and he'd sit up sipping V. O. on Banbury Street and think of Maddy, his lover in Melbourne, and those few blissful weeks before they shipped out to New Guinea and New Britain and the actual war.

Maddy would be his first. He was nineteen, not yet a killer, and he loved her for it, even if at an impossible distance. He never wrote or phoned or went back, but he knew, of course, that he'd have gladly considered it, if Sally hadn't quit dating Rodney after his dad took over the ring by proxy and got her to say yes to the future they planned, and if the survivors of New Britain—the one out of four of them who weren't killed or wounded—hadn't been dumped on that hellhole Pavuvu, if they'd gone back to Melbourne instead, he might have found Maddy again and settled down with her or had her come to the States like so many of her countrywomen would. It was a thing that always made Doyle wonder about the theory he had first learned, "for every Jack a Jill."

Maybe it was even more random than that, a series of contingencies and happenstances that landed him and Sally in the same bed, in the same room, in the same house, in the same place, after all the bullets he'd dodged and bayonets and mortars and blades, both of them in the same happy and fruitful marriage that lasted all of forty-three years, not counting the years of their courtship and engagement.

"We were all just whored out for the violence in us," Wayne said. "Our willingness to kill and die for the cause, whatever the cause, we were nothing but whores for the Corps. No different than those poor women on the brothel boats in Tientsin harbor. We'd kill and risk being killed for less. We let them pimp us out in trade for what? A place at the bar at the Legion Hall? The honor roll? The VFW? The grave?"

Wayne Primo Ally, Doyle thought, was badly damaged. Still, try as he might, he couldn't rise to a contrary argument. What his old buddy said rang true. He had felt like fodder for a killing machine that took young men to the far reaches of the world and set them down proximate to the young men of other nations, freighted with their own lethality, and let them go at it until someone quit or declared victory or gave up the war.

Wayne Primo Ally seemed like he still had a foot in the sucking mud of Cape Gloucester or in the black sands of Peleliu or on the high cliffs of Okinawa. God knows, by the time he made China he was certifiably nuts. And he damn near killed Doyle with his craziness. He got by now on poaching game, gill netting, and growing pot, which he sold to the students at Michigan Tech and NMU. He wanted to talk to Doyle about what he'd done.

"You could've had me drummed out, Doyle. What I did was horrible."

"We both made it home, Wayne. There's something to be said for that. There's a lot that didn't."

"I might have killed you. It was pure reflex; I was blind drunk."

Wayne Primo Ally, who in any other life might have risen through the ranks of Ojibwe braves to lead his own band of Chippewa through the woods and river tributaries of Gitche Gumee, went on to tell Doyle of how his soul had been hobbled since the night in January thirteen years before when he and elements of the Fifth Marines, Doyle Shields among them, survived the battle for Aogiri Ridge—a jungle rise hidden by dense foliage where the last of the Japanese infantry at that western end of the island of New Britain were defending their weapons cache and supply route to their headquarters at Rabaul. That this ridge and the creek that ran along its northwestern perimeter into Borgen Bay appeared on none of the maps that anyone had simply underscored for Wayne the sense that he had that whoever was in charge of this chaos had conspired with the gods of war to send young men to their miserable deaths in pursuit or defense of the godforsaken. It was mindless mayhem and random killing and not the defense of liberty or defeat of the evil empire or revenge for Pearl Harbor or a noble cause. It was, rather, a decision taken by the higher ups—the old, the rich, the white, the powerful, to rid the world of the young, the poor, the colored and powerless by pitting them against one another over places no one would ever see again in trade for idiot glory and faux nobility. Suicide Creek, as they gamely called the little river where so many of them died or were wounded trying to

94 • NO PRISONERS

get across under the strafing fire of the Japanese bunkers tucked into the high banks on the other side, and Walt's Ridge, as they would rename Aogiri, after Lt. Colonel Lewis Walt, who helped muscle a howitzer up through the mud and enemy fire, thereby saving K Company's bacon, were where Wayne Primo Ally had slipped his moorings and gone adrift.

His soul was scarred. He was never right after the night of the ninth and morning of the tenth of January 1944.

He was a supply runner in Doyle's squad of the machine gun section of the weapons platoon of Company K of the Third Battalion of the Fifth Regiment of the First Division of the Expeditionary Forces of the Marine Corps of the United States of America. He carried two metal boxes of thirty-caliber cartridge belts, two hundred and fifty rounds per box, with a carbine strapped over his shoulder, a .45 pistol he'd brought from home, and the combat knife he'd been issued at Camp Elliott strapped in its sheath to his belt behind the canteen. His job was to keep the ammo coming, a job he did with PFC Benjamin A. Romero Jr. and Pvt. Anton J. Haas Jr. in league with Corporal Horace E. Goodwin, their able squad leader, and Corporal Louis L. Schafer and PFC Doyle Shields, their gunner and assistant gunner, respectively.

Wayne was saying these names, there at the bar, as they'd appear on a manifest or roll call, and each of them corresponded to a face Doyle could see in his own version of that horrific night. Doyle remembered the typed sheet of their names he'd made on Okinawa, the whole platoon, a machine gun and a mortar section, each made up of three full squads, six men to each machine gun squad, five to each mortar, plus two sergeants to serve as section leaders—Harry J. Rader was his, John Marmet led the mortar squads, and the gunny sergeant and second lieutenant who led the platoon and two buck privates who did their bidding. He remembered wanting to remember them, and the handwritten notations he'd made next to each one: "wounded leg," "malaria," "dead," "rot," along with the weapons they carried, "TSMG," "M-1," "carbine," ".45." He nodded to the barman to refresh their drinks and wondered if he should check on the boys sleeping upstairs or the corpse in the car in the parking lot outside, but Wayne Primo Ally was somewhere else now, deep in the holes they'd dug in on the ridge, just below the crest of it, and Doyle wasn't going to leave him alone. It was pitch dark and getting noisy.

"Maline! You die!" and "Raider, raider, why you no fire?" And beginning at around half past one, they came screaming and howling, "Bahn*zi*!" And the rain, torrential and permanent, adding to the noise and the long-range artillery coming from God knows where blowing up more or less in our faces. Lonnie Howard blown away. And Tex shot dead, and that's when Doyle saw Wayne Primo Ally slashing his Ka-Bar knife at shadows because except for some silhouettes when the shells lit things up, all they could do was aim at the voices and Doyle knew he now occupied the story Wayne Primo Ally was telling about that godawful night in '44 when the Japanese kept coming in wave after wave of Banzai charging.

After the third or fourth charge, they were out of ammo— six boxes of it, fifteen hundred rounds, and the cross fire Doyle and Billy Swinford Smith on the left flank had kept up after their gunners got hurt wouldn't be able to repel another. That's when Wayne Primo Ally was dispatched, as the fastest and fiercest of the supply runners on hand, to head to the command post fifty yards back in a mangrove glade and grab a couple boxes of belts. That's when it seemed to Doyle like forever, waiting for Wayne or the enemy to charge and him with his M-1 and bayonet against half-crazed Asians with their swords and madness.

96 • NO PRISONERS

That's when Doyle began to reckon his life was about to be over for good, that death was little more than running out of ammo on a ridge in a monsoon in the middle of nowhere while the woman of his dreams was back in Detroit on that side of the world where it was still the day before, or maybe in Melbourne, ready and willing, it hardly mattered now because in just a few minutes it would all be over. He could hear the voices over the rise, the low din of them beginning to work themselves into the frenzy of blood lust and futility that would get them up and over the ridge again, for closer combat than any of them had ever planned.

That's when Wayne Primo Ally reappeared, huffing and puffing from his race through the dark and the rain and the rear echelon to return with two boxes of ammo in time to ready for the fifth and last attack. Four minutes to spare, Colonel Walt would tell them later. "All the time in the world for my marines."

It was the half-light of predawn on January 10, when the shooting was over and the screaming and running and artillery, into which Wayne Primo Ally and Doyle Shields emerged from their hole with Julius Labeau, Bob Marsden from theirs, and those few survivors along their front lines to see the field of enemy troops laid out before them—a tableau vivant of corpses and corpses to be. Carrying their M-1s with bayonets affixed, they stepped from body to body, checking for souvenirs and signs of life. In the former case they would remove them—the flags or photographs or documents or rings—and in the latter case they'd work their bayonets under the sternum and into the heart, thereby abiding by the Old Breed's decision, observed since the horrors of Guadalcanal, to take no prisoners.

This was the morning, according to the booze-sodden Chippewa slobbering his story to Doyle Shields in the hotel bar in Ishpeming years later, this was the morning of his moral injury, made the more permanent with every wounded soldier he dispatched, leaning on his rifle to deepen the blade of his bayonet in the enemy chest. The wheezing they made, like the moaning bellows of blacksmithing works, and the gurgling of their final demise was replicate in what he could hear in nature, so that he never forgot that morning's horrors and triumph. If there were two hundred and fifty bodies in the tableau, near half of them needed further assistance with death. Not one of them gave it a second thought. No surrender was the rule the enemy lived by. No prisoners, the code of the US Marines.

It was the first time someone told Doyle that his own long-hidden guilt made sense, that there was something evil about what they'd done that morning in the mangroves, stepping from body to body, checking for signs of life or grotesque trophies of their victory. The hatred and deep contempt he bore toward the enemy was giving way to the gathering sense that they were, like Doyle and his fellow marines, fodder for the same forces of war that none of them had any control over. They were all victims of the same machine of mayhem, the interests of nations and leaders and influencers long distanced from the fields of battle where men like Doyle followed orders that degraded and defiled themselves and their likewise powerless enemies. He'd become evil and animal and performed outrages to survive. He had tried his best to keep it deeply tucked away from the world he now occupied, so wholesome and blessed with Sally and their children. A boozy night with Wayne Primo Ally brought all the darkness forth again. Blood and violence, peril and fear made brethren of all combatants, regardless of flags and nations, faith claims and causes.

Doyle Shields didn't sleep well that night, fitful with vivid, vexing dreams, and he woke groggy and hungover and summoned the boys to hit the road for the last hundred miles to

98 • NO PRISONERS

Houghton. Coming into town, in accordance with something he'd heard in mortuary school, he looked for the grove of cedars and Scotch pines that uniformly signaled graveyard to him. Once all of the players had assembled, the honor guard and American Legion and the locals who had known the corpse or his people, Doyle stood at the head of the grave and read out the words of Psalm 51, as Pastor Allwardt had instructed him,

> *Have mercy upon me, O God, according to thy lov-*
> *ingkindness: according unto the multitude of thy*
> *tender mercies blot out my transgressions.*
> *Wash me thoroughly from mine iniquity, and cleanse*
> *me from my sin.*
> *For I acknowledge my transgressions: and my sin is*
> *ever before me.*
> *Against thee, thee only, have I sinned, and done this*
> *evil in thy sight: that thou mightest be justified when*
> *thou speakest, and be clear when thou judgest.*
> *Behold, I was shapen in iniquity; and in sin did my*
> *mother conceive me.*
> *Behold, thou desirest truth in the inward parts: and in*
> *the hidden part thou shalt make me to know wisdom.*
> *Purge me with hyssop, and I shall be clean: wash*
> *me, and I shall be whiter than snow.*
> *Make me to hear joy and gladness; that the bones*
> *which thou hast broken may rejoice.*
> *Hide thy face from my sins, and blot out all*
> *mine iniquities.*
> *Create in me a clean heart, O God; and renew a*
> *right spirit within me.*
> *Cast me not away from thy presence; and take not thy*
> *holy spirit from me.*

*Restore unto me the joy of thy salvation; and uphold
me with thy free spirit.*

*Then will I teach transgressors thy ways; and sin-
ners shall be converted unto thee.*

*Deliver me from bloodguiltiness, O God, thou God
of my salvation: and my tongue shall sing aloud
of thy righteousness.*

*O Lord, open thou my lips; and my mouth shall shew
forth thy praise.*

*For thou desirest not sacrifice; else would I give it:
thou delightest not in burnt offering.*

*The sacrifices of God are a broken spirit: a broken
and a contrite heart, O God, thou wilt not despise.*

*Do good in thy good pleasure unto Zion: build thou
the walls of Jerusalem.*

*Then shalt thou be pleased with the sacrifices of righ-
teousness, with burnt offering and whole burnt offering: then shall they offer bullocks upon thine altar.*

Then the honor guard did the rifle volleys, sounding more like the
turkey shoot than the drill squad. Then the flag, the taps and sa-
lutes. They gave the shell casings to the dead man's family. And
then the pallbearers lowered the box on ropes, while those gathered
tossed flowers and sang a common doxology, then turned from
the grave and walked away. The brief obsequies were attended by
a swarm of black flies, drawn to the sweat and the perfume and
putrefaction, the faithful waving them away from their ears and
ankles. Bees buzzed amid the gladioli. Ants, dislodged by the sexton's shovel, returned to their industry in the earth. Doyle waited
till the grave was closed, paid the sexton, and called to the boys,
who were chasing a hatch of mayflies at the edge of the graveyard.

And here now these decades since, easing the nose of his old Chris-Craft into its berth at the City Marina, Doyle Shields could not shake the sense that sooner or later its moorings would be permanent, the dry rot would get it, much as the bad heart or blood sugar or prostate would get him in the end, and get him to his permanent grounding. They were, as he had read once, all terminal cases.

Time to ready for the inevitable end. Hadn't he had a grave dug for Bill, back in the woods behind his place, on the better than even chance that the winter would take him? And not wanting to dig through the frosthold of winter, he'd had his man dig and cover a grave with a sheet of plywood against the day when old Bill quit managing the dog's life and times. Maybe he'd be chewing a soup bone out in the snow and simply not get up. Doyle prayed he'd get such a death. No drama, no alarms or surprises, just easing into the nothingness or some-thingness as into a bed of fresh linens and good pillows for a long anticipated, well-deserved slumber.

Here on the Feast of All Souls, having kept his boat in the water longer than any of his neighbors, he had managed to make it up the river on a day that was windless and coolish but not without its attributes. Doyle was heavy-laden with all that was mortal before him and about him and out in front of him, the dead who occupied, he reckoned, a heaven or limbo or plu-perfect tense, or a piece of the sky from which they beckoned him to follow in his own good time. The bald trees, the brown-ing wetlands, the migration of waterfowl, the water clarity all pointed to an end of days.

Surely, that time would come. Its certainty shuddered in him as he looked at the old boat moored to its stumps under the roof boards of the marina. It looked like nothing so much as a coffin, opening its lightly bobbing embrace to the old man. Time to join his uncle, the dead priest, the Lindbergh baby, the boys he left dead in the South Pacific, Sally and the daughter who, if not entirely dead to him, was gone. Time to align with the dozens of friends and acquaintances, dead and buried or dead and burned, but gone and more or less forgotten. Time to take his allotted spot at Holy Sepulchre next to his dear dead wife, their dead daughter's ashes, the remains of neighbors and friends and perfect strangers. The weather was unmistakably changing. The light of days was shortening, the chill more needling, the forecast short of any relief. Time to get his affairs in order. To batten down the hatches. To ready himself for the longest haul.

He contemplated the instructions he might leave his sons and their children on the matter of his obsequies, his preferences and plans, but then it came to him that these were among the things that mattered least—the box, the blather, the accessories. And pending death meant an end to planning. The boys would tend to the essentials, he was confident. They would get him where he needed to go. His son had had his name cut into the stone at Holy Sepulchre in Section 24 that he would share with Sally. It was cut in stone: Doyle Shields 1924—awaiting only the final date. Maybe 2015? Had he another Christmas in him? 2020? He couldn't see himself at ninety-six. Still, hard to know. He knew where he was going and how he'd get there. One day in the none-too-distant future, as every generation and iteration of his species had since soon after the Creation eons ago, he would simply cease to be. There'd be a cause and contributing factors assigned to his case. November was in him with its penultimacy. The impenetrable chill of it spread, like the shelf of ice soon would from the shoreline out to the deep middle of the lake. It was good that he got the boat put away, the dock out of the water, the dog out of the weather, the outdoor furniture up on the porches, the fallen leaves raked and bagged and everything ready as it could be. He would use whatever time he had left to make known how life had been for him. In keeping with his promise to Sally, he was resolved to write it all down, how it had come to pass: his water crossings and river journeys, his voyages and adventures, their love and longing and correspondence through the worst of times, how he had come to be who and where and how he was. Was it meaning enough, a worthy purpose? He would leave it, like a guidebook, for his children and their children and hope that it would help them make some sense of their own coming and going in the sparkling future that, it hurt him to know and acknowledge, he would not share.

Chapter Three

PREPUCE

1 January 1990

It was the first of January that Doyle quit smoking. That first winter after Sally died, late in October, the year before. The blink of an eye, the moment and twinkling—as if it were yesterday, and there he was, in the film always flickering out in slow motion, the matinee version of his life and times, sometimes in living color, sometimes black and white, and there he is, stretched out in the old tub on New Year's morning, soaking in the bubbles, trying to work up some excitement and contemplating the Feast of the Circumcision.

Sr. Rose DeLourdes had always kept them alerted to the everyday feasts in their daily missals, and taught them to pray to the saint of the day for guidance and good counsel and something she called *continence*. By which, they gathered, she did not mean pissing the bed or shitting themselves. Though it had to do with their "nether regions." He had to hand it to Sr. Rose DeLourdes, she sensed what bedeviled the sixth-grade boys. And what would bedevil the old farts they would grow into, obsessed with their bladders and bowels, their eructations, ejaculations, emissions, and erections.

For most of the years of their marriage, Sally would give him one of those word-a-day calendars to keep on the desk. The idea was to use the daily word three or four times before lunch in the normal course of your morning rounds. He'd say *imbroglio*, or *codswallop*, and folks would roll their eyes a little, thinking to themselves, he must've got another of those vocabulary calendars for Christmas, but sure enough, he'd find himself talking way over his pay grade, and Sally liked that. And she liked the way it disappeared, one page with the day's date and the good word and its meaning, and on the back, a more fulsome explication of its etymology. How's that for a handful of calendar words? "One day at a time," she would say. "No need to get ahead of ourselves."

Continence, Doyle still said to himself; where is Sr. Rose De-Lourdes when we need her? Dead as a mackerel, he answers rhetorically. They're all dead—Sally, Major, the old nuns and priests, saints and sinners. And Sr. Rose, always telling the girls they were not to dress in such a way as to lead the boys into the "occasion of sin," which is, of course, all they ever thought of, such occasions, getting their hands on the fine new breasts taking shape under the uniform blouses of their classmates, safely ensconced in their brand new brassieres. Doyle always said *tits* back then but learned that girls didn't like being called *girls* and preferred that their chests be called *breasts*. But how that nun could make it sound like Saint Catherine of Siena, the sad, anorexic mystic who lived for years on the communion wafer she had every day, could relieve boys of their newfound urgency, is hard to know. Saint Catherine's feast day was at the end of April, and even in Michigan the winter was sufficiently banished by then that the whole sexy, muddy, miracle of mighty nature was pushing itself up through the soil, budding and busting loose—was there forsythia then?—

and chirping and shoving itself into being, and even the fourteenth-century Dominican looked fetching in our *Lives of the Saints* in the mauve-toned likenesses that occupied the page next to the little biographies of their holiness. There was Saint Catherine, in her halo and chaste habit, bearing the stigmata and a crown of thorns and holding a crucifix and sprig of lily whilst gazing on the nearly naked, crucified body of Christ with a look on her face of such longing and piety. And even though among her several patronages—firefighters, people ridiculed for piety, nurses, and sick people—there was one that said her intercession would save them all from "sexual temptation," it didn't entirely work on Doyle's crowd, whatever Sr. Rose DeLourdes prayed for with her beads. They were all mad-anxious to cop a feel, and, according to what Sally told him years later, one night well into their marriage when she'd had too much champagne punch at the K of C dance, the girls really wanted to be felt up too. She'd never have spoken so brazenly without the drink. And she was a cheap drunk. A glass of champagne, a whiskey sour, a rum and coke. She'd get giggly and chatty and fondling.

Of course, he wouldn't be lounging in the tub, smoking the last of his cigarettes and playing with himself to visions of his late wife in her girlish, preteen beauty if, by the grace of God, she were still alive. Still, a man has to conjure what he can. He let the ashes off the end of the smoke fall into the suds of bubble bath, then doused the hot tip, put it in the ashtray, and lit another. His limp member fell into the suds.

For years he'd been a closet smoker, ever since Sally quit. She used a rubber band around her wrist, and every time she felt like smoking, she would snap it. The little pain produced an "operant conditioning"—her words—against the impulse to light up another Pall Mall. Doyle felt it only fair to keep his continued smoking hidden from her. He went out to the garage, where he'd kept packs of Kent 100s hidden among the bicycles and garbage cans. He'd smoke in a hurry and try to wave the smoke away into the air and keep the smell of it off his clothing. He never smoked in the house or car or at the office. He was always outside, in a hurry and huddle. He'd say he was taking old Major out to do his business—their golden retriever—and once down the block a little he'd light up. So to lie there in the soapy water without a worry over who might catch him at it was oddly luxuriant, just one of the mixed blessings of bereavement. He was alone.

Saint Catherine hadn't much of a chance. Late April in northwest Detroit, in the hub of southeastern Lower Michigan, the light of the vernal equinox lengthening into the rest of the day, bright on the sides of the brick bungalows they all lived in—Sally on Eileen Street and Doyle on Montevista—under a canopy of elms and sugar maples, littering the air with their preleafiness, up and down the street. He could see that light now, and Sally in it, if he closed his eyes, angling its way through the tall windows of the classroom at St. Francis De-Sales, and the smell of chalk and Murphy's oil soap, as the afternoon edged toward liberation and all of the girls in their blue uniforms and white blouses and anklets and saddle shoes and the whiter still outlines of their satiny bras and the certain air of detachment they all suddenly adopted because there was some form of knowledge they had recently acquired, coincident with their new breasts, that none of the boys would ever have and it made them, however chaste, however determined they were not to be provocative in their manners and dress, all the more objects of desire, each and every one of them, and the look on sweet Saint Catherine's face as she contemplated the broken body of Christ, nailed to the cross, for the sake of our sins did nothing but fan the flames of that desire, thus, no doubt, her patronage of firefighters.

But April is a long way off on the first of January, and the snow everywhere and the bitter cold and the Feast of the Circumcision is one that Sr. Rose DeLourdes never mentioned in school. Of course, we'd still be on our Christmas break, not going back until the Epiphany—the little Christmas and the three kings that Sr. Rose DeLourdes celebrated more than the big one. But really, what's to celebrate about circumcision? How to make any sense of it at all? It always made Doyle wonder.

When he asked Fr. Clement about it—this was later, he was in high school, and everyone got a kick out of how uncomfortable it seemed to make the priest talk about penises and other body parts—he said it was probably best not to bring it up with the nuns but that the reason we celebrated "the octave of the birth of Christ," which meant eight days on from Christmas Eve, was that it was the first time Jesus's blood was spilled and therefore "the first episode in the story of our redemption." He was blushing when he told Doyle this. Somewhere Doyle'd seen a holy card with a painting of the incident replicated. The rabbi with his little knife, the infant with himself exposed, the helpful parents trying to hold him. And to say the look on our savior's face was, well, not exactly four square in favor of the proceedings would be the truth of it. Doyle's mother was a convert to "the one true faith," which she took instructions in before she could marry his father, and she had books at home that listed the rubrics and liturgical calendars and the various devotions and novenas and all the details of the magisterium.

Doyle had interrupted religion class to ask Fr. Clement about circumcision and the holy prepuce and how many churches claimed to have the relic, and the priest counseled Doyle to see him privately after class. He could call in at the rectory.

"As you yourself know, Mr. Shields, we are redeemed by the sacred body and blood of Christ, who loved us so much he died for our sins and rose from the dead and saved us from eternal damnation and left us the gift of the blessed sacrament."

"Yes, yes, Father, but why circumcision? What was so special about the end of a penis?"

"Of course, you have to understand, Doyle . . . ," he was turning bright red, "you have to understand it was the Law of Moses. It's all there in the letter of Paul to the Galatians . . . the Jews . . . the Gentiles . . . it's all there in Paul's epistles, a longish disquisition on the power of the law."

When he thought back on the episode, Doyle reckoned that priest got *disquisition*, whatever it meant, from a calendar. No telling which of the nuns might have given it to him. He'd learned all the churchy words at seminary—*cardinal, venial, transubstantiation*—but he took special joy in deploying words like *factotum* or *indefatigable* in the normal talk of the day. He'd pepper them throughout his Sunday sermons and stressed the importance of *etymology, exegesis,* and *hermeneutics,* which were words the curious could look up in their own good times.

"Yes, Father, of course, but why, I mean, who exactly, whose idea was it in the first place?"

"He writes elsewhere to the Corinthians or Ephesians, I cannot be certain, except that he broaches the topic with them of 'spiritual' circumcision. It's in the Bible."

"But whose idea was it at the start?"

"Idea, Doyle?"

"Yes. To slice the skin off the ends of little boys' penises in the first place?"

"Yes, of course, Mr. Shields, now I see . . ." He was beginning to sweat a little now, and he brought a white handkerchief from the sleeve of his cassock and wiped his forehead and removed his eyeglasses—the fragile, wire jobs with octagonal lenses—and gave them a quick wipe with the cloth, then returned them to their place on his face, wiped his pursed lips with the kerchief, returned it to the sleeve of his cassock, and proceeded.

"Of course, that would go back to the very beginning, to Abram or Abraham, as he was later called, as we call him now. God was always changing names like Simon to Peter for example, the Rock of the Church. Saul to Paul. So, it was with Abraham in the Book of Genesis. It is all in there, Doyle, how he had a dream and God spoke to him about how his wife Sarah was going to have a child, though she was herself a very old woman at the time, going on one hundred if I'm not mistaken, well past the age you'd expect such things, but Abram, that is Abraham, was told he'd be the father of the nation and his heirs would be as many as the stars in the firmament, or, shall we say, the sky."

Doyle reckoned that *firmament* was one of the calendar words until he went and read it all himself in Genesis, all the begat and begetting and the deal they made—God and Abraham when he was ninety-nine, that his ancient wife Sarah, whose name got changed from Sarai, would bear him a son, Isaac, and God would keep his testament with him so long as all of the kinsmen would be circumcised. Doyle wondered momentarily if Abraham had to look that up—circumcision—or if he knew exactly what God had in mind.

And there was the part that always had flummoxed him, how the scribes in charge of the Book of Genesis fell upon penis foreskin snipping as the sign of the deal between this little itinerant tribe in the desert and the Creator of the Universe. Why not a tattoo or cleft palate or pierced ear or eyebrow? Maybe a secret handshake like the Freemasons were said to have. Wouldn't that be sufficient for the Jews? How is it they went right for the penis?

110 • NO PRISONERS

Such was the nature of his contemplations that starlit, pre-dawn morning, twenty-some years ago now, the first of the year, the January after Sally died, lonesome and lazy and out-stretched in the bathtub, smoking with impunity, considering the uncircumcised end of his miserable dick, which he was trying to get stiff in his sudsy right hand, only to say that it might be a sign that he was still alive, if not the father of na-tions, at sixty-five, widowed and heartsore, sleepless with grief, that here at the opening of another year, another decade, the last of the twentieth century, the new year of the new life he'd been living without her, that he was nonetheless someone to be reckoned with—a man who, despite age and hard miles, type 2 diabetes and a broken heart, had a member in good working order, sufficient to the few if any tasks it might have to perform.

When that didn't work out the way that he wanted it to, he contented himself that cleanliness was still next to godliness. He got out of the tub, dried his parts, dressed himself, and made his way in the darkness downtown to the Main Street Deli, where old farts like him had talked the proprietor into opening up on New Year's morning to keep the routine of their daily offices of coffee and talk. They promised her a big tip and no mess if she'd open on the holiday.

That's where he heard that Ron Gillies and Joe Baker, the last of the smokers besides himself, had taken it into their minds to resolve to quit smoking from this day forth. Maybe, Doyle told himself, this was meant as a sign, which is something he'd been telling himself a lot since Sally died, not incidentally of lung cancer—a slow eighteen-month subtraction of herself, first her fitness, then her comfort, then her voice, then herself, after the cancer moved itself into her brain so that she died within a few days of Halloween after a horrible night of sei-zures and visions. It was just after daybreak, and she was gone.

Doyle could remember coming home from the club where they had the funeral luncheon, even though the ladies at the church had offered to do it; he wanted it to be first class, like Sally, so after the graveside at Holy Sepulchre and after the club with its condolences and cocktails, he came home to the house, which had never seemed so empty, and hadn't been there long enough to make coffee when the first little trick-or-treaters, ghosts and goblins, came shouting for candy at the door. And his daughter, who thought of everything, had thought of that, because on the straight-backed wooden chair by the side of the door where he always threw his coat was a clear plastic bowl full of miniature Baby Ruths, Sally's favorite, to give to the beggars on All Hallows' Eve. Surely, he told himself, it was a sign.

And so he said he'd quit with Ron and Joe. They'd make a clean sweep of it. All the other old farts were smoke-free. The three of them were the last to carry on. But he'd take the pledge with them that day. No more smoking from that day forward.

"What the hell, God loves a chancer," is what he said, and they put the ashtray that used to occupy their end of the row of tables back up on the counter and began being nonsmokers.

"We'll see," said Bert, doubting their resolve and launching into a story that no one was listening to about how he'd quit smoking years before. Bert had a memory like a steel trap, never forgot a name or a detail, and he could make a story that ought to be told in thirty seconds last for twenty minutes. He had the Irish gift for talking all day and never saying a thing. Still, as old farts go, he wasn't the worst. He sat at the end of the table with guys like himself who listened to talk radio in their shops all day, working on some project they dreamed up for themselves. Cleaning a gun or carving a block of walnut into a model truck or whittling a walking stick out of some windfall. Bert had been a machinist's mate in the navy and had a deft touch with little engines and other oddments. George did up-holstery and had turned the business over to his daughter but still worked whenever she asked him to. He was hard of hear-ing, so Bert's retelling of the same story never bothered George that much. He'd just nod and smile and ignore what got past the low volume settings of his hearing aids.

It was the first of January, 1990. George Bush the first was partway through his only term as president; the Dow Jones was holding above twenty-eight hundred. Gas was a buck thirty-five a gallon. As good a day as any to quit. Doyle hadn't planned it, but there it was. He'd said it in front of all those people, albeit they were old farts, and he was nevertheless resolved. So he left the deli and drove up the street, north of town to Dr. Rozella's office, the osteopath, and asked him to write him a script for the patch. He'd heard—was it that idiot Bert who told him?—the nicotine patch made it so if you smoked you'd get nauseated. He hated puking. The helplessness. The cold sweat. The toilet bowl.

Puking was, for him, sufficient deterrent. He was still pray-ing for continence: to get more piss in the toilet than on the floor and not to dribble it out in his shorts after zipping his fly and not to be caught short needing to take a shit, as sometimes happened. He'd get out of the car, feel his bowels move, and have to race to the toilet. He couldn't count on his sphincter the way he could in his youth. He'd get loose shits from good grease and some dairy products. If he had, just for old times' sake, a greasy burger and chocolate shake for lunch with the alchies, he'd have to plan his departure and make his way home before he'd get what he called *the sharts*—half fart, half shit—and mess his trousers. Hell to get old.

He didn't smoke that day and put the patch on at night and couldn't believe the vivid, cinematic dreams—like going to a double feature back in the old days—and he woke wishing he was still back in the dream, which involved his beloved in ways that were none of anyone's business but his own. Suffice it to say, he'd, in fact, quit smoking and was glad he did. His wind got better and his appetite, and the dreams remained sumptuous and memorable. He quit the cigarettes but never the patch. He still kept a box of them in the drawer and still saw Rozella if he ran out. He renewed the scrip out of habit, though it'd been twenty-some years now and more. "Don't quit quitting, Doyle," is what he yelled from inside his office, while his gal brought out the prescription. "Right, Doc," Doyle would shout back. "One of these days the cure will take." Whenever the dreams disappeared, he'd break out the patches and get back in the dreams and feel alive.

Of course, one had to take the good with the bad. Some nights it got a little too intense and seemed more the nightmare than an apparition. Probably it was the same for Abraham, the father of nations, the man who dreamed up that first deal with God—his tribe's foreskins for the ancient covenant, the promised land, the chosen people part. Doyle tried to imagine the following morning. His tribesmen gather like old farts do, for no apparent reason, just to chew the fat, and Abraham announces that God has spoken to him. There's some good news and some other news. He's determined to tell them.

"I'm going to be the father of nations," he tells them. "My descendants will be like the stars in the night sky, as numerous, you'll never be able to count them all."

Of course, his tribesmen know there's some trouble with this. His tribesmen know he's been trying for years to get old Sarai impregnated to no avail. They know—because like this place, it's a small town and people talk—they know that eventually he got the servant girl, Hagar, knocked up, and she has

114 • NO PRISONERS

given him Ishmael as a kind of consolation prize, a son and heir and someone to teach the religion to. But the wife of his heart, old Sarai, remains as barren as the desert. Until this dream about which he's telling them now, the good news of it. He and Sarai will have a son.

"And the other news?" one of his pals now asks. "You said there was something more to it."

"Yes, yes, I was only just now coming to that. God wants all of us to have the skin cut from the tops of our penises. In exchange for which we are to be his chosen people."

"His chosen people?" They're looking at each other now, kicking the dirt with their bare feet or sandals. "Cut our penises?" Their eyes are widening and rolling now.

"Yes, as a sign of our agreement with God, our covenant, our testament."

At this point Doyle was always trying to picture what happened next and didn't think Fr. Clement could tell him, and there is no mention of it in the Book of Genesis in the Bible. How many of Abraham's tribesmen do we see running into the desert as fast as they can to get away from this crazy old sonofabitch who wants to slice their penises? They want to get away and start another religion, another covenant with a god who doesn't think like that. This is before even those who would become the chosen people had come to understand that life is about learning to take the good with the bad. And that for every night old Abraham dreamed about Hagar and Ishmael, banished with blessings into the Jordanian hinterlands, he probably had some nightmares about killing Isaac, how close he'd come to it. Or the pharaoh fucking his wife, Sarai, who Abram had claimed was only his sister—chickenshit that he was, frightened of the Egyptians.

In much the same way as every night poor Doyle dreamed of dancing under the stars, the firmament, at the Walled Lake

Pavilion to Glenn Miller or Tommy Dorsey tunes with Sally in his arms and her pressing herself into his tightening embrace that summer after their high school graduations, between the day of infamy and his signing up and taking off the day after Thanksgiving in '42: that perfect summer of their brand new lives when after the music and the moonlight and the rest of the gang, they'd drive his father's '36 Chevrolet out to Middle Straits Lake, down the bumpy dirt road to the clearing in the woods by the lakeshore, where they'd lie on a blanket and look up at the stars and try to imagine the life they could have if only there wasn't a war and Doyle wasn't going to be fodder for it. That's when Sally would take his hand and place the palm of it on her breast and pull him down to kiss her on her mouth. They would do that for most of an hour or more before it was time to head back home on Grand River Avenue. Every dream Doyle had of reaching under her blouse and getting under her bra and holding the soft globe of her breast in his hand, his finger tracing circles around it, and the catch in her breath and then the heaviness of her sighing and the increasing difficulty with which she would plead, "Please, Doyle, not yet, not yet . . ." and he could tell over time how her resolve had been shaken by the pleasure of it, their touching, and kissing, their chaste embracing. "Don't go driving that bumpy road, with anyone else but me," they would sing to the tune of "Don't Sit Under the Apple Tree," which is all they were hearing that summer from the Andrews Sisters and Glenn Miller. That clearing in the woods by the shore of Middle Straits Lake is always turning up in his dreams, and Sally is always willing but not quite ready. And Doyle trying to tell her that they mayn't have time, what with the war and its contingencies, they mayn't have time to take their time and wait for a wedding in the easy future, that sooner than later he'd be having to go and do his part.

For every dream like that there are darker, violent dreams in which he's utterly terrified, afraid for his life and certain he's going to die horribly and alone. But the dreams of Sally keep him coming back for more, and even though he has some in which she cannot be found, or when he finds her, she's dying of cancer and her oncologist is saying there's nothing more he can do and there's really no reason to take her to the hospital, just keep her comfortable as long as we can at home and to hope for an easy end to her struggle and she's only sixty-five and Doyle can't imagine a moment without her ever since coming home from the war, those forty-some Januaries back.

Now, in his advancing years, it has gotten well-nigh impossible to separate dreams from memories. So whether they ever got naked out there at the lake, both of them eighteen and eager and earnestly in love, and went for a swim and lay on the blanket afterward drying and whether he ever actually held her naked body with his naked body before he went off to the US Marines is not a thing he can actually say for certain now. But he's dreamed it and knows the tune he's humming in the dream as she lets him trace her formerly secret places with the fingers of his right hand as he lies next to her, propped on his left elbow and the moonlight shines on the lake and their bodies and they have the rest of their lives before them. Whether he dreamed it because it happened or whether it only happened in a dream, he can't tell. Still, it is real and part of his settled memory of her.

Whether that happened because she wanted him to have something to live for when he was thousands of miles away or it happened because on the Feast of the Circumcision the year after she died he quit smoking cigarettes with the help of a patch that gave him the most vivid dreams of his life is impossible to say.

Prepuce • 117

Possibly it's like those matinees they'd go to on Saturday or Sunday afternoons. His father would take him into the bars on Fenkell Avenue. Bumming, he called it: After Sunday dinner, they'd walk up Montevista to St. Francis DeSales, cross to the far side of Fenkell Avenue, turn left and stop in the first of the three bars he'd always visit—the Italian, the Irish, and the Polish one. He knew the barkeeps and the patrons, who all called out his name, "Hey, Frank! Whadaya havin?" or "Who's that good lookin fella with ya?" He'd introduce Doyle all around: "My son, Doyle," he'd tell them, and buy the boy a soda and give him a quarter and tell him to come back when the movie was through.

"If I'm not in Carmello's, I'll be at Mike's," he'd promise, and Mike's was most often the one Doyle would find him in, glad for the excuse it gave him to tell his buddies he'd have to get the boy home. He liked a couple beers and maybe a shot off the top shelf, but times were hard, and he couldn't afford to settle in for the long haul and certain headache of routine excess.

Doyle would settle into the plush green velvet seat of the theater with his two slowpoke suckers and bottle of pop and wait for the cartoons to begin. When the theater darkened and the projector cast its first light toward the stage from the little square windows up behind them, the first images hit the velvet curtain, which slowly began to open so that the light and the colors rippled with the ripples of the curtain's opening, then the white linen curtain underneath, almost sheer, so that they could see the big screen behind it, but still the images were undulant with the wave of motion in the opening curtain. It was like the word *apocalypse*, the etymology of which Fr. Clement once told them had to do with the removal of veils, as in a dance when the face of the dancer is eventually uncovered, revealed—thus the Book of Revelations—at the end of the Bible and, he supposed, of life, when everything finally becomes clear to us. Such is the nature of his memory and dreams now: It is impossible to know where one ends and the other begins, and the older he got, the worse he was getting, and the better the dreams were, like going to the theater on Sunday afternoons while his dad killed a couple hours in the bar, then walked him home in the fading light naming the constellations he knew—"Orion, the dominant winter constellation," or "there are the seven sisters, the Pleiades"—or talking about the Tigers and their chances this year, his hand on his son's shoulder, the world in order, the curtains and the veils shimmering with light and glimpses of images, promising that in the fullness of time, everything would become clear and known and certain.

Still, all Doyle knew for certain now is that he'd quit smoking on the first of January, 1990, twenty-some years ago—we don't feel the time going—and he'd been dreaming ever since.

It was Saturday, the first of January, 1944, when the marines came ashore on the beach at Cape Gloucester, New Britain, in New Guinea. Doyle's outfit was the last of the division. They'd already secured the airstrips at the north point of the cape, the west end of the island. They followed the battalions that'd been landing all week and bivouacked just north of Borgen Bay. Yellow Beach on the operations maps. There'd been talk about scouts from the Seventh Marines, three of them, who'd been ambushed a couple days before and never got back to their outfit. They'd come upon an injured Japanese foot soldier and chased him up the trail to have a look-see when a platoon of screaming enemies rose out of the green with bayonets and rifle butts. Apparently, they didn't want gunfire to alert the company from the Seventh a couple hundred yards away. Only one made it back to tell the story, so Doyle's battalion, the 3-5, hardly slept all night there on the beach, knowing the enemy was out there, before moving out on the morning of the second to the southwest to join up with the Seventh Regiment.

It's crazy how it all gets smaller and smaller as you make your way to the actual business of battle. When Doyle left Detroit on the Grand Trunk Western out of Michigan Station for Chicago, everything seemed to be opening up—the future, the world, the possibilities. Even the war was a big-picture event, a wide canvas of good and evil ever since the Japanese surprise attack at Pearl Harbor the year before. After passing the back ends of Michigan's small towns—Ann Arbor and Tecumseh, Niles and St. Joe's—to see the skyline of Chicago finally, so much bigger than Detroit's, then out across the great space of the nation, prairies and canyons, the damn purple mountain majesty and fruited plain of it all, before arriving at long last in California and the ocean, which he'd never seen before, and the distant mountains, and the southern turn from LA to San Diego for boot camp. It was a month before they gave out the M-1s, and it only took him a week to make sharpshooter. The bayonet drills, truth told, were harder. Then to Camp Elliott, where he qualified as a general clerk, then to Camp Pendleton for serious drills, jungle warfare, scouts' and snipers' eyes, hand-to-hand combat, machine gun school. He got scraped up on the amphibious landing drill and spent a few days in the base hospital, while the rest of his platoon, Lou Rogers among them, shipped out with the Second Marine Division. He'd met Louie on the train and gave him Sally's sister's address because Trisha wasn't going with anyone, and Louie seemed nice and needed someone to write to back home. Doyle got assigned to K Company of the Third Battalion, Fifth Marine Regiment of the First Marine Division and shipped out on Friday, June

25, 1943, from San Diego on the SS *Lurline*, a luxury steamship turned transport, en route for the Pacific Theater, which they told them meant catching up with the Old Breed of the division in Melbourne, where they'd been regrouping and retraining since Guadalcanal. It's a big war on your way to it—crossing continents and oceans, meeting guys from every state of the nation, Billy Swinford Smith from Paris, Kentucky, and Donald Crescent Coe from Galesburg, Illinois, learning to stab and shoot and survive the elements, learning to keep from puking on a ship, watching out the portholes for signs in the firmament, the night sky and the shape of clouds, as to what the future might hold, the V-mail and postcards back to the old neighborhood, to Sally and his parents and younger sister, the distance ever widening between them, so that when Maddy from Melbourne made it known to him that no man should risk dying before he'd had sex with a willing woman, Doyle was happy to hear it and dove right in. That was something that made the war smaller—her lovely body moving beneath him with its tidal, undulant pleasuring. He'd just turned nineteen not four months before, and here he was, a little buzzed from the Aussie beer, glad for the heroes they all took them to be, and grateful for Maddy's manifest eagerness to relieve him of his virginity. Suddenly the great adventure seemed a poor substitute for this actual pleasure, her dark brown hair and darker eyes, her pale white body, its actual chrisms and benedictions. After that baptism he knew two things immediately. The nuns and priests were wrong about sex, and old men bereft of it were the ones who waged wars, even if young men were required to fight them, because no human wrapped in such an embrace could work up the intention to go out and kill or conquer. He supposed it was from Maddy he learned such things. By the time he'd left Melbourne, it was clear there'd be no turning

Prepuce • 121

back, that those two months of relative ease and easy pleasure were compensations for what was coming next, the two months of intensive training on Goodenough Island and the horrors of the jungle war on New Britain. When they left Milne Bay on Saint Stephen's Day, with only three hundred miles of the Solomon Sea between there and Borgen Bay, he was thinking how tiny the sea seemed with their fleet setting forth and their days numbered right down to the moment they came across that maggoty corpse of that poor gyrene scout from the 1-7 who'd gone out a couple of nights before looking for the enemy and a way through the jungle.

And Doyle's outfit were really in it right away. Japanese patrols they could only imagine in the thick green rainforest, and because it was always raining, they couldn't hear them, the noise of the rain made double by the leafy fronds of overgrowth. It was like fighting ghosts because you couldn't see a thing for sure, only some movement in the canopy of green, the low ground growth or vines at eye level or trees rising at various heights toward the sky or snipers in the higher trees rising above a patch of kunai grass. Doyle saw one dropped like a box of rocks after Romero, who qualified sharpshooter with him in San Diego, dropped to one knee and squeezed off five rounds just as the Japanese were taking aim at someone in the First Squad up ahead of them. It was not long up the path they came upon one of the scouts from the Seventh who'd never made it back two nights before. It was horrible what they'd done to him. He'd been tied to a tree, where they'd clubbed his head to smithereens and apparently used him for bayonet practice, the thick lacerations in his thighs and thorax making him look like Saint Sebastian in the *Lives of the Saints*, who'd been shot full of arrows by Diocletian's archers. This was in the third century, somewhere near Rome. Of course, Sebastian had been found by a Christian widow and taken down from the tree and back to her house, where he was nursed back to health. This seeming reprieve was soon reversed when Sebastian continued to insult the emperor, who had him beaten to death and thrown into a privy. He was known as the saint who was martyred twice, and it looked much the same for this poor gyrene, limply hanging from the tree they'd bound him to. No one could say if he was dead from the clubbing before they started bayonetting him, whether the beating or the bleeding finally finished him. Nor could it be determined at what point in the proceedings his captors had dropped his dungarees, castrated him, and jammed his genitals into his mouth, which is how we found him, wide eyed and full of maggots swarming his wounds and orifices.

That's when the war got proper small for him, down to a dose he could fairly manage. The Japanese hated the marines, lay in wait for them, were watching through the rain for the chance to kill them, and from that moment onward, from finding that poor defiled corpse of a man, never mind he was a countryman, Doyle wanted to kill some Japanese in return for what they had done to him beyond the necessary bit of killing him. It wasn't about Pearl Harbor anymore. That was long ago and far away. Doyle had no grudge with the Japanese people or the Japanese nation or the Japanese version of current history. But he hated the ones who had done this thing and were doing things like it every chance they got, and he wanted to rid first this jungle, then this island, then this hemisphere, then this globe of them. And he feared such an end for himself. Worse than death, to be dismembered and defiled and left out to rot. The fear was like a dry prickling heat at the back of his throat. It was fear turning itself to hate. He quit watching for snipers to save himself and started watching for snipers to kill. He hadn't, as it turned out, very long to wait.

Prepuce • 123

McMahon, their platoon leader, asked for volunteers to square away the dead guy and hump him back to the CP for graves registration.

"We're not gonna leave the poor devil here like that," the lieutenant said. He knew they'd already reconnoitered some high flat ground near the airstrips for a cemetery. A couple runners from the mortar section said they'd get him back the mile, maybe less, we'd advanced if someone else would get him "squared away." Doyle said he'd do it.

The smell was awful and the maggots, but he got some kerosene from the corpsmen and soaked some cotton in it and stuffed it in the nostrils and the gaping wounds from the bayonetting. And then laid some cotton over the pelvic incision by which they'd removed his genitals and poured more kerosene on it. The maggots that didn't drop off the open wounds or orifices quit wriggling and died. Doyle was glad of that. It wasn't exactly a medicinal smell—the kerosene—more like a gas station, but it was better than the rotting. The corpsmen brought him two extra ponchos, and they laid them out, wired the eyelets together to make one huge winding sheet, cut the poor man away from the tree he'd been tied to, laid him flat out on the ponchos, and folded his arms across his chest. The poncho would make a serviceable shroud, tied with three belts—one for the neck, one around the hips, one for the ankles. It would make the handling easier. That's when the corpsman offered the needle and thread. He actually threaded the needle and set it on the thigh of the corpse. Not the kind you'd sew a button on with, but thicker, like butcher shop twine, and a needle curved like a long S shape. Doyle knew immediately what he had in mind and carefully pried the dead man's jaw open, slipped his genitals out of his mouth, and quickly jerry-rigged them back where they belonged with four or five quick, looping stitches to hold them more or less in place. He was weeping now. And it was raining. It never stopped raining. Even so, Doyle could see he'd never been circumcised.

He swabbed the maggots out of his mouth best he could, stuffed it with cotton and kerosene, repacked his nostrils with the same, then yanked up his dungarees, buckled him up, retied his boondockers, wrapped him up tight, and sent him on his way, feet first, covered by a flag. A man of parts, in part repaired. Dead as dead can be.

Chapter Four

OLD DOGS

2004

A re you possibly projecting, Doyle?" is what Dr. Clarke said, when Doyle told him the old dog was getting anxious about its mortality. He'd gotten the first appointment of the year. Said he'd have to see him today so that he could get back up north before the weather turned worse.

"No, really, Doc," Doyle insisted. "He gets this faraway look in his eyes, as if he knows it's out there. And he's barking at nothing and perpetually restless, inconsolable. I've seen it before."

"In Bernese mountain dogs?" the vet asked, while rubbing his hand up in the old dog's groin and along its belly in search of tumors. "We humans are, if the science is correct, the only species of sentient beings that comprehends our own mortality. There's some talk about chimpanzees and elephants, and God knows the dolphins and whales are in a class of their own, but as far as I know, Doyle, old Bill here hasn't a clue about the future or wherever his demise is hiding. He'll know when he hurts or is sick. He'll find a quiet place to call it quits." He winced with sympathetic pain as he came to the cluster of lumps in the old dog's belly. "But it would require a more comprehensive grasp of time. A sense, as Aristotle reckoned, of a beginning, a middle, and end, Doyle. But maybe you? Anything going on with you, Doyle? Do you see that look in your own eyes now? Do men who've seen what you've seen fear death, like the rest of us? Or are you immune?"

The thousand-yard stare, they called it in the Corps, the way some guys got Asiatic, dopey with incessant rain and the mud and mosquitos, the rats all night, the enemy everywhere, though those islands killed more marines than the enemy did. Sure as shit they were goners then. Some killed themselves. Some asked others to do it for them. The vet's question put Doyle back into his ruminations.

It's what kept Doyle driving downstate to Dr. Clarke for his old dog's veterinary care. He knew Clarke kept an eye on the bigger picture, the large-screen, panoramic sweep of things. Still, he was worried about the dog's increasing anxiety.

"He's well past his expectancy—ten years plus. His breed's supposed to live six to eight years, nine tops; I looked it up on the internet. The bigger the dog . . ."

"Maybe he's worried about you, Doyle. Maybe it's your impending doom he senses, your own fears about it; they have a keen sense of fear in others, I believe. There's a contagion to it, a look, as you say yourself. You're a tad past your own prime and expectancy, aren't you, Doyle? What are you? Pressing eighty? That's more than biblical. That's more than the 'three score years and ten' we Methodists are always angling for."

Doyle had memorized the psalm, in the King James version, the time their Bible study was doing the psalms. "And if by reason of strength they be fourscore years, yet is their strength labor and sorrow; for it is soon cut off, and we fly away."

He was nearly fourscore years and, like his dog, well past expectancies.

"For fuck sake, Doc, just give me his meds. I'm taking us both back up north where all he has to bark about is snowmobiles and ice-fishermen. Not the daylong procession of designer babies and fitness buffs and their pampered dogs. He seems to think he's saving me from them all—the yummy mummies in their yoga togs, the daddies with their strollers and Yorkshires, all named Murphy or Quincy or something cute. Long as he can jump into the car, he's good to go. After that, he'll be a goner."

"You've both got some time left on the meter, Doyle. Carpe diem, my friend. And safe on the road. Is one of the grandkids driving you?"

"No, I can drive myself. The car knows its own way. Less than four hours, even if I stop for coffee."

"Haven't they taken your license away yet?"

"Hell no! I get it up north where the old gal that runs the secretary of state is nearly as old as me."

"Careful going, they're promising snow."

"Shocking in January, in Michigan, Doc. No worries. We could all be alive tomorrow!"

All the way up the interstate he was thinking how much he had begun to identify with the old dog on the floor in the back. How they both slept more, napped more, dozed off in the middle of things; how they shared Doyle's cooking—a pound of bacon, a cup of oats, a bag of perch from the fishmongers, two strip steaks fried up in the skillet, potatoes boiled or baked or fried with eggs. Bill took his meds with a slice of cheese. Doyle took his with a slurp of water from the tap. They both liked asparagus and soft serve vanilla cones, and where Bill had a staple of kibble, Doyle ate a bowl of popcorn most nights. Neither were crazy for kale, though Doyle liked onions on everything, fresh garlic, radishes in season. When he had a grave dug for Bill last November in the northwest corner of the yard, it was only to avoid being caught in midwinter with a deep frost in the topsoil and a dead dog on his hands. Lately he wondered if the dog might outlive him. He hadn't planned for the contingencies. First come, first serve, he figured for the grave.

He had survived the Advent and the solstice and the Christmas and the New Year downstate with family, and he had made it back before the little Christmas and the last gasp of holidays gave way to Martin Luther King Day and Valentine's Day, which would herald, once they were done, the brink of another springtime, and everything seemed right with the world when he woke that morning to blowing snow and the cold breath of winter bouncing the tree limbs outside his south-facing bedroom window. Bill seemed agitated by the noise of the storm, huffing and puffing with anxiety the way he did around the Fourth of July or the opening of rifle season, when the bombast made him drool and pace. Doyle yanked the blankets up over his exposed right shoulder and resolved to sleep it out, but the dog's disquiet made him think that he had to shit—Bill, not Doyle, who nonetheless got up and pissed and brushed what little was left of his hair and his yellowing teeth. Sally used to give him lemon juice and baking soda to brush with to keep them white, but he had fallen out of that praxis. He wrapped the bathrobe around him and slipped on the fur-lined boots he wore as slippers and told the old dog to follow him downstairs, where he opened the kitchen door into the breezeway and opened the back door out onto the day, which was drifting and blowing the fresh foot of snow that had fallen overnight. He went back up to bed, crawled into it, and assumed the position, determined to lay up a few more hours.

His was the nocturnal journey of the premodern. He imagined an age of fires on dirt floor, mud and wattle walls, holes in the thatch to draw the smoke out. Or rooms equipped with chamber pots and shitting bowls, heated by wood fires, lit by lamp oil, lives that could not abide or afford eight hours of rest in a row and thus accustomed themselves to vigil and wakefulness, watch and insomnia. Simpler lives, he liked to think, made so by the performance of simple tasks, common chores, primal contingencies: shelter, food, water, and fuel. It was a day's work, and the fatigue of it was sweet, the discipline and purpose. No need to wonder what to do. No time to meditate or contemplate the options, just one foot in front of the other, forward progress. Nothing to procrastinate over. Home fire and stewpot, bucket and stonework, the everyday hold on the rudiments of survival.

Once he returned to sleeping alone, he found himself, after four or five hours, widely awake and well-enough rested. Before his widowhood and retirement, such wakefulness was a source of panic. And the panic made him all the more sleepless. Then he found an article on the way our ancestors slept in shifts, segmented sleep, it was called, giving in to their bodies' apparent rhythms. They would go to sleep when the dark made work impossible, then wake after four or five hours to feed the fire or visit neighbors, to pray or check the animals or read a book. Then they'd go back to bed. He started doing the same. He'd get up, sit on the loveseat in the bedroom, maybe turn on the TV or his laptop to check his email or google something. On the big-screen with the multiple channels that he'd had installed some years ago, adding the cable service with the high-speed internet and landline package he'd heard about from the boys at coffee, he'd watch the TV preachers or the cable news pundits feeding the crazies in the various echo chambers. He wanted to be a contrarian on just about every topic that might

130 • NO PRISONERS

come up at coffee, finding it more interesting than the predictable positions of the old farts who joined him in the morning
for talk and caffeine and breakfasts.

Or he'd read from one of the many books that Sally had left
him, *The Big Book of Alcoholics Anonymous* or the *Oxford Book
of English Verse* he'd bought at the library sale, or, when all else
failed, an old Douay-Rheims translation of the Holy Bible. He
kept these three texts on a table next to his bed. In the latter, he
liked the Book of Sirach for its straightforward wisdoms and di-
rectives. Among poems he favored the Romantics. In the former
he was especially fond of the fourth step, which called for a searching and fearless moral inventory, and the fifth, which required
a good confession. This put him in mind of the examination
of conscience he learned from the nuns before making his first
confession in 1935. He was eleven. They taught him the mortal
and venial sins. He was making his first communion in June. He
liked taking this moral inventory and writing down the list of
his transgressions on a pad of paper he kept near his bed. The
fourth step took him to parts of his past he had otherwise limited
access to. Eventually, the secret he had never listed or confessed,
the amends he had never made, involved Maddy in Melbourne
in 1943 who had schooled him in the pleasures of sex, the giving
and getting of it, the give and take. Sex was a subject that had
become part of the correspondence he'd kept up with Sally all
through the war, when toward the end, in August of 1945, after
the Japanese had surrendered and he was heading home in his
heart, unbelievably alive, after all he'd seen, his letters began
addressing the intimate life he hoped to share with his true
love, his fiancé, his wife when he got home. He'd been eighteen
when he saw her last and was returning to her a different man—
skinny and malarial and experienced in ways he could not exactly tell her about.

The First Marine Division, damaged in mind, body, and spirit from combat on Guadalcanal, had been sent to Melbourne to be restored to order. They were in tatters—if not casualties of Japanese warriors, then casualties of the bugs and the jungle and the rain. Few of them didn't suffer from malaria, jungle rot, or fevers. It was there he'd caught up with them— the Third Battalion of the Fifth Marine Regiment of the First Marine Division. After boot camp and basic training in San Diego, he'd shipped out on the *SS Lurline*, a luxury liner refitted for the war, on Friday, June 25, 1943, out to Australia to active duty. He was part of the Ninth Replacement Battalion. After nineteen days at sea and stops in Honolulu, Figi, and New Caledonia, they arrived in Port Phillip harbor off Melbourne, and Doyle, freshly minted and shipshaped in his starched khakis, stepped off into a city teaming with life. He was nineteen. The Fifth Marine Regiment was billeted at Camp Balcombe near Mount Martha, half an hour southeast of Melbourne Central. Liberty began at 1 p.m. and lasted till 5 a.m. the next morning. There was a beer party at the cricket grounds with the Aussies and the Yanks bellying up to the same open bar, and if this was war, Doyle was for it. "HiYa Digger," the sign read over the grandstand, welcoming the local soldiers. The local girls did not much distinguish between the heroes of Guadalcanal who had saved their nation from the Japanese and the newly minted marines being delivered at the docks, off-loading from luxury liners conscripted to the war effort, fresh from boot camp in America. Their gratitude, the approved national policy of it, gave license to their youths and urges, which spoke the same language, if in a local patois, as the Yankee boys in the bars and dance clubs in their crisp khakis and spit-shined shoes. They needn't be wooed or spooned, on the contrary, these girls had grown up with the boys gone to war. They ran the trams and the post office, the shops and the civil services. They'd spent their teen years longing for the love they'd read about in novels, waiting for the attention of men. When the dashing young marines showed up, "Overpaid, oversexed, and over here," as the local bromide held, the Melbournian girls were more than ready for them.

To the beauty of their youths and the chemistry of desire could be added the big band music and cheap booze, which made life in Melbourne in 1943 bacchanalian in all ways. The romance was seasoned by youth's unshakeable sense of immortality, in relentless tension with war's constant looming shadow of death.

Outstretched under the Southern Cross that rose over St. Kilda in Melbourne with Maddy, fearful of pregnancy but eager for intimacy, fellating him to ecstasy while he returned, as best he could, the favor, it came into his brain for the first time ever, how sad it really was that they were mortal, that someday they would die. He reckoned whatever heavens there were or weren't out past the facts of death could never supply a bliss more generous than the one he felt there in late summer of 1943 with Madeleine Lee. Walking with her through the botanic gardens, dancing at the Dug Out or jitterbugging at the Palm Grove or Trocadero, drinking with her in the bar of Young and Jackson's Hotel, where they first met, under the nude portrait of Chloe with her leggy beauty and bald pudenda, before going up to their room or making for the beach for the night and aligning their young and shameless parts, Doyle felt entirely alive and well and able for whatever the future held.

"She died for love," she had said to him, in a voice like velvet, as a way of opening their conversation. She was sitting at the bar, and he had ordered a beer but couldn't take his eyes off of the naked girl on the canvas under glass. "How very sad," he said. "I think I'm in love." He was glad she had started the conversation. Doyle never knew what to say. Once he got started he could go with the best of them, but the first move with a girl was impossible.

"She was in love with the painter, Jules Joseph Lefebvre, a Frenchy, who was, of course, seducing her. And who could blame him?" She nodded toward the canvas of the standing nude. She sipped her drink. "But he married her sister. Her real name was Marie, not Chloe. She was nineteen. By twenty-one she drank poison, a tea made out of match heads, heartbroken for the artist who had debauched her."

"The cad," Doyle said. "That's no way to treat a lady."

Maddy smiled.

"Can I get you another?" he asked.

She rubbed her small hand along the bar until it came to his. She looked up at him with the same look as Chloe or Marie or whoever the naked girl was on the wall of the bar, and in every rendition of his memory of it, there was a catch in his breath when she said, "Please."

Their romance lasted the two months he was in Melbourne waiting to ship out to New Guinea to train at Milne Bay and then join the assault on Cape Gloucester, New Britain. He had arrived a boy and departed a man, ever grateful for the carnal tuition of Miss Maddy Lee of Melbourne, Victoria, Australia. She had taught him to love life, fear death, long for another's flesh, and eat chop suey. Ignorant and virginal, he had joined the marines in a spasm of gung ho youth, willing to fight and die for a cause, glad to be a hero, even a dead one. She taught him to want to live forever, basking in the approval of another human whose body wanted to be with his own body. The nuns

134 • NO PRISONERS

and priests had taught him the fear of God. Maddy had taught him the fear of death.

He'd never mentioned any of this to Sally, when, thanks be to God, he got home from it all, late in January 1946, and not at any time in the forty-three years of their marriage did he ever break his silence on the matter. And such nights as he found himself taking his searching and fearless moral inventory and making the list of amends, this lack of candor and the dark he'd kept his wife in always appeared on the top of his list. Sometimes he would speak into the night as if she occupied a heaven nearby from which she could monitor his night visions and full confessions. "I'm sorry, Sally," he would say. "Forgive me, please."

Other nights he'd make a shopping list, including the ingredients for chowders and stews and pots of chili. He liked the kitchen filled with the aroma of simmering things—the medley of flavors he imagined comingling through the low boil and the blue flame flickering under a pot. And the size of the enterprise always made it seem like he mightn't be eating, as he did, alone. He would email his alchie friends and widowed sorts, announcing a shrimp boil or fish chowder or beef stew or pot of chili in hopes that one or more of them might show up hungry for a free meal, which was, if he did say so himself, not the worst of the entries in the local cook-offs. Peeling and quartering potatoes, chopping onions, carrots, and celery, and dicing the variously colored peppers made him think of the way of the world—how it took all kinds and we were all God's children, all of us the same but different, each with a distinctive flavor and texture and style. He kept frozen peas and corn and mixed legumes in bags in the fridge to add to the brews. He would throw in a cooking sheet of buttermilk biscuits, which he reckoned were near enough homemade to give some sense of a feast to the feast he prepared. The composition and construction of these meals made him think of the creation narratives in Genesis.

What he kept trying to replicate in the kitchen was that cover of the *Saturday Evening Post* that his mother sent him at Camp Pendleton, California, when he was finishing his basic training and turning nineteen. It looked like their home on Montevista in northwest Detroit, his mother in her blue-print dress, her hair in a bun, wearing a starched white apron, and setting a platter with a huge turkey on the table in front of his father in his good dark gaberdine suit, the cousins and aunts and uncles all there. "Maybe they'll let you come home for Christmas?" she'd written in the birthday card in the same envelope. It was the middle of March 1943, and she was hoping the war would end before Christmas, in nine months' time. He spent that Christmas aboard a coast guard manned LST in Buna Harbor in Papua New Guinea as part of a convoy, readying for their assault on Cape Gloucester. None of them were going to be home for Christmas. No turkey, no cousins, no bowls full of cranberries or mashed potatoes. On the eve of his first actual combat, he was nineteen and frightened and far from home. He was missing Sally's smile and Maddy's lips and wondering if there was anything other than either of them worth dying for. He wanted his mother and father and his own bed and to be anywhere but here, huddled among hundreds of likewise frightened boys from all over America, with their M-1s and helmets, about to go into battle with the Japanese.

These were the years of his life—between his late teens and early twenties—when the things that most shaped him had happened. From falling for Sally, to sex with Maddy, to killing enemy foot soldiers and cooling his heels on Pavuvu and Okinawa and Peiping for the months in China, the return to safety and Sally and the future he'd have, from December of 1941 through January of 1946, when he and his nation had been at war.

136 • NO PRISONERS

And here in the latter chapters of his life, living alone on the lake with his dog, hours of every day were spent in hapless contemplations of how he had come to be the man he was. Unfailingly his mind would wander to a vision of Sally, in her thirties or forties, riding him in the moonlight in their upper room. Or kneeling before him when he'd come out of the shower to give him a blow job while he was shaving. The sexual abandon and play of these scenes, long lodged in his most intimate memories of love, never failed to excite him to some degree. Even in his advanced years, while he couldn't exactly rise to the occasion, whatever the occasion wasn't, he could at least get stiff enough to play along with himself and quicken his breathing toward a climax. He had been alone so long he regarded it as all a little ridiculous, having nearly forgotten the undulant, soul-bracing pleasures of sex. And still he kept on checking, every so often, against the day when it would be outside the range, another loss to be chalked up and lived with, like hair and muscle mass, hearing and night vision. As long as he was a dangerous man, he thought, as long as he could do the necessaries on his own—pissing and shitting and the rest—life would be, albeit marginally, still worth living. The thing is, he told himself, to be more homicidal than suicidal, though he reckoned the impulses toward either proceeded from the same region of hopelessness in his brain.

After an hour, maybe two, he'd be sleepy again and a little chilled, and he'd slip back under the covers for his second sleep, which would take him past daybreak, often into the middle of morning, till ten or eleven o'clock. He would wake feeling rested but would often slip into napping sometime in the afternoon.

As an entrance into his second sleep, Doyle could not resist the impulse to meditate on times gone by and the lessons that might be learned from them. Before Melbourne and Maddy he'd never known what it had felt like to be an object of desire. But worshipping at the altar of the full-frontal nudity of Chloe, or Marie, or whoever it was, all those years ago now, he was momentarily recharged with the unmistakable sense that Maddy wanted him in the flesh, wanted him to want her, wanted them to be friends and lovers with no strings attached—but attached, nonetheless, in every way that human bodies could be.

Schooled by the nuns for the twelve years at St. Francis, and having pursued, within the acceptable boundaries of the big band era, a Catholic girl from his own tribe and neighborhood, he'd had the impression that her body was somehow more precious than his. And that the gift of her virginity was a treasure dearer than the gift of his and that nothing in her conduct would ever betray anything more passionate than her approval of him and of their consortium so long as it fell within the precincts of good Catholic family life. The pleasures of sex were, in her worldview, an inducement to parenthood and a compensation for the hard work it was to make a household and raise a family. Sex was something to be endured, even enjoyed, but never longed for or eagerly sought after. Whereas with Maddy, and Doyle's memory of this was unimpeachable, she found every aspect of his being beautiful, and she craved it and would tell him how wet it made her just to be proximate—to hold hands or dance or to speak in low voices. Most all of their lovemaking began with her sucking him nearly to climax, then riding on top of him until she came and then thanking him profusely for making her so happy. This made him feel like he imagined women felt when it finally came to them how crazy they could make men feel by merely turning to or from them with the proper reticence or willingness. Her desire for his person and his parts mitigated the growing sense he'd had—ever since the twenty-fifth of November in 1942 when, moved by the news of marine heroics on Guadalcanal, he'd enlisted in the USMC—that he was in all ways expendable, one of a kind but still one of many, each of them fodder for the larger purpose. Nor did this sense do anything but intensify when, arriving at Camp Elliott in San Diego, he joined what appeared to be an endless marching supply of men in their prime, men with homes and little personal histories, girlfriends and hopes for the future, who were dressed in dull colors and taught to move like a school of fish in the water, in unison. To eat, sleep, shit, and shower at the same time, say the same thing, abandon any personal feature or foible that set them apart from the corps. That *the Corps* read to him like *the marine corpse* was not lost on Doyle—seen one you've seen them all. Nothing, now that he'd had seven decades to think of it, had removed from him that keen knowledge of his own ordinariness, his oneness with the masses of men of his time who went off to try and stay alive in the maw of world conflict. Nothing, except those two months in Melbourne when he was the recipient of Maddy Lee's grace—the abundant, undeserved pleasure she gave him and the unambiguous pleasure she took by doing so. It made him feel precious and full of grace in a way he seldom had in the lifetime since. He replayed in his illumined memory, as he fell into a second sleep, the episodes of their long-ago lovemaking and could still remember the prickly heat at the back of his throat the first time he ever climaxed inside of her while wearing the rubbers his CO distributed to cut down on the unwanted pregnancies. Now, long into his anecdotage, the sleepless old gyrene found himself devoutly lapsed in the ways that most mattered, religiously, sexually, temperamentally. And though lapsed and indifferent, he was not yet free, he had to concede, after all these years, from desire. His appetite for intimacy, all kinds of intimacy, spiritual, intellectual, emotional, sexual, remained.

Bill thrust his muzzle deep into the snow and seemed to be supping from it like it was a cream pie, then, working his way up the hump of the septic field, dropped and rolled in the cold wakening of it, no doubt remembering the dog of his early days who loved the snow and the winter and cold, a love bred, Doyle thought, in the bone of the old Bernese. Bill had outlived the expectation that a big dog of a breed beset by tumors and dysplasia would make it six or eight years with good care but rarely the ten years that Bill now marked. Over the grave he'd had dug on the lake side in November, sure that old Bill would not make it through the winter and not wanting to fight with a frost line and frozen topsoil to get him in the ground, Doyle had set a stone cut by a company in Petoskey that read, "William Wordsworth aka Bill W. 1987–1999, Always a good dog, seldom a great one. RIP." Still, to see another Bill rolling in the new snow on the septic field, then easing into the woods to take a shit, regular as an old Ford, thought Doyle, then pissing on the rocks and tree stumps and boundaries such as he knew them to be, made Doyle think that if he made it till spring he might see another year. The warm summer would comfort his old hindquarters, just as the new snow felt like a return of youth in the depths of his thick black fur.

This was the second or third Bill that Doyle'd had. He'd lost track. The first one he got before Sally died. More than once he thought it might have been what killed her, but then he'd remember her kindness to it, subtracted, Doyle had to admit, from the kindness she used to spend on him.

Doyle had always wanted a dog, ever since the kids had grown and gone and moved into their own lives. He wanted something to piss and moan about, to give a grudging care to, to commiserate with. "You need a dog if you're married to a sensitive woman," he'd say to his friends. "You can say things to a dog you couldn't say to a wife. They'd never forgive you. But a dog could care less. Long as you feed 'em and scratch behind their ears and take 'em out to shit." This he'd demonstrate to whomever was handy by addressing the dog thus: "You miserable sonofabitch." And he'd point out the dog's unchanged demeanor. "Ya fecking gobshite," he'd say, to no apparent response, whereupon he'd rest his case about the dog's indifference to his master's moods.

He couldn't say now, these many years since, if she'd ever really forgiven him for bringing the dog home as a puppy. Oh, she had, in fact, come to love the thing, brushing it, seeing to the heartworm meds, inspecting it for fleas and ticks and ear infections and, eventually, tumors, after she'd read up on the breed, insisting that Doyle take it to Dr. Clarke, the local vet, for its shots and rabies and distemper vaccinations. But Doyle always thought that whatever care she heaped upon Bill she subtracted from the care she'd formerly spent on himself. There were fewer shared dinners, less gratuitous episodes of rollicking sex, no certainty about her participation in his life, or he in hers. Then she got cancer and eventually died, forty-three years into a marriage he'd planned would only end with his own sudden, pain-free, possibly heroic death in a noble cause or selfless enterprise. "A real curveball," he called it—Sally dying before himself. Something he'd never planned on. He thought they'd be lovers forever and that he'd get out of life long before she did.

Instead their romance ended a little when he got that first dog. And that it outlived Sally, albeit only by months, made good the truth she would often speak, bending to pick up a clump of the dog's fur off the hardwood floor or pushing the vacuum endlessly during shedding season, "That dog'll be the death of me." And while Doyle couldn't say that that first Bill had killed her, he did outlive her, for which, nonetheless, Doyle had forgiven the dog, if not his dearly departed wife. He'd felt utterly abandoned, rejected, left out in the cold, as if she'd chosen lung cancer over any more time spent married to him and tending to that big old dog.

"Bill du jour," he sometimes called the current iteration. He watched the current Bill through the windows as it made its way around the house, pissing on trees, on the firepit stones, on the woodpile, sniffing at the legs of lawn furniture Doyle was too lazy to bring in for the winter, the flagpole and other markers, until he achieved the edge of the pond of well overflow that never froze because of the moving water, and there the dog drank deeply of the fresh artesian water, then stared out at the frozen lake, which was blurry with the blowing snow that had fallen all night and was now rising and drifting into its undulant, spotless topography. An eagle and its juvenile hatchling flew out of the neighbors' tree stand, balanced like any windhover—Doyle thought of the kestrel in Gerard Manley Hopkins's poem the Jesuit had dedicated to Christ our Lord and the visitation of the magi following a star through the desert, then opened the door for the old dog to return to the shelter and the warmth. Though he had lost his faith, he remained, at least, religiously literate, reading the Bible Sally had studied with and memorizing, then forgetting, then memorizing again, the poems in the anthology she'd given him, bought at the Salvation Army one Saturday before their first anniversary. "I caught this morning morning's minion, kingdom of daylight's dauphin, dapple-dawn-drawn Falcon, in his riding . . ." He poured himself another cup of coffee and sat at the counter to contemplate the day, staring into the bright abyss outside the window.

142 • NO PRISONERS

This put him in mind of the moment, cinematic in his memory of it, like something out of *Doctor Zhivago* or *Lawrence of Arabia*—could it be thirteen winters ago already?—when he first spied an upright figure moving on the ice amid the blowing snow and shanties, like desert sandstorms or the whiteout David Lean had the heartbroken medico stumble through: an epic, passionate journey of pursuit. It seemed to have come from Topinabee, though Topinabee was hidden behind the gray haze and snow squall. Doyle grabbed the binoculars from their perch on the window sash and tried to focus for a better look. The figure, in a gray greatcoat with a plush white collar, red boots, and what looked like a billed cap such as a railroad man might wear, was working its way bent over by the northerly wind and into the easterly wind, stopping to shelter behind shanties, occasionally trying the doors of same. Doyle watched the flags on his flagpole, one American, one Irish, one USMC, billowing between directions, and he reckoned the figure was surely looking for shelter.

That is how she'd come to him, quite literally out of nowhere, across the frozen lake, out of a blurry blizzard on Little Christmas, marching as if to that whistled tune from the River Kwai. In his memory the cinematography was epic and laden with drama and metaphor. It was the type of happenstance that might make him believe in, or anyway doubt somewhat less, the possible existence of a loving God, who sends us the very help we need when despair seems nearly to have us on the ropes. How else to explain the appearance out of nowhere of just such assistance as he was in need of? Or how, he crawled into his bed wondering that night, how to explain the coincident math that added up to the ever-elusive win-win situation: that she was a traveler in need of transport, and he had transport but needed a lift, a driver, some good orderly direction, someone to take him along for the ride. He fell asleep dwelling on such mysteries. What are the chances, he asked himself, that a girl and an old geezer might be for each other the way by which each gets where they needed to go?

Nights like these he fell asleep with the gathering sense of a loving God in charge; others he felt entirely alone.

It was her rump, serendipitously glimpsed, shapely and snuggly tucked into the leggings she must have slept in, or slipped on or into to come downstairs, with the sleeveless silken camisole that gathered around her ample breasts to articulate her girlish curves, the tights women of her generation wore to show off, albeit modestly, the particulars of their figures—the thin sinews of their upper thighs, the thigh gap they all strove for, the intergluteal cleft between her buttocks, the smooth shelf and bald round of the pudendum, the bones of hips, the twin peaks of the iliac crests he remembered from his study of the pelvic girdle in mortuary school after the war, the flat plane of their lower tummies. It was this glimpse of her, pressing her morning coffee at the kitchen counter, the way she turned and looked sleepily at him, the immediate intelligence that this girl, this child, this granddaughter of old Boatwright was in fact a woman with a woman's parts, which put him, for the first time in what seemed like forever, in mind of the man he had once been and the shape of the woman his wife Sally had been in her girlhood, her twenties, her thirties, in fact well into her fifties: a small and exquisite beauty, of fine haunches, sweetly shaped particulars, and an ever-present, high-grade sexual energy.

He banished from his thoughts, of course, the idea that she might be trying to gauge what effect she might have on him, in this or any apparition, as a provocation to a man Doyle's age, and Doyle did his level best to seem unperturbed, but he did admire, though an old man well past desire, her manifest, unabashed beauty, her fine form, her tonic body, her sinewy, well-wrought bottom giving way to legs still fit for a long haul and longing look. He knew the powerlessness younger men would experience in the gravitation of her body's hearkening to them. He and they could never be the same after glimpsing, however momentarily, such form, such beauty. It was nature, mighty nature, that would cause an electrical impulse in younger men's imaginations and genitals, and in himself a kind of catch in the breath, a flash of memory, a gratitude for living long enough to appreciate such perfections of form without the awkward desire that once attended same. Still, he blushed and turned away, as if he'd beheld something he had no business beholding. And might have looked too long upon, as if he'd trespassed her youth and beauty. But he spent the day seeing Sally in his daydreams and smiling, for no evident reason, at his guest.

At noon he went upstairs to take a shower and to see if he could get an erection. He could not. He thawed a bag of perch fillets for dinner, and she made what she could of the few greens and vegetables he had on hand. He boiled some red skins, and they dined at the kitchen counter. He had a dusty bottle of Chablis, which he uncorked and poured for her. He liked watching her drink and after dinner suggested a glass of Oban, a pricey scotch he kept as a conscience bottle—he hadn't had a drink in years and still attended AA meetings—and she drank it neat. He watched her closely, sipping it vicariously, feeling its warm wash on her tongue and in her throat by proxy, and for a moment got the rush he used to get when he was taking spirits. When she poured herself another, they adjourned to the morning room, though the sun was gone, and she sat in the dark leather chair and told him about her mother's death, which was the only thing that he remembered about her family. He remembered the summer several years ago when word spread among the houses, how the pretty woman, the daughter of old neighbors with the young family, was killed when her car went into a culvert on the Straits Highway north of Cheboygan, and how the family gathered that autumn for a memorial service at the lake.

"We went down to the point and scattered her ashes," she told him. "I tucked some into the sand and mud at the water's edge," she said, "thinking it could be her grave, hoping that they'd always stay where I could find them." They washed away, like everything. Still, that's what put her out on the lake, wandering among the ice shanties, looking for shelter or safety or someplace she could hide out on her own, out of the cold, away from the ogling and cloying advances of boozy guys. "I really don't know where I was going," she told him. She'd left her work at her uncle's gallery in Cheboygan, tired of that life, after her education in Detroit at the Center for Creative Studies. It was clear she wanted to tell her story, how she'd grown up in a small town in Southwest Michigan; her father worked for the development department of a seminary. Her brother was a toddler when her mother died, so at thirteen she'd felt like the surrogate mom.

After a few glasses of scotch she told Doyle about her first sex, a "sort of" rape. And before Doyle could figure out for himself whether it was better to hear her out, on the theory that she might need to unburden herself of a long-held secret, or whether he should insist that such talk between them was inappropriate, she was well into her tale about two older boys with whom she'd had sex when she was fourteen. "I never told them to stop. I let them do it to me," she said, but seemed to agree when Doyle said that it was rape because of their ages and hers.

146 • NO PRISONERS

"Well, I didn't stop them."

There was beer and pot and pills, and she'd tried a little of everything.

Before the boys asked her to come with them out to the pool, she'd been aware of their interest, their attraction to her. And it excited her, the way it would silence them and focus their attention as they imagined the form of the body they beheld. And while she knew even then that they could not see her hopes or dreams or thoughts or soul, the person she knew herself to be, the parts of her body were sufficient to cause the hush and clumsiness of boys much older than she was. Her sense that her breasts were too small, her hips too narrow, her legs not long enough, her face not comely enough, her hair too strange gave way to the pleasing, tidal wash of approval when they asked her to take a swim with them. And their nervousness when she said she hadn't brought her suit and they suggested they just go skinny dipping—how it seemed a dare, as they started getting out of their jeans and T-shirts, and before she knew it were both standing in their jockey shorts before her. When she removed her bra and panties, she understood immediately the power she now had over them, their attentions and desires were suddenly and ineluctably hers. Touch was only moments away and increased the intensity of their regard, and as they fondled her breasts and kissed her nipples and neck she could see the erections her acquiescence produced in these boys, these men, and though these were awkward and frightening, they were likewise exciting and a kind of balm against her worries about whether she would be good enough or pretty enough or sexy enough to be wanted by boys.

She seemed to Doyle lost in the narrative she was determined to tell him, and he wondered whether she might regard him as postprurient, too old to find stimulation in the sexual history of a young woman, or whether she meant to titillate him with a story she could later claim to have invented or blamed on drink. She had continued to refresh her tumbler from the bottle of Oban Doyle had perched on the table next to the leather chair she folded her small self into. Or maybe it actually was invention, made up to deepen his interest in her and his grand-fatherly instincts to provide shelter and safety and wherewithal. Maybe it was from a book she'd read or movie she'd seen or fantasy she nursed. It was impossible to know.

"My mother named me from a book she read in school. She always was reading. Me too."

It had happened again when she was eighteen, and a man she'd gone out with gave her pot laced with heroin and then took advantage of her. Again, she could not say whether she consented or not. "I was very stoned. It was over before I knew it." After that she'd grown accustomed to sex and drugs and rock and roll. She smoked dope through college every day and on occasion worked for a studio that filmed brief episodes of girls doing a striptease or pretending to masturbate, to help pay for her tuition and board. "I'm still strapped with a fortune in student loans," she told Doyle. "My father helped with the rent for a while and then said I was old enough to be on my own." The money she made doing scenes was added to what she was paid as an artist's model. "Those were the first times I really felt like I was beautiful," she said, pouring more whiskey into her glass, "when I was paid to be . . . you know, beautiful, comely. Or sexy, you know, wanted, all right, not for who I was, but for what I was, but wanted all the same, by total strangers. I was happy to be objectified. Removed from the actual reali-ties. It's why I had to get out of the Breakers the other night. I could feel myself cruising toward trouble there. I could feel the distance creeping in. Between me and myself."

148 • NO PRISONERS

Doyle asked if she'd ever had sex with fans of her films, and she said no. Only pretended on camera for them to watch. "I got over any sense that I'd been mistreated," she told him, "by learning to use my control over it all. I could dictate what I'd do and what I wouldn't and with whom and when and when to stop. They'd stand on their heads and whistle 'Dixie' if I told them to." She laughed, and Doyle noticed she was getting a little tipsy now, but he was taking more than a little vicarious pleasure in watching her pour the amber spirits into her mouth, swishing a little as if she was savoring their dark heat, swallowing and then opening her pursed lips for air. He found it mildly suggestive and watched closely every time she put the rim of the tumbler to her mouth.

"The sex meant nothing," she told him. "It wasn't a big deal."

He asked Patty if she'd ever told her father. "About the body modeling and stripping?" she asked him.

"About the rapes when you were a child, a teenager, the drinking and drugs attached to, let us call it, your 'sexual precocity'?"

"Never," she said. "No way," and he wondered if she'd wanted to tell someone all along and that he just happened to be the right old man for the job—too old to consider in any sexual context, well past the point where even modern pharmaceuticals might help. An old man who liked to talk and ask her about herself but was otherwise harmless to a young woman, no more excitable than an old Hoover or a table lamp.

He did not say to her how he thought she was lovely or had really swell tits or a fine ass or great gams, or any other idiom of mannish praise that women of his generation, accustomed to being treated as objects by the nitwits they shared their times with, would hear as a stupid compliment. He knew better than that. But he told her how nice it was to have another human on the premises and how fine it was to find her so damn easy to talk with and how it put him so suddenly in mind of the man he'd striven to be in his youth and middle age and the partner Sally had been to him during the forty-some years of their marriage, about which he was suddenly flooded with precious memories. He would have shared with Patty the lives he and Sally had led in private and the dark, the details of their long intimacy, how different it seemed from the hook-up culture the young were reputed to have now. He'd been thinking about how some things change and others don't, and he was sure it was due to the presence in his home of a bookish young woman with a woman's perspective, and that is where he left it.

He asked her if she thought that the early loss of her mother, so sudden and unexpected, just when she was entering puberty, had left her disadvantaged in some way when it came to her relationships with boys and men.

"I do just fine with boys and men," she told him, and said that she didn't think of herself as disadvantaged in any way.

"What are you, twenty-five or thirty?"

"Twenty-seven. And you?"

"I was old before you were born. So, years older than old, I suppose. I'm going on seventy, sixty-seven. Enough gets, eventually, to be enough. Maybe that guy was right who said less is more."

"Easy for you to say. Now that you've got everything you need."

"Not everything, Miss Patty, not everything."

"What's left to want? A great send-off?"

He admired the quickness of her, her contrarian impulse, her refusal to be cowed by her much elder host.

"I'd like for it to have meant something. My having been— that it meant something; something came of it. If not memorable, then meaningful. Does that make sense?"

"Sure, Doyle. The meaning of life. I'm looking for that too. What's it all about, Alfie, my mother used to say, whoever the fuck Alfie was."

"It was a movie."

"Everyone wants to be in a movie." She paused to consider a life two times longer than hers and how it could still lack something in the way of purpose. The old man had seen wars and riots and new technologies. He'd heard big bands and the Beatles come and go. Her own life often seemed to mean nothing, the latest of the species just coming into their own. She figured it would all make sense in the fullness of time, as she'd heard it called. Time would fill up with obvious meanings, what you would do when you had grown up, how you would know what it was all about. She had some causes she believed in—sustainable farming, family, the politics of food, community gardens. Art and music gave her inklings of a deeper end of the pool she was eager to swim in. She wanted, like all Sagittarians, adventure, surprise, challenge, and change.

That this old man, her dead grandfather's contemporary, could hunger for meaning the way she seldom told anyone she hungered too cast her further into the ambient noise of mystery.

"Were you in the war? The Greatest Generation? Didn't you save the world? That's in the history books."

"It meant nothing," Doyle said. "Less than nothing. A waste of lives."

He asked her if he could smell the drink she had just poured in her glass. She held it to his nose. He closed his eyes and breathed deeply.

"I was a coward, and a killer. I'd have shit myself if they'd ever fed us. I did things I could never be proud of."

"War is hell," she said in a whisper, wanting to be a comfort.

"So they say," said the old man, and rose to go. "Goodnight and God bless you, Miss Patty," he said, "whoever God is these days. Who's to know."

He took with him up the stairs the lifelong failure to resolve his thoughts about glory and cowardice, mortal terror and moral lapse, which were for him the permanent themes of his combat experience. The day and night of January 9 and the morning of January 10 of 1944 on Cape Gloucester meant in his personal history everything and nothing at all, at once the worst time of his life, and then again an unremarkable hell in the history of none-too-special hells. The Bismarck Archipelago, but a jot in the litter of islands in the vast expanse of the Pacific Ocean, no less in the oceans of time on either side, the before and after of the species, yet so overwhelming were the small facts of what had been the worst time of his entire life up until the night that Sally died, that when he died, Doyle knew, no mention of either of those horrors would get into the small ink of his obituary.

He thought of Sally. How he found it harder to conjure her voice or her touch or a memory of her being. How he had made his father propose to her by proxy and front him the difference between the money he sent and the money it took to get a quarter-karat diamond to make the deal for him. His first response to combat was to secure some anchorage, a piece of the rock of real life back home in the form of a formal engagement to his steady girl, Sally. He thought of their correspondence through the war, how at the end of the war, after the bombs, there on Okinawa, he kept writing to tell her how much he loved her and wanted their lives together to be free of any of the nonsense the nuns had taught them both in grade school and high school before he went to the war and was taught killing.

152 • NO PRISONERS

In the course of their dialogue, Doyle had asked Patty if she'd ever loved someone with whom she'd had sex. The alignment of body, soul, heart, and mind had been, in his long intimate life with his late wife, a mystery and a gift.

"I'm sorry," he said. "It's none of my business." The nuns had taught Sally that sex was a thing you did about love. That sex that did not make babies was unnatural. Coupling with someone you did not love but wanted nonetheless to pleasure was meaningless and immoral, animal and wrong. But Patty seemed joyously free of such formulations.

"What's the big deal with it all," she said. "It's nature, nothing more or less." She'd been taught by experience to see herself as a vessel or dispenser of it to men for whom enough would never be enough.

"It's not a zero-sum game," she said. "What I give to one, I do not subtract from another. Nor is it removed from my own store or inventory. There's an infinite supply of it we can give away and take away and share with one another. Only the marketplace requires the lie that it is finite, and we might be running out. How else would it sell us cars and perfumes and fashions and drinks? By pretending there's a code or currency or shortage of love or pleasure. It's just not so. Sex is just sex, nothing more, nothing less."

Of course, making little of it made less of the loss, Doyle thought to himself. It made what was taken from her, by rapists and opportunists, less of an abuse. Nothing special or one-off or bespoke. Nothing that was hers and hers alone to give that had been taken from her by thieves. She'd become a woman for whom there would never be the one and only. Only the one and lovely, the one du jour.

These were the things the old man took with him to his night's repose—a night made notable by his conversation with

Old Dogs • 153

a woman who, though possibly under the influence of drink, was nonetheless willing to share some details with an older and amiable perfect stranger about intimate matters of her body's story, how it was she came to be who she was and how she came to be his guest, intersecting with him this January in their vastly different lives.

Chapter Five

HYPATIA

The Epiphany

She thought she'd better come in from the cold. And the figures on the big porch, blurry through the snowsquall and frost fog—an upright human and a big black canine—were the first signs of life she'd seen that morning. A big black dog with a white chest next to a brown-robed and bare-legged specimen in brown boots and what looked like one of those fur ushanka hats with the ear flaps down—the whole ensemble the color of a turd or a dead squirrel and a figure of plane force wrapped in it and apparently enrapt in some sort of morning office, sipping something from a mug and looking her way with that thousand-yard stare, whether at Patty or past her, impossible to know.

The dog started barking when it saw her moving out on the ice among the shanties, none of which were unlocked. When did ice-fishermen get so hung up on locks? It was a big deep guard dog of a bark. The sidekick just kept sipping and looking through the little huddle of shanties, so Hypatia felt only mildly scrutinized and moved accordingly, as if she belonged there or was harmlessly lost. Except to gather the top of the robe more tightly round his chest—and it was then that the specimen became a man to her—there was no extra movement on his side of things.

As well him as another, she told herself, and started toward the shore after he'd gone back inside. There were shards of ice shoved up like the sharp scales of beached whales, tectonic and gunmetal gray, one on top of the other. But she kept moving forward toward the shore, like the blurry sister of the Pleiades, chased by Orion, over the ice impediments and up the snowdrifts in the yard, her lungs filling with the cold and the uphill trudging and exuding steam like the little engine that fucking could.

Where there's light, she told herself, there's hope. The sun was winking through the wood lot behind him, off his right shoulder.

Or so her mother had told her. She would always correct her.

"Life, Mom. I think it's *life* and *hope*."

She'd roll her eyes at her daughter's precociousness.

"You're ahead of your time, Patty!" she'd say, and laugh. "May it ever be thus."

The morning she died she was ahead of her time, mid-June, years back, not yet forty, and there was neither life nor light, nor any hope. It's hardly dark in June in Michigan. But it was black that night, that morning. And where was she going? And why? How suddenly she ceased to be. She wasn't, anymore. Her body, what was left, got so warm. Patty remembered thinking, is that all there is? Where has she gone? What now? And everyone saying everything had changed.

"Do tell," she remembered thinking. Not that much changed for her. "Do tell's" a thing she always said, and "there's a science to everything."

It had come to Patty the previous week, on New Year's Eve, a few of them doing shots and blunts and pairing off for the eventualities—the sloppy kisses, the zipless rubs—that she was into the fourteenth year since her mother had died. She'd outlived the less than thirteen years she had a mom. And had lived longer now as a motherless child. Seemed like a long time since she was a girl.

The guy wasn't long on the porch. He turned sideways and pressed himself between the spindles, then arranged himself and waved to let her know he saw her, and went back inside, splashing the dregs of his coffee in the snow on top of what Patty imagined was the piss he'd just taken. A lamp went on in the interior, brightening a side window. She was still rummaging among the empty ice shanties that formed a little ghost town on the lake, four or five hundred feet from shore. They were vacant and secured with locks and latches and lengths of small chains, awaiting their occupants' return on the weekend. She really didn't know what she was looking for. Just her habit to want to have a look inside.

Patty's grandfather always kept a shanty on the lake in winter. Long before power augers and snow machines made it easy. He'd drag her out to it when she was a girl, pulling the toboggan with his gear and his granddaughter in tow. He let her sit on a box and look into the holes he'd cut with his old blue corkscrew auger and ice spud. He jigged wax worms and pulled perch out into the cold air, where they flopped to death on the ice. He'd set tip-ups around for the odd pike. He had a transistor radio tuned to the Traverse City station, right-wingers and religious crazies, a thermos of coffee. He'd talk back to the radio as if he were arguing with a guy in the bar. He'd flown more missions over France in WWII than any other American and never would get in a plane after that. He drove or stayed home. He loved his fish dinners Friday nights. He'd scale them, fillet them, dust them in seasonings and flour, and sauté them in a cast-iron pan with lumps of butter, garlic, and onions. That was the other side of the river mouth on Grand-view Beach, where a point of land made from the fill dirt from the digging of I-75 divided the river and the lake. "Mind the moving water underneath," he'd counsel, and he'd often point to the crowd over on this side and say it was the stony shore and deep weed beds and the two rivers emptying into the lake—the Pigeon and Indian—that made the fishing good over here. His people were boat builders in the old country—Germany or the Netherlands—and he would give out with the Dutch or German of it, which Patty couldn't remember, but by the time they got over here it was Englished as Boatwright. That was her mother's name; she was one of the Boatwright girls, famous, to hear her tell it, for their fine lines and red hair. And for their "heavenly bodies." "We're guided by stars and the tides, moons and times," she'd tell her daughter. "It makes us seaworthy." Maybe it's how she got named Hypatia. Hard to know. There's a science and mystery to everything. Either way, she was Patty if anyone asked. Patty Casey. A name for plaid gymslips, knee socks, and patent leathers.

Her dad said she favored his side—Northern Italians with fine features, great teeth, dark eyes. They were scholars, artists, roustabouts, suited to the circus of the world. His grandfather gave the name of their town's saint, Cassiano, to the clerks at Ellis Island when he landed, thinking there'd be a good omen in it for him. The "mackerel snapper" at the desk made it Casey.

"Porca miseria," her dad would always cuss, quoting his forefathers, "the pig's misery," and if it got especially dark, "porca Madonna," meaning "the blessed mother's a pig," a curse that could get you struck dead by lightning. In the story of their naming it was "the fucking mick!" who turned them Irish.

So Patty Casey is who she came to be, named after her mother's longing to see the world, how it worked, the science in everything, the stars and seas. She never got there. Maybe Patty would see it all for her. Even now she was crazy for horizons, sunsets, seascapes, beaches. Gardens, mountains, open spaces, distant cities.

She couldn't say how long she'd been crossing the lake. Things were a blur from the night before, which was likewise a blur from the day before, which was the Monday she left Cheboygan, first day back to work after the holiday break.

"Why open up for all the returns?" the uncle reasoned. He sold oddments no one could afford or appreciate in hard times. "Everyone thinks art's an accessory, optional. It's the essential thing." So he took off after Christmas for someplace in the Carolinas and came back in the first week of the new year, saying the winter was shortened by a dose of the sun.

She couldn't start another day, another week, another year in that "art gallery," as her uncle called it—handmade jewelry and artsy crafts—in what was left of the main drag in a down-market resort town ravaged by recession and Walmart and snowless winters in what he called God's country. *Godforsaken* was always the word that came into her brain whenever he said it.

She'd been restless for months, knowing that this was not the life she could possibly settle for or into. The job kept body and soul together well enough and even left some to buy a few beers on the weekends. She'd moved from the room over the store into a place with a guy, Richey, who cooked short-order at the WigWam bar. Margarita Mondays, Taco Tuesdays, fish fry on Friday, and karaoke on Saturday. He cooked and cleaned for her like a hireling or wife, and soon enough they were having serviceable sex, and he was talking about maybe a "getaway" weekend in Petoskey or Traverse City and asked her what she thought about kids. "Maggots," she told him, "aliens," which put an end to that sort of talk.

She supposed he saw a future with her. It was his upbringing—straitlaced, evangelical, altar calls and personal saviors. Sex meant love and visa-damn-versa, and marriage was the thing one did about love. But he was just another port in the storm that Hypatia had existed in since she got out of college and noticed the American Dream wasn't coming true, which was, of course, the fucking fact of the matter and the sad tale of woe for her generation—top of the class in high school, early acceptance to a prestigious art school, six years of pricey education on credit, and when it's over, nothing. No job offers, nothing, just a crushing debt and no prospects so that finally when her dead mother's brother offered her a job in his gallery in Che-fucking-boygan, she told him, sure, why not. Temporarily. She was more into access than ownership, comingling rather than commitments. Eventually her only desire was to leave. Her only lust was wanderlust.

Her mother's only brother, he'd come up here with his metal sculpture and ceramics and opened a gallery in goddamn Cheboygan, with its Christians and Tea Party white trash and Walmart, and of course he was going out of business like the rest of the main drag because no one thereabouts was in the market for one of his metal sculptures. All the same he felt obliged to give his dead sister's girl a go-nowhere job, and she took it because it could be faked on a resume to sound like something more substantial than it was. *Gallery Manager and Arts Advocate*, it read under *Professional Experience* on the curriculum vitae. It was, after all, a good art school she'd gone to. Gallery work, selling the handmade papers and books she'd learned to make in Detroit, it all sounded like a life going in the right direction. That was more than four years ago.

Hypatia • 161

But she couldn't take it anymore, going nowhere: the mindless locals, the crummy food, the sense the uncle exuded from every pore that she was a thankless kid, those days he'd go off to have lunch with the Rotary or Chamber of Commerce and come back at closing time tipsy from their boozing and leering at her in the way men do. Like she owed him something. Like when was she going to show him some gratitude? His wife was an attorney who worked for the county and made more money than he did, a thing for which he would never forgive her—damned if she did and if she didn't. She worked late and left early and stayed high whenever she was at home. And who could blame her? He was fit, she'd give him that, even handsome in a quirky sort of way, so Patty could see why his wife stayed with him, for the flat-bellied, hard-body love he made with her, with his topknot and tats.

But Patty needed earth and a purpose and some kind of plan. Fresh roasted coffee, her own vegetables, a place to read and write and meditate. She needed live music, big vistas, open roads, and some adventure. Not the day-to-day subtraction from time that life in Cheboygan had become. She'd been choosing the blue pill long enough. She needed a dose of the red, the real, the depth of the rabbit hole exposed.

And worse still, the simpering profession of love and the half-baked proposal of something, if not exactly marriage, still exclusivity, that Richey had worked himself into the night before last; he could have kept that to himself. They were doing fine as housemates and fuck-buddies. He cooked, he kept things tidy, he'd go to the coin laundry and market. He paid his share of things. And he was pretty to sleep with and would even put up with the boys Patty brought home sometimes because, as she would tell him, acting high and dreamy like she imagined her aunts and her mother did in their hippie days, "the more the merrier." Her mother's favorite movie was *Jules and Jim*. It was a torment to her father, the fear that she might not be entirely sated by him. A fear that he would never possess her because even a man with himself inside you cannot claim you with another man inside you elsewhere. The all and forever, one and only, and entirely his is so utterly impossible when one's divided by two. And however you've another fellow in you, in the palm of your hand or the back of your mind or imagination, the refusal to be possessed is a power women all possess. And then Patty brought the Pilgrim home—that's what she called him because he was hitching his way around the nation with all of his belongings in a backpack and a budget of no more than twenty dollars a day for food and shelter and anything else that might happen. And because he had this prepossession about him, an aura of innocence and anointing, it was sexy. He was from Nova Scotia and had been out to Vancouver and back through Winnipeg before he got work and transport on an ore carrier that dropped him at the Soo, where someone drove him south of the bridge—so, when Hypatia brought the Pilgrim home, poor fuck Richey tried to go along with it, fearing what might happen with an ultimatum. Sometimes he even seemed to get into it, so that for a while there, most of the three weeks the Pilgrim stayed, she'd come home from the store to find dinner, something veggie and fresh, ready on the table, a bottle of Merlot or a glass of scotch and the two of them in bed, naked and waiting, like cocker spaniels, or a pair of plural wives gone rogue, eager to pleasure themselves by pleasuring her, eager to do whatever she told them. And it pleasured her, to be doubly wanted and never totally had by either one, and all the while having both of them at her beck and call. That was beyond the pale of the poor fuck's evangelical upbringing. Still, he got into it. She'd come out of the shower all shining in her cleanliness and put on that porkpie hat like the one Tom Waits wore that time she saw him with her husband in the Chicago Theatre. Only got married because it got her foot in the door of student aid at the art school, a marriage of convenience, though God knows there were times she thought it might be the true love girls of her generation were never quite sold on. She still has a romp if she's in Chicago. He won't divorce her, and she can't afford the paper shuffle, so, according to some paperwork in Wayne County, she was still Mrs. Osborn. Made Patty, Mrs. Osborn, smile. Made Larry laugh out loud as if he couldn't care less. But she knew he cared, and he cried when she left, though they'd both agreed it was only a marriage of convenience. He got someone to talk with and to sleep with and share the rent with. Patty got two points off the usurious student loan rates and a refund on taxes for filing jointly.

Of course, they never promised, as part of their nuptials, the traditional agreements about intimate exclusivity. And maybe it was a reoccurring theme, it occurred to Patty: multiply your options, divide and conquer. Anyway it worked for her, to keep any man she wanted in pursuit, chasing the myth that there's a shortage of sex, as if there wasn't an inexhaustible supply, to be doubled and quadrupled, increased anyway, algebraically by simply sharing and sharing alike. So when he thought he'd got it, finally got it, her undivided attention, she liked to rock him back on his heels, uncertain of his claim. They mostly wanted to know how they measured up. She'd tell them size doesn't matter, except when it does. But they were fairly one-dimensional. Most men, she had come to think, believed in prime numbers and upright digits and longed for exclusive rights over the favors of women. They were possessive but not eager to be possessed. Divisible by one and by themselves, as if they were the center of a woman's universe. Look heavenwards, is the

164 • NO PRISONERS

thing she'd say, whatever kind of star we are, we're one of bil-
lions, not one alone. And variety was, indeed, the spice of life.
She'd read an article and began to identify as a polyamorist. It's
a thing they could look up in the dictionary or encyclopedia.
Doyle asked if it meant having more than one lover in your life
at the same time, or more than one lover in your bed at the
same time. It could be either, Patty supposed, the more, she
further supposed, the merrier.

"It changes the looks on their faces," she said. And Patty
learned to read the looks, constantly watching for approval or
indifference or contempt or love. When she'd be doing one guy,
he looked like he owned the world; when she was having two,
they each looked like a double mortgagee. A little furtive, helpless, wondering about each other's credit score. Worried that
the card would be declined after he'd passed himself off as such
a big damn shooter.

It has to do with power, she theorized: a shift of that
dynamic—who's in charge. Of course, it was like that thing
she'd read in one of her mother's feminist books: "The weakness of men is the façade of strength; the strength of women is
the façade of weakness." Something like that. There's truth in
it; it's all illusion and pretense, the expectations of a romantic bias. She hadn't much appetite for that. She liked sex and
power and pleasure and flesh. She liked the way nature made
us and didn't make her satisfied with any one man. Nor any
one man, she reckoned, pleased enough with just herself.

And it made her feel twice as desired, twice the woman,
to have two of them working away at giving it their best and
each of them half the necessary man. It was beginning to
dawn on them, maybe, because it was soon after that the Pilgrim hit the road south, away from the winter in Northern
Michigan, just stopped in the shop, the gallery, gave Patty his

thanks, then walked out, turned left and kept on walking; it was after that, after a couple nights not sharing her with anyone, that Richey put forth the harebrained plan of them "pledging their troth"—he actually said that, without irony, like the way he'd wear old-fashioned hats, he'd looked up the word, troth, like truth—a "commitment of loyalty" to one another. She looked back at him, tilting her head. And to tell the truth, the Pilgrim had caught her a little off guard because she loved his being, his body, his waifish, lost-boy sense of adventure, and she thought he loved her some too, the regular comforts, enough to stay on for a while. And poor fuck Richey looking hangdog and needy and Patty knowing he would never be sufficient, nor would any man, not himself alone.

So, when she turned the key in the door of the store that night, her car already packed with her worldly possessions, a tool kit, some pickles and peaches she'd put up, shoes and clothes, a box of books, her portfolio, now there's a laugh, and poor fuck Richey weeping and pleading with her to stay, he was sorry, he'd never press her again, she just started heading south in that old beater Toyota, thinking she might catch up with the Pilgrim—that Tom Waits tune "Shiver Me Timbers" playing like her anthem over and over on the Bluetooth from the iPhone to her car radio—and only got so far as Topinabee, where she pulled into the Breakers because it was starting to snow and she needed a drink.

Her dad used to take her mom there when Hypatia was a kid. She could remember them dancing summer nights between the bumper pool tables to something he'd tee up on the jukebox. The Righteous Brothers or old Motown hits. Her dad was a little crazy for Motown and lived a portion of his life as Lance

Laskey of the DC Dynamites—an alter ego who had boogie moves like the backup doo-wop line of those Detroit quartets, Temptations and the Jackson brothers, and was cooler than her dad could ever be in his own incarnation of himself. He quit that after her mother died, and Hypatia missed that sometimes as much as her. She'd loved watching them box step among the tables and half drunks, the taxidermy heads of elk and moose, beaver and skunk, brown trout and bluegills sailing round the room, her sister with her chicken bits, Hypatia with a burger. That was before her brother was born, before the car crash, before everything.

And after a couple shots of bourbon at the Breakers, she could see the male gaze of the bartender—deer in the headlights, mindless and dull—settling on her and her attributes: fetching, toothy smile, perky breasts, fine ass, and, if not a skinny lizard, nicely curved. And the old feeling, a prickly heat, like a leopardess or lioness began to rise in her, and the sense that she could have anything she wanted from him because he couldn't escape the soft velvet bait dance of her predation. So when he asked her into the back room to share a joint after the last of the weeknight barflies left, and after the two of them got a little baked and Hypatia asked him how she could get her hands on a smallish stash, he said he'd be happy to take it out in trade. He'd been staring at her chest, and he leaned in to kiss her, and she didn't mind his tongue in her mouth or his hand on her ass and another on her breast, but she didn't really have anything else in mind, so when he started to unzip himself, she just got up and made for the door, no hard feelings, you understand, and thanks for the good ganja, but she'd had enough and told him so before he could start exposing himself. He felt bad then, and she meant him to so that he'd give her the rest of the bag he was rolling from, and she took it and thanked him, and when the car wouldn't start, what with the cold, she didn't dare go back and ask for a jump, so she just locked it up, grabbed her heavy coat, crossed the road, and walked out onto the frozen lake. The first light was winking across the lake and the snow was swirling everywhere, everywhere, and for reasons she was not entirely sure of, all she could think of was her dead mother and the car wreck she became at the end. And maybe she was just tipsy enough or sufficiently stoned or still pissed at the guy thinking she'd give him some head because they'd talked over the bar and shared a joint, and she'd been half hoping he would offer her a job, though she had no idea if she would have taken it. But there she was, could it be daybreak in the middle of winter, walking across a frozen lake going nowhere for no apparent reason? A car with a dead battery, a life without prospects, a frozen lake they'd scattered her mother's ashes in. And she was thinking, for fuck sake, Patty, how do you get yourself into these pre-fucking-dicaments? And it occurred to her that maybe one of the ice shanties off in the distance might be open and give some shelter where she might get a nap or get a look, through one of the holes they'd made, into the world of the water where her mother's remains, her ashes, might come floating up with some good counsel or free advice. Hypatia missed her so. She needed to ask her mother things.

She'd been there for Hypatia's first bra at ten, mostly to feel like one of the girls, she really didn't need it, and first period at eleven; there to let her know everything would be just fine, all part of nature, hormones and histrionics, while the nature in her, her hysteria, made mayhem of their family, her discontent, her stymied dreams, whatever it was that put her up on the Straits Highway that June night, driving like a banshee, maybe weeping, maybe looking to hook up, then gone. But what about the sudden attention of men when her chest, by twelve, had grown fleshy and round, and hips widening and hair everywhere? And suddenly, the scrutiny of men staring for no apparent reason, not at Hypatia but at her changes. Where was her mother then? "Out with friends," classes at the college, doing aerobics? Then dead, her ruined dad, and not a word since. Radio fucking silence. She thought if she could see into the lake, which is where they'd dumped, though they kept saying scattered, her ashes, down by the point, that August after she died that June. They kept saying scattered as if they'd float off on the breeze instead of plop, plopping like kitty litter into the sandy shallows. Wish now she'd kept some for her own. She tried to bury some in the mud at the shore and piled gravel over the top of them. They make ankle bracelets, pendants, earrings, things like that. But she had nothing. Hypatia's dad never said a bad word about her, and wept like it really hurt him, but she could tell he was pissed. That his wife, the mother of their children, just couldn't settle for the regular life he was trying to give them all. Two kids, two cars, a double mortgage, two weeks every August up at the lake with the grandparents and cousins. Enough, he would sometimes say about her—and Hypatia never knew if he meant it as something bad or good— was never going to be enough.

And maybe she was still high or hungover, but she had the idea that if she could just get a look into the bottom of the lake through one of those holes men fish through in ice shanties, huddling up with their booze and nothing better to dos, maybe she could see something that still looked like it might be her. Even if they weren't really that close. What with her perpetual discontent, her always searching for something more. Why, she wondered, why did she still miss her so?

Precocious is the word she kept hearing about herself, from the aunts and grandmothers. What did she know? Curvaceous is what the uncle called her, thinking maybe she wouldn't know the meaning of it, staring like the others did. Nowhere was safe. Not church, not the mall, not school, especially not school, where she thought it was because she was the girl with the dead mother when in fact she was the girl with the figure. She was thirteen, straight A's, 34 B's, red hair, blue eyes, sinewy legs, and a butt boys couldn't keep their eyes or their hands or their imaginations off of.

"Do you have a license to carry that?" or "Isn't there a law against concealed weapons?" Hypatia was turning heads, not because she could recite Emily Dickinson and understood game theory or could name the dominant winter constellations, but because she had become a woman with a woman's parts, though she was still a girl. She sometimes felt like a freak of nature. Other times she felt like a predator.

When she was fourteen, she discovered sex, drugs, rock and roll, and the truth in the bromide about the more the merrier.

Which is no doubt why, however loving he was and good at making love, however good a cook or cock, however tidy poor fuck Richey was, he would never amount to man enough for the likes of her, and she knew she simply needed to move along and go find the life that was sufficient to the being and the beauty and the body of Hypatia Casey because, as her mother highlighted in the book she left beside the bed she no longer would share with Hypatia's father:

> *Now I have only to hear the neighing of horses and the cracking of whips and I am seized with amorous trepidation: in Hypatia you have to go to the stables and riding rings to see the beautiful women who mount the saddle, thighs naked, greaves on their calves, and as soon as a young foreigner approaches, they fling him on the piles of hay or sawdust and press their firm nipples against him.*

170 • NO PRISONERS

> *And when my spirit wants no stimulus or nourishment*
> *save music, I know it is to be sought in the cemeteries: the*
> *musicians hide in the tombs; from grave to grave flute trills,*
> *harp chords answer one another. True, also in Hypatia the*
> *day will come when my only desire will be to leave. I know I*
> *must not go down to the harbour then, but climb the citadel's*
> *highest pinnacle and wait for a ship to go by up there. But*
> *will it ever go by?*
> *There is no language without deceit . . .*

Was her mother bound for the harbor or the bridge? The hinterland or citadel? Was she running from the family, her father, the brother, and Patty, or to someone else? Was she at her pinnacle or in deep despair? Might she have driven herself off the road? Flipped the car? Shattered herself? Never felt a thing? That's what the mortician told her father, meaning, no doubt, to be a comfort.

"She never felt a thing. It was so fast."

Which is maybe likewise why Hypatia felt so fucking stupid, once she made it off the lake and across the yard and up the porch steps and in the door of the old guy's place, even though the coffee was good and he offered her a bowl of oats with cinnamon and dried cherries because she hadn't eaten since God knows when and he built a fire and told her to sit in one of his big leather chairs and she told him she had to get her car in Topinabee and could he give her a lift and a jump and she'd be on her way and he said to take first things first, to warm herself and to take it easy, and before she knew it, she was fast asleep in the easy embrace of that big leather chair by the fire, and when she woke she was covered with a quilt and it was dark outside and he was working away at his desk between the bank of windows on one side and the wall of books on the other. So much for the being and the beauty and the body of Hypatia Casey. After everything, she was fetched up with an old guy in his old manse in Northern Michigan's frigid midwinter on an icebound lake and her derelict car in the drive with a flat tire and bum battery, no job, few prospects, and whatever she had going with poor fuck Richey, well, like the car, a shambles. So for all her romance and taste for adventure, her "only desire will be to leave," she hadn't gotten far. Not far at all.

"You must've needed the sleep," he said, hardly looking up, still typing whatever it was he was typing.

She asked what he was writing.

"Memoirs," he told her. "It's all I can do now, the past is alive, long ago. No one will read it, but what the hell. It passes the time, trying to make sense of it all. The places I've been to. The ones I've met. The few lessons I've learned that still ring true."

She told him sometimes she kept a journal, and he said it was good to have a record of it all, that writing it down gave him some sense of mastery. Not in the sense that the past did his bidding but that having it in words kept him from being overwhelmed.

"Sometimes I wonder if anyone will ever experience things the way I did, sometimes still do. I tell you some things seem like one-size-fits-all, and others seem entirely one-off, meant only for me, the happening of them."

"I'm down with that," she told him, but she was just marking time, wondering how she'd get her car and herself fit for the road.

He brought her a bowl of stew and a biscuit.

"You ought to be hungry after the long walk, the long nap, the long day."

All she could think of was the car and all her earthly possessions in it.

"The keys were in your coat pocket," he said. "The battery's shot, a tire flat. I had it towed. It won't be going anywhere tonight. It was still locked up when the wrecker got there, but you can check it out yourself after you eat. You're welcome to stay here. There's plenty of room. Tomorrow is another day."

That no one knew where she was felt suddenly a sort of comfort to her. Lost in the world, an improbable route had brought her safely, it seemed, to what looked like fairly cushy shelter. A separate bed in a separate house with a separate bathroom and windows to boot on the second floor of a snug house at the south end of the lake of her youth—it was at once beyond the pale and fairly familiar. Even the old guy was more or less the age her grandfather would have been were he still alive. Or somewhere between her father and her dead grandparents. What's more, he seemed safe enough. He didn't stare at her chest or sneak looks at her crotch and seemed actually concerned with her well-being, kind for no especial reason, apparently well past the age when men seemed utterly driven by the force of their balls, he was instead patriarchal, fatherly, rather than kinky, kindly, rather than lustful, glad for someone to sample his stew.

"Tell me about your life," he asked, while she traded the bowl she'd emptied of stew for the plate with what looked like store-bought cheesecake on it.

"It was my Sally's favorite. She's been dead a while. But I still can't pass it by in the shop."

"What put you out on the lake at dawn?" he wondered. "Where did you come from? Where are you going? Have you everything you need?"

"What's a girl got to do to get a drink around here?" she said.

"Say 'Doyle, set 'em up.'" He extended a hand and said, "Doyle Shields." She shook it and smiled and told him, "Patia, Patty Casey."

Hypatia • 173

"I haven't had a drink in nearly fifty years, Patty. It got to where I was spilling too much." He faked a kind of stage-Irish accent as he poured the whiskey in a glass.

"Saint Patrick's holy water," he said.

"Spirits," she said, to let him know she was game for snappy repartee, even with a man her dead grandfather's age.

Doyle had connected the dots between the Boatwrights and Caseys from just the other side of the river mouth. He'd known her grandparents and known of her parents, if she was a Casey from the other side.

From the top of the bookshelf, he'd brought down a bottle of J. W. Dant bourbon and brought her a glass of ice and a small cruet of water and set it all on the table next to the leather chair.

"That was old when I bought it. It's older now," he said, and kindled the split logs in the fireplace with paper and cardboard and a handful of sticks. The sour mash made Hypatia feel warm and well inside. The flames in the bottom of the glass tumbler with the amber spirits seemed alive. It made her feel looked after, ample and replete.

"So what is it you want to know, Mr. Shields?" she asked.

"Doyle, Miss Patty, Doyle will do."

"How is it being you?" he said. "I'm stuck here with an old dog and my own long but lackluster history. I'd love to hear another story. So tell me everything, anything, so long as it's so. Think of yourself as an artist's model, and me an amateur sketcher, but you can keep your clothes on. I want to know what a young person thinks and knows and feels. I had a daughter near enough your age, well, in her youth. Fiona, the bed of heaven to her."

The sudden introduction of the past tense of a dead daughter lent gravity to his query. She tried to imagine the contingencies, and seeing that long-drawn look in his eyes, she decided against pursuing them, instead answering the question he asked.

"Actually, I've been an artists' model, a figure model, when I was at art school, in Detroit. It paid well, and I felt artsy doing it. It's the first time I ever remember feeling beautiful. All of those eyes on me, scanning my person, my posing. To be paid to get naked. I started eating right and working out. Some of those guys were really cute, apart from their artistic affectations. And they looked at me as if they were looking for the person inside me, not just the flesh, though they would spend as much time on a shoulder as they would my butt. Naked as I was, some of them looked at me like I was really there. They saw things about me I had never known. Their work amazed me, flattered me. And I was getting paid for it. Like going to the shrink and not getting a bill. Getting paid instead for showing myself, just as I am, telling my story. I guess I was looking for some kind of meaning, something more than the daily grind. All my generation seems to want is to get to work on time, make enough to get buzzed on the weekend, hook up every now and then, and keep their batteries charged. Lately I've known it wouldn't be enough. I'm always restless. I had to move."

She told him the lake is where they'd put her mother, how her father was a wreck after she died when she was twelve, going on thirteen, just starting a new school, her little brother just a baby, and how she tried to keep things going at home. She told him about the megachurch where they had the funeral and how she went to school with the pastor's son and for a while after that how she thought she was saved and wanted to spread the good news everywhere. How she found it hard to believe in anything now, but still she lived in hope. Where there's light, or life, there's hope. She didn't know.

He poured the last bit of the bourbon into her glass and said she could sleep at the top of the stairs and not to be frightened if the old dog, whose name was Bill, wound up in her room sometime in the night. She could see he wanted to shift the subject. She really couldn't tell if he had blushed or become excited talking to a young woman about her intimate life in person, in the flesh. Maybe he was just too old for all of that. Though he didn't seem that old, not yet seventy. Maybe there was simply no context in which he could allow himself to think of Hypatia or anyone else as a sexual being. She didn't know. But she could tell he wanted to change the subject before it got any more awkward. She wanted to change it too. Talking sex with an old man seemed inappropriate. It was the whiskey and the fire and the leather chair, the momentary sense of a safe harbor. For Patty it was fairly empowering, to be in charge of the facts of her life, to be free of the boundaries, the bindings of a traditional marriage.

She had only married for convenience. She loved him well enough at the start, he was pretty and he wanted her, and to be wanted is a balm and seduction, isn't it? To feel a man's urgency and panting and involuntary thickening inside? She was twenty and in a city for the first time, and it seemed the thing to do, adventure. And, just like poor fuck Richey, now that she thought of it, they were good partners, a more or less equitable division of labor, no power trips, share and share alike, and they might have made a permanent go of it, grown old together, except it was never really in the cards, and the passage of time more or less told them both all they needed to know about the difference between the marriage they had and the one they might have imagined. That's one undeniable thing about their demographic, their generation: They travel light, hunger for adventure, don't want to be anchored or freighted or weighed down by the until-death-do-we-part sort of deals. No, they resist equity and permanence, would rather rent

176 • NO PRISONERS

than own, more catch as catch can than hotel reservation. If their grandparents were the Greatest Generation, as they kept hearing growing up, the young and restless were the cheapest. Couch surfing around the country, the planet, hooking up en route, crossing paths, ride-sharing, rent sharing, access not ownership, stowing away, and always jumping ship.

Whereas Doyle seemed old-school, that's what he called it, still pining for his dead wife, Sally, still figured whatever happens it's fine by him because he's ready, he said, for a big date in heaven, a heaven in which he claimed he no longer believed, but hoped might be there, where Sally and he were both about Patty's age again, and made for each other and no other. There's a smarmy romance to that, all right, a real sweetness and sadness to his missing her, but it's never going to happen for her. Nor for Richey and her, nor anyone and her. The one for her is the one to hand, the few or the many, whoever she meets and is attracted to on the journey. Her mom had it right when she hummed or sang along with that old song that proclaimed, "If you can't be with the one you love, honey, love the one you're with." And just like her book said, the time came when her only desire was to leave. That's how the job in Cheboygan came to be, her aunt and uncle sensing she needed to change her situation. She got out of the city with a little nuisance case of chlamydia, a marriage still on the books but otherwise nothing, and her sense of adventure still intact.

"He'll just flop beside you on the floor, and after a while, he'll leave again." Doyle warned her about Bill and asked would she turn off the lights when she went up. "Good night and God bless you, Patia, eh, Patty?"

"Either way," she told him. "It's actually Hypatia, but that's another story."

"Good night and God bless, then," he said, and slowly made his way up the stairs. She could hear him huffing and puffing some, and that's when he really seemed the oldest to her. And the old dog huffing and puffing behind him. When he talked he struck her as au courant, curious about curiosities that were real to a younger demographic. He asked about consent, consortium, pleasure, and commitment. He shared what seemed like intimate details of the life he had spent with his wife, with whom he remained in love after her passing from cancer. In a younger man, such loyal devotion would have been endearing, even sexy, whereas in this old guy it just seemed so sad, his pathological isolation and loneliness, the resignation he so evidently felt, the sense that he was just killing time waiting for time to return the favor and kill him too. He said that his life was incontrovertibly—that is the adjective he used—devoid of real meaning or purpose and that all he hoped for now was that his death might lend some iota, some smidgen or scintilla, she loved the way he could throw words around, some jot of purpose to his purposeless life.

She heard his footfall upstairs go the length of the hall, and the door close to his bedchamber, and, presently, the stop-and-go piddle of his piss in the toilet up there, and then the toilet flush, heard the toothbrush and the squeak of the tap water and the bed creak when he took to it. She heard what sounded like a police scanner or talk radio—a kind of white noise that he must've used to fall asleep—and soon enough, the faint and rhythmic snoring of a mouth breather in a shallow slumber. And everything was calm and, if not quiet, quiet enough. Hypatia was safe and warm and a little tight and lodged for the night with a harmless old guy and could begin her adventure in comfort rather than in crisis mode. She went up, found the suite at the top of the stairs with a big bed of striped linens, a

178 • NO PRISONERS

clean bathroom, soap, and towels. She showered and toweled dry, then, standing in her altogether, admiring her fine breasts and flat tummy and further attributes, gave thanks for them to whomever gave them to her. Then she crawled into the cool sheets, happy in her panties and bare skin and clean hair and blank slate and that her unlikely odyssey had brought her here, for the time being. She could smell the fabric softener and figured that Doyle must employ someone to clean and launder, market and maybe check on him, maybe cook a dinner from time to time, something he could pull out of the freezer and warm on the stove, small comfort foods, stews and casseroles, or something he could heat up in the microwave, chicken and rice, peas and carrots.

Anyway, she further reasoned, he seemed to have a working household here in the worst of seasons—someone to plow his drive and shovel his porch and the path from the garage to the back door, someone who stacked the firewood and got it handy for him. No nearly seventy-year-old lived unassisted in Northern Michigan in winter. It was no country for aging men.

And lying in the freshly laundered sheets beneath the plush comforter, Hypatia considered the topic the old man had broached about her hiring on as his assistant on a temporary trial basis, in exchange for lodging and meals and a reasonable stipend. An easy and agreeable sort of side hustle, he called it—some light housekeeping, an occasional trip to town for groceries or his meds. Another human in the house is what he claimed to be after, someone to dine with and discuss the evening news. No heavy lifting or hanky-panky. Mostly company and conversation. A stay against old age and infirmity for himself and his dog.

She didn't know which or who he was betting on to go first, himself or the dog. There was a hole big enough for either of them by the lake, he told her. First come, first serve, he supposed. He said he wouldn't mind being burned up and his ashes put in the grave with Bill or with his dead wife. "Together forever, either way," he said. "Old School. Semper fi."

This is how the prospect of Doyle's employment of Hypatia Casey came to pass, the way one thing seems always to lead to another. He offered to hire her for company because he'd been living dangerously alone on a lake with a dog, both of them aging inexorably and running out of reasons to rise to the occasion of another day, another season, the same old same old situation they had gotten to. The old man had more money than time and discerned that the young woman had more time than money. Possibly, it occurred to both of them, each could be of use to the other.

The big dog came in the middle of the night, just like Doyle said he might: pushed the door open with his snoot and began to sniff around and then eased himself down by the side of the bed like Poldy Bloom in that book she'd read, beside his Penelope, landing with a thump on his poor old hips. Whatever he'd smelled in her crotch when she first came into the house, he apparently approved, because he assembled his aches and pains and fitful sleep beside her bed as if he'd been doing it for years. She thought, head to foot with Molly at the end of a long day. And she, like me, just out of the bath, and fondling her lady parts, dusted with powders and perfumes and wondering which of her suitors she'd bed with next. "Yes, yes, as well him as another . . ."

He was gone in the morning—the dog. Hypatia had dreamed of distant battles, storms at sea, safe harbor, a sandy beach, and that little seam between the lapping lake water and the beach. Possibly it was all that talk with the old man, how

180 • NO PRISONERS

he knew her grandfather and how the poor man was never the same after her mother died and died himself soon enough after that, now all of their ashes, relics and selves, out there in the lake under thick layers of ice.

She couldn't remember when she'd last slept like that, twelve hours, rich dreams, a little groggy. The dark and quiet and the whiskey, maybe. Anyway, she was eager for coffee. She pulled on her tights and tiptoed downstairs, hoping the old guy was still in bed.

But he was back at his laptop at the desk, typing away at the story of his life. She never looked at him. Feigned the morning grogginess. Just walked to the kitchen and turned the kettle on and spooned some coffee in the French press and stood there looking out the kitchen window up the hill that walled the world off from him.

Her derelict car was out in the drive, covered with overnight snow and going nowhere. As good as it had felt last night to have a snug bed, a deep sleep, a harmless old guy snoring down the hall, and an old dog breathing on the floor beside the bed, she didn't like being stuck there. Like being trapped. A sliver of the old panic began to deepen in her. She wanted to get back on the road and needed to tell Doyle thanks but no thanks for the job he'd offered. It would just be too easy to settle in, well paid and well lodged, to fetch up with some old guy company through a few weeks of Michigan's winter and then drive him to wherever he needed to go. She needed to get back on the road south. Harbor or citadel. She needed to go. Everything was going to be all right, she told herself, this too will pass, everything is going to be all right.

"Ya want a cup of coffee?" she called to him, still staring out the window at the deepening snow on her poor car, and she was startled to hear his voice close behind her reply, "No thanks, Patty. I've had enough." She turned to find him standing and staring at her, a little embarrassed at having startled her. She smiled and took herself and her coffee back upstairs to meditate on options.

Sometimes she just had to tell herself to stay in a room and see what came out of it.

Chapter Six

NEW YEAR'S EVES

When Johanna came to invite him that year to join her for New Year's Eve, to see the back of 2014 and the fresh face of 2015, he was in the midst of plotting the end of his days, the trip he would have to eventually take, out to Tulsa, to enact what he'd come to see as his surpassing gesture, to make of himself, of his death, a spectacle and enactment that might change the world or a portion of it for the better.

His plan had been taking shape for weeks. He had become by default a dangerous man with nothing to lose; he couldn't give a fuck, he liked to say to himself, and a man without a fuck to give was a peril to others. While harmless in most every way, he was not entirely harmless. He had achieved a new sense of fearlessness and futility. Someone who would be undeterred by the fear of death and would not be taken prisoner. A sort of old fart jihadi, the ultimate weapon, no longer afraid of the worst that could happen. The worst, so far as Doyle could make out, had already happened, to wit, he had outlived his own hunger for life or love or adventure. If happiness seemed out of range, meaning and purpose still might be possible. He

184 • NO PRISONERS

had begun looking for missions and causes worthy of his surpassing gesture.

It was an item on the evening news that gave him what he came to regard as some good orderly direction—a sense that whoever was in charge of things might have placed before him a mission to accomplish, a job for the doing, a purpose worthy of his dying for.

In mid-December the Clay Hunt Veterans Suicide Prevention Act was being held up in Congress by a senatorial hold placed on the bill by Dr. No, the retiring senior senator from Oklahoma. Dr. No, known for his stinginess with the taxpayers' money, believed the act just threw money away on more psychiatrists for veterans suffering from PTSD. Doyle could not, try as he might, imagine a public servant more in need of correction than the senior senator. The honorable Thomas Coburn, MD, of Oklahoma, soon to spare the nation any more of his stingy wisdoms by retiring early from his second term as a US Senator with his hundred percent congressional pension intact.

He knew the senator was not a bad man, an ordinary, garden variety ideologue, a self-described citizen legislator, opposed in practice and principle to government waste. It was that he put his stop on this bill because it was his last chance to burnish his legacy as a skinflint, to hold the spotlight on himself as a hard-nosed humbug when it came to the government purse. That twenty-two veterans a day, mostly warriors from the stupid war in Afghanistan and the criminally negligent one in Iraq, men and women who knew that they had fought and killed and displaced and maimed in a war waged for no apparent reason and that their comrades in arms had died in same.

"It would be good to see you, Doyle." Johanna was smiling, stamping her feet in the cold. "You survived the Christmas downstate, thank God! And everyone well?" He could see the small path her footfall had made, coming from her car, each small socket of her high boots articulate in the deepening snow.

"Good to be seen and not viewed," he said, no longer trying to keep from repeating himself. "They're all fine, automatic pilot."

"Oh Doyle, stop it. We're not corpses yet. I came to invite you for an early dinner and maybe a movie if there's anything decent on. No need to be alone on New Year's Eve. We'll play a few hands of gin rummy. Who knows, we could kiss at midnight!"

Doyle was staring at the patch of yellow snow next to where Johanna was standing. He'd pissed in the raised flower bed by the door, the tall dry stalks of last summer's hostas sticking through the snow. Whence the hummingbirds?—he thought to himself. Whither the snowfall?

The new snow hadn't yet hidden the stain of his urine. He liked to unhitch his riggings, let his pants slip open and bare his ass, and piss into the out of doors as an exercise in what he thought of as liberty. The neighbors on the west side, from Findlay, Ohio, were seldom up in the offseason. Still, he tried to maintain, to honor his dead wife's memory, what she would have called decorum. Pissing out of doors meant he didn't have to clean around the toilet in the house.

"Come in," he said, and backed inside the breezeway, hoping she hadn't seen his dribble.

"I bought a bottle of sparkling cider and a couple of strip steaks. We can watch the ball fall in Times Square." She stamped her feet on the flagstones, pulled the hat from her head, smiled.

"Shouldn't have gone to any expense, Johanna. I'm nodding most nights by nine, asleep by ten. I'm lousy company."

He was a little mortified now at the orange cast of the pissy snow, the color of the montbretia he'd planted in front of the grandkids' long vacant sandbox by the lake last August. He did not know if it signaled blood in his urine or blood sugar that was too high or too low or incipient kidney failure.

"Let's do something maybe sevenish, Doyle. Don't be an old stick-in-the-mud. Come on over to Topinabee. It'll do you no harm. Go into the new year with a home-cooked meal in you and some conversation besides that one-sided talk you have with Bill. Don't worry, I won't kill you."

Was she referencing their history?

They were both private people, year rounders among fair-weather and weekend cottagers, locals, Doyle supposed, but still distant enough, in age and habits. He fished and read and walked some, puttered around the place. He could make a day out of patrolling his small estate for Bill's dog shit, shoveling the small heaps into the woods on three sides of his lakefront lot.

If asked, and he seldom was, he claimed to be working on his memoirs. He carried a notebook and a pen, wrote down words to look up later. He visited the library to use the internet. He liked Google and YouTube and the Sunday *New York Times*. When he discovered a free porn site, he bought a laptop computer, got high-speed Wi-Fi installed at home, and sometimes sat up watching fit and oddly tattooed twenty-some-things pleasuring each other for cash and fame. He hadn't had an erection in years but sometimes wept quietly at the beauty of their entangled bodies.

Johanna gardened and marketed and volunteered at the Topinabee library, in the former railroad station painted bright red, which Doyle could spy across the lake. She'd been widowed in her mid-forties. He'd been sixty-five. Her Carl's suicide and his Sally's cancer had dealt them both, respectively, a pair of crummy hands, albeit one too sudden and one too slow. She played solitaire. He tried crossword puzzles.

He'd been prepared to go it alone for whatever was left of his time. She wanted company but was unwilling to occupy a stool at the WigWam on Taco Tuesday, at the Pinehurst for Thirsty Thursdays, or at the Breakers on the nights the Intoxitones played for the local singles who assembled themselves in crude line dances and endeavored to drink enough to grope each other through the slow waltzes. No, if Doyle was that bit older, he was close at hand, balding, a little paunchy but otherwise fit, not sexy but sober, bookish if a bit of a slob, and no one would know whatever might come of their private business. There'd be no gossip—out of sight, out of mind. If not anxious to kiss, he was less so to tell—a gentleman of the old school, he held doors and coats and took the garbage out. What's more, if he had a suicidal impulse, she reckoned he'd already wrestled it into submission by the time she came calling on him. She'd had her fill of depressives and crazies.

It was a casserole, tuna noodle, Doyle remembered, she'd brought by all those years ago, garnished with pine nuts and dried cherries. She had heard him on the radio, speaking about being a widower. There had been some correspondence; then they had met at an AA meeting near her home in Topinabee. She had offered to bring him a dinner. She was wearing shorts and a summery top that showed off her chest to some advantage. She still colored her hair. Her legs were girlish. He admired her gumption. He invited her in, flattered by the straightforward advance. She asked how he was doing. Was he sleeping? Eating? Getting through the days? They talked about their dead spouses, their grown and distant children, their sense of the mixed blessings of being alone after years of marriage—no reason to bathe with regularity, nobody to cook for, nobody to talk to when you'd rather say nothing, whole days spent in the bathrobe and slippers. For the widowed, they concurred, the good news was often the bad news: no one farting on your leg, the bed to yourself, no other body to warm to, no fear of death. The press of isolation brought the silence in which your own voice became clearer to you, along with the sense that you could die alone and no one would notice.

There was a certain liberty in it. You could piss off the porch, squat in the garden. No one to answer to.

Doyle had his coffee with the old farts, mornings at the the deli, his AA meetings on Sunday night at Transfiguration Episcopal, Wednesdays at the Strait Gate House of Prayer. She had her women's Bible study with the Methodists, where she helped organize potlucks and funeral luncheons and sang irregularly with the choir. "Just when you think you've got it rough, you find someone who's got it worse," she said, in the maw of some heartbreak or vexation.

She worked three mornings a week in the dollar store, helped at the library book sales every month, and sometimes gave workshops on gardening and cooking. She didn't have to, she assured Doyle. Carl had left her well provided for, considering he was a Methodist minister. Even the policy, taken out in his twenties, had to pay out, despite him shooting himself. "He died of depression, undiagnosed, not treated properly, but depression nonetheless," she told anyone who asked. But she liked being out in the world. Doyle helped out on occasion at the funeral home when their young embalmer was off or on vacation or needed assistance with a difficult case. He'd done trade work downstate and had a reputation in the tri-cities of Midland, Bay City, and Saginaw, where he was known as a real artist when it came to restorations, before moving upstate for good after Sally died. He was more political than Johanna.

New Year's Eves • 189

She was more religious. He had opinions. She had beliefs. She gardened a lot; he golfed a little, mostly to have something to talk about at coffee with the guys. She put up peaches and pickles. He stacked the firewood he got delivered by the dump-truck load. "It takes most of a year to season properly," he said. "Like grief," she said, and smiled. "A year of mourning." "More if you need it," he reminded her when she showed up with the casserole.

After their third visit, she performed fellatio on Doyle, a thing that his darling Sally rarely did because she'd been instructed by the nuns, who insisted it was "unnatural" because it avoided the possibility of impregnation. Johanna seemed to have no such reservations.

The first blow job he ever got, in Melbourne with the First Marines, he knew it was a gift from God, akin to grace as it was described in the catechism, abundant and underserved, the free and unmerited favor of God, or a girl, like the first time he beheld a pair of breasts.

He was in the fifth grade at St. Francis DeSales, and it was Lent, and Sr. Jean Therese was discussing the passion of Christ when she turned to the blackboard to emphasize something she had written there, tapping the chalk next to it and underlining the cursive sentence, and Doyle observed the bulge of her bodice beneath the long scapular the IHM nuns wore back then as part of their blue habits. Sr. Jean Therese was twenty-something and spoke French to her students and was beautiful in all ways, Doyle thought, and moved like a dancer, with grace and elegance, and when he saw her sort of swivel toward the board, quickly so that her long rosary rattled and the deep-blue habit and black veil swirled around her, with her arm upraised to tap the chalk on the subject of our dear lord's passion, he saw, unmistakably, the

190 • NO PRISONERS

protuberance of her breasts, like Euclid's sketching of parabolas, and it was then that he lost his beliefs in exchange for what he would ever after consider the grace of beholding.

He no longer cared if Christ was raised from the dead or died for our sins. He believed little of what he was taught to believe. He lost interest in Capernaum or Nazareth or Bethlehem, the Annunciation or the Last Supper. He had beheld as a boy, not yet a man, the unspeakable beauty of a woman's form, albeit hidden by her raiment and modesty, and he could hope that some such creature might, in the fullness of time, let him get ahold of her breasts. And nothing in the intervening years since he had first caressed Sally's lovely tits, as he came to call them in his own irreverent but loving vernacular, disabused him of that certainty. Beholding, he knew, was beyond belief. And he beheld any chance he got.

Thus beholding Johanna's head in his lap that first time, as he sat on the sofa after the pot roast with roasted potatoes she'd brought him, after their conversation, during the third inning of the Tigers game they were watching on the TV, as she first unzipped him, then undid his belt buckle and unhitched his trousers, then pulled him out and kissed him and took him slowly into her mouth, he leaned his head back and, looking at the pale-white ceiling and letting his gaze follow the curves and turns of the crown molding, he began to thank aloud his lucky stars, which he assumed occupied the firmament above the tree line outside and out over the lake in the dark in constellations he did not need to name. He could feel himself resisting the impulse to weep aloud, while his eyes nonetheless slowly moistened with tears. He wondered whether it was grief or gratitude. He couldn't say. It was, unmistakably, he reckoned, that form of grace he'd known before when something utterly unearned, unwarranted, and gorgeous happened.

New Year's Eves • 191

The next thing he knew he was coming to in the ER at the hospital in Cheboygan, and some medico was asking him what day it was and who was the president of the United States and then about his cardiac history and was there any incidence of heart disease in his family.

Doyle said it was Friday, the thirteenth of April, and George Bush was the president of the United States. He'd voted for Bush because he'd been in the war like Doyle and, though he'd been Reagan's factotum, he knew enough to call that trickle-down bullshit "voodoo economics," which Doyle agreed with. "Trickle down, my ass," Doyle was fond of saying. "That's just 'piss on you' policy if you work for a living."

As for the heart disease, he further informed the doctor, his father had died one night at their home on Montevista, in northwest Detroit, after a chicken dinner in Frankenmuth, where he'd driven with his wife to dine at Zehnder's, famous for their family-style chicken dinners and their tidy faux-Bavarian town, with its souvenir shops and handmade candies and Missouri Synod Lutherans. That was, however, in November, as best he recalled, of 1964, a couple weeks after the landslide when Lyndon Baines Johnson won over Barry Goldwater. Doyle had no use for Texans but knew Goldwater was a head case, so he'd voted for Johnson. His father had been sixty-four and loved the Interstate Highway System that Dwight D. Eisenhower built from coast to coast after the World War, ostensibly to move missiles around for the public defense against the Russians, who had been our allies against the Germans. His dad, Doyle told the doctor, always had a new Pontiac Bonneville, which he drove ten miles an hour faster than the speed limit and sometimes would get up to a hundred miles per hour just to hear Doyle's mother, Geraldine, give out to him about his daredevilishness—a thing she'd loved, Doyle always thought. The two hours it took to get from northwest Detroit to

Frankenmuth was an easy ride in the Bonneville, and Doyle's dad loved cruising the highways with his Geraldine, and there was no traffic in November and no lines at Zehnder's, so why not get out of work an hour early, pick her up, and hit the road north; it was on the way home that he first felt oddly about maybe something he had eaten and the pain in his arm after he'd puked once followed him the way home, so Doyle's mother called the priest and the fire department and the doctor and Doyle saying something was the matter with his dad, and by the time they all got there and his old man sat on the edge of the bed in the bungalow on Montevista, in his undershirt, the fire department had hooked up some oxygen and the priest had given him extreme unction and the doctor was listening to his back and his front with the stethoscope that he pulled from his ears to tell Doyle's mother, "Mrs. Shields, I can't find a thing wrong with your man," whereupon her man, in Doyle's memory of his father's demise, turned a shade of purple that started in his earlobes and neck, inhaled quickly, a catch in the breath Doyle would always remember, and slumped to the floor dead as a mackerel, thereby proving, as Doyle reminded the medico in the ER in Cheboygan, that it was only the "practice" of medicine they all were dispensing.

"I've already outlived the old man by a year," Doyle informed them. "It's all gravy now! Bonus time."

Johanna was more than a little mortified, by Doyle's loquaciousness and by the way she'd been questioned about what was going on before the "shortness of breath and the passing out." She'd had the presence of mind to phone Doyle's eldest son to say that "something had happened" while she and his father were having dinner, and she got him to the hospital as fast as she could. "The doctors say it could go either way," she'd told him, and he told her he'd drive up right away.

New Year's Eves • 193

"Just blame it on the pot roast, Johanna," Doyle had told her when he first came to in the emergency room. "The other is no one's business but ours."

Doyle was a week in the hospital that time, while Dr. Po tried to get his meds right and his vital signs stabilized. After the cardiology workup, they got Doyle on some blood sugar medicine and a daily aspirin, and he and Johanna enjoyed a more or less irregular consortium for nearly six months before another episode, another perfect storm of satiety and breathlessness, conspired to put him into cardiac arrest, though Doyle noticed that she had seemed less passionate about their foreplay, performing a much abridged version of her first kindness on him, while he took up a regular worship at the altar of her pleasure until he'd gotten the launch code to her climax, or she became sufficiently convincing in her pretending same. To Doyle, it did not matter. He was grateful for the meals and the good company and occasional sex, and when the ER resident, after the second episode, coincident that August with the Iraqi invasion of Kuwait and the president's saber rattling over Saddam, told Doyle that he'd gotten himself into congestive heart failure and would be, based on the whooshing backwash sound he heard in his heart, a good candidate for an aortic valve replacement and suggested during the pendency of their diagnostics—there'd be some other tests, an echocardiogram, a heart catheterization—that Doyle only have sex with "familiar" partners, Doyle didn't bother explaining that he'd only been familiar with one woman for forty-three years and that she was dead and that his kindly young neighbor was doing him a huge neighborliness in sharing her lovely if unfamiliar and potentially lethal intimacies with him.

"You've gotta have something worth dying for, Doc," is what Doyle told him, CNN's coverage of the gathering storm of war, the international coalition, flickering on the TV, to which the young intern replied, "Of course, Mr. Shields, and what a way to go!"

"You know, Doc," Doyle said, "I saw plenty of dead soldiers in the war—our own, the others, the dead were everywhere. And it wasn't, in the end, the flags or causes they were fighting for. They just kept shooting to keep from getting shot. They cared about the guy in the line next to them, the ammo runner or the rifleman. In the end, when the dead were laid out like so much cordwood in the morning, and we'd be rummaging among them for souvenirs, the only thing we'd ever find is notes and photos, wives and women friends, they all had them, some beauty they'd not be getting home to."

The third episode was the following winter, when the First Marines were off to war again, assembling in the desert in Saudi Arabia for Operation Desert Storm. The air campaign had already started, with scenes on TV like video games of buildings and convoys being blown apart somewhere in the desert.

Of course, those were the days, still in his sixties, Doyle still feared dying, whereas, at ninety, he feared a life that seemed to have come to nothing more than he feared mortality. The love of his life long dead and gone, their children grown and preoccupied with their own lives, his work life finished, he was biding time without mission or purpose, like a can of beans too long in inventory, that had outlived his use or sell-by date. He'd taken up smoking again, though infrequently, and always out in the garage where he used to sneak them when Sally was still alive. He even thought maybe he should take up drink again, but after years of sobriety, he was convinced there was no trouble that couldn't be made worse by the addition of class A depressants.

"How long might I have if we do nothing, Doc?"

"Six weeks, six months, who knows? It's up to you, Mr. Shields."

With the broad view of his life, now punctuated by the shadow of death, Doyle became increasingly aware that what he'd considered watershed moments were little more than puddles and potholes on what seemed, in retrospect, a long road to nowhere, a journey without direction and of little consequence, a pilgrimage that meant nothing and would soon be over, not as the end of a noble and lifelong quest, but only the end, unremarkable from every angle and vantage—his being and his ceasing to be competing for the greater meaninglessness.

Eventually he had the surgery, recovered from it, felt somewhat better, quit smoking, and did not take up drink again, easing into a harmless and easygoing senescence that stretched through his seventies and now his eighties, not joylessly, but still with few excitements and dwindling company.

Thus, the eve and night vigil of a new year meant little to him. In his working life it had always been a busy time. Those stingy morticians who'd never call a trade man because of the share it might subtract from what they'd make on a service would pay a retainer to keep him on call from New Year's Eve until a few days into the month, leaving them with the liberty to party hard and tie one on and sleep it off and show up in fine fettle on the second or third day of the new year. Doyle would do the removals and preps, car wrecks and misadventures, and meet with the families on New Year's Day, while the name on the sign slept off the night's reveries. There were always, he'd noticed around New Year's, a few of the elders, one side or the other of a hundred years, for whom the new year must have seemed to them a kind of border that once crossed they could let go, give in to the death that they'd known was always in them. He remembered especially a tiny German woman from

Reese, in the Thumb, who lived to be 104 and died on New Year's Day after celebrating the night before with her children and grandchildren and great-grandchildren, all of whom gathered at the farm to give thanks for the old lady's long and healthy and, by all accounts, happy life. "She never strayed from the house she was born in, nor the farm she was raised on, nor the church she belonged to," her youngest daughter, who was herself older than Doyle at the time, told him. "She was still sitting in the same pew she had as a girl and weeping when they sang 'In the Garden.'"

"You must feel really good about the death she got," Doyle said to her, wanting to comfort and console, "what with her long life, her good health, the night spent with the ones she treasured most. And then to slip away in her sleep without pain or trouble."

"Actually, sir," the daughter said, "we're not feeling that good about anything today. Our mother died this morning."

Doyle winced and returned to the collection of vital statistics and survivors' names and obit details, then took them into the showroom, where they bought a cherry casket and a better than average vault. Old Man Woolever, still hungover from his carousing at the K of C dance, gave him an extra twenty for selling such a pricey unit. Years later, Doyle would read Montaigne's essay, number thirteen in book two of his complete works, to wit, "Of Judging of the Death of Others," and wish that he had read it years before. He could still remember lifting the little corpse of the old woman, who couldn't have weighed more than eighty pounds, dressed in a high-collared, long-sleeve blue dress with lace trim, into the bed of that polished cherry casket. Who, he sometimes wondered to himself, would embalm him and dress him up and put him in his casket.

Time had come to seem a meaningless construct of meaningless men who had, like him, lived without singular purpose.

What day it was, who the president of the United States happened to be, what incidence of what disease might be part of his eventual history was of no discernable import. As one of the last who were hailed as the Greatest Generation, Doyle felt that all he had left from which he might exact some inkling of meaning and purpose, some sense of mission or quest, was the death that had seemed for some time now overdue and ought to be just around the corner. And while he didn't think of New Year's Eve as a particularly suitable time to die, one day seemed as good as any other. He'd survived more than his share of them, outlived his own expectations, and only wanted to accomplish one last thing, one surpassing, worthy, and, he hoped, memorable gesture.

The way into the woods behind Doyle's had a trail that ran along the base of a ridge, maybe thirty or forty feet high, wooded with poplar and basswood and evergreens. It formed a rim around the basin that rounded downward to the lake and never failed to put Doyle in mind of Walt's Ridge on Cape Gloucester and the portion of himself he never brought home from there when he was nineteen.

New Year's Eve of 1943 he huddled in a troop transport off of the northwestern shoulder of the largest island in the Bismarck Archipelago of Papua New Guinea, checking his weapons and rations and gear, waiting for the predawn amphibious landing on Yellow Beach. He'd been away from home more than a year by then.

By the time he'd turned twenty everything had changed. He'd lost his virginity, killed men in combat, learned how to drink and smoke, hate and fear and pray. Walking through the snow in the dark, he tried to imagine what it would take to get a fifty-caliber canon to the top, up the muddy slope after a week's rain, under enemy fire from the other side of the crest. How Colonel Walt had gotten it done by dint of will and grit and a handful of gyrenes that January in 1944, for which they'd eventually name the battle and the ridge for him. How the worst night in Doyle's life, until the Friday night his Sally died, was Sunday the ninth of January, 1944. And the worst morning, Monday the tenth. Nothing in the more than seventy years since, nothing save seeing his Sally seize and convulse in the final stages of her miserable dying. Watching the life go out of a body was terrible, worse than the fear of one's own death, he thought.

"Maline you die!" he said into the cold and dark, aping the way the Japanese foot soldiers could not pronounce the *r* in marine. "Bahn*zi*! Bahn*zi*!" The frost from his hushed shrieking was like the steam in the inferno of those awful islands all those years ago.

He remembered the quivering in his Sally's face, involuntary, a sign that the cancer, having spread from the lung she had left to her spine and brain stem, had made its way more deeply into her nerve center, and her eyes rolled back into those sockets as she trembled like a dying fish at the end.

Now, nearing ninety, he wore his high boots and wool socks and carried a flashlight as he made his way under the sliver of a new moon through the insular quiet of the snow and dark. The old dog was working its way ahead, following the base of the ridge, sniffing and pissing and sniffing some more. These were the woods into which the dog took cover on those nights around the Fourth of July when the suburbanites who came up north couldn't keep from blowing up cherry bombs and M-80s and sending up flares to replicate the bombs bursting in air they had never seen from the wars they all got deferred from fighting in.

Doyle was glad for the solid footfall of progress he was making in the snow and the ease of his breathing—a sign that the pig valve was still working—and the light of the flashlamp. Johanna, he reckoned, had been good for him, getting him out of the house and out of his own head and alive to the possibilities those years ago when he might just as easily have sat in the leather wingback chair of his bereavement waiting for the other shoe to drop after Sally died. He had, in his own way, tried to return the favor, looking for chances to gainsay the guilt she sometimes mentioned over her Carl's suicide. That she'd done or failed to do something that might've made some difference. "The poor man," she always called him, and Doyle never questioned it, though he thought survivors of a suicide were more the victims than the victim of it.

"I know it had nothing to do with me," she'd always say, in a voice that left open the possibility that she hadn't seen it coming when maybe she should have.

"It wasn't about you, Johanna," Doyle would counter. "It was a despair so deep it didn't know it was despair." He'd heard that from a minister at a funeral once.

When they first got together, he'd told her he wouldn't be marrying again. "No paperwork, no mortgage, no long-term lease. Come and go as you please," he told her. That didn't go over very well with her until he added he was happy to have her be the same to him. Not a thirty-year mortgage, he told her. Rather a condo, seasonal or off-seasonal use, a couple weeks a year, when all was said and done, where the lawn was cut and the gutters cleaned and the snow shoveled and there were no school taxes. We're not looking for equity or exclusivity, only access every now and then, comfort à la carte, a familiarity this side of contempt, come and go, here again and gone tomorrow sort of thing. Someone for dinner now and then, maybe a movie. We can take each other to the grandkids' weddings. But we can keep our own main premises and only use each other for vacations and holidays, long weekends and road trips. To get out of the winter. A little sunshine in the Februaries and Novembers of a life.

"It sounds like you just want to use me." Johanna looked at him warily.

"And I want to be used myself," he told her. "You want someone to take you to church or shove up to your rump at night and cup your tits in my hand. I'll be your huckleberry. Same for you. When I don't want to cook or clean up, I'll take you to Petoskey for a proper dinner. If you get horny, I'll come on the run. No courtship required. I'll be on my knees. No duties or dowry rights. Or death till we part. Just what suits your purposes or mine and only so long as they do. If something better comes along, go for it. I can be taken or left as you see fit."

"How romantic," she objected.

"You want romance? Run an ad in the paper. Hang out at the Breakers or Inn Between or the WigWam. Time's a-wasting, Johanna." Doyle had already outlived his father by a year and figured the overtime clock was ticking. "Come as you are. You're fine by me. No need to put on a face or dress up or fake anything. Succor and comfort. It should be enough. I can't make you happy, but I can keep you company. And I can pleasure you, if you want. And you me."

It was the case three of diamonds he discarded, he was fairly certain would give her rummy. It had become part of their New Year's ritual, gin rummy, and they knew each other's game so well there could be no bluffing or pretense. The year about to surrender to 2015 made time—his ninety years in pursuit of ninety-one—seem a blur, entirely. The years had made them so familiar to each other, and yet free of the contempt familiarity was said to breed. Possibly it was his recollection of her determination and resolve, when she first came to him, the sense that he still had these years since of her intimate pursuit of him, the forthright desire to have her way with him. He never quite got over it. That sweet remembrance undid the passage of time and restored his sense of the man that he had been and the lovely seductress Johanna had been. Nonetheless, he found himself inclined to occupy the present moment, which did, indeed, seem such a gift.

Doyle Shields, in the long arc of his life, had become a live-and-let-live sort, free for the most part, of bile and rancor, unencumbered by the relentless grievance of his demographic, the whinging, why me, give me, show me self-absorption that was both a feature and flaw of old white men. He got breathless and rheumy eyed at the mention of his dead wife, Sally, or his lost daughter, Fiona, and joyous in the company of his sons and grandchildren. He craved the intimate knowledge of women—intellectual, spiritual, physical—a craving satisfied by his unlikely and longstanding consortium with a woman of surpassing goodness and fierce beauty. He was sexually a little hobbled, morally uncertain, religiously lapsed, spiritually alive, and socially curious. He had learned that women liked to be referred to as women and treated like humans possessed of their own agency, that all adjectives subtracted and all pronouns were risky.

He attributed the better version of himself, toward which he seemed to be inexorably evolving, to the promises read out at every meeting that he'd ever attended of the fellowship of Alcoholics Anonymous, as a kind of reminder as to what to

202 • NO PRISONERS

expect to reap through years of sobriety, to wit a new freedom and a new happiness, neither regretting the past nor wishing to shut the door on it. He intuitively knew how to handle things that used to baffle him.

He woke some mornings after the sweetest of dreams, all his family reconciled and together, maybe standing knee-deep in the shallows, just off the shore, seeing great fish swim among them, amiably, passing through their own lives and times much as Doyle and his people were endeavoring to pass through theirs. This struck him as evidence that the end was near and that, come what may, he was ready for anything.

The three of diamonds did make for gin, fitting as it did between the deuce and four of diamonds in her hand. She laid it down in triumph with a smile of someone with too few triumphs in her history.

"Just like they had eyes, Doyle!" Johanna sang. "I was thinking of the card and the card just came."

"You're playing outside of my league tonight, my dear," he said. "Bodes well for the coming year." And then, while she was still beaming, still gathering the cards up for the next shuffle and deal, he said, "Would you take a little road trip with me, Johanna, sometime this winter? It will shorten the worst of the season. I'd love some company on the road."

"Tell me you're not going to the Villages, Doyle. You've not thrown in that towel, have you?"

The Villages, in West Central Florida near Disney World, was a sprawling retirement community where the elderly Northern Michigander could go to replicate the *Leave It to Beaver* neighborhoods of their youths. It was 99 percent white, steadfastly Republican, free of the young and godless. It was the preferred winterage of the old farts with whom Doyle had coffee most days of the week, what with its pickleball and free golf courses and predictable politics. What's more, there were more women than men by 10 percent, which fed into the old-fart fantasies about free love and multiple partners.

"Mitt Romney singing to those Tea Partiers queered that place for good for me. No, I'm thinking Memphis for ribs, New Orleans for oysters, pre–Mardi Gras. I want to see the World War II Museum there—there's a Higgins Boat just inside the door; then points west, maybe Austin for some music, then Tulsa in mid-February. Chicago for jazz, then home again before the ice is off the lake, but in time for spring. We could share the driving, the dinners, some double rooms."

Johanna looked at him. "Restless legs syndrome?" Her eyes narrowed to focus closely. She thought a road trip at ninety out of character. The Doyle she knew was a famous homebody.

"Are you looking for a chauffeur or a partner in crime?"

"Some of each," he told her. "Someone to spell me behind the wheel, to navigate, find a good eatery, and reserve a room. Someone to talk to. Someone to go along for the ride."

"I'll let you know, Doyle. But these old bones aren't great for long hauling. I need to stop too often to use a loo. I fall asleep too easy. Hell, I nod off between here and town sometimes and catch myself or get startled awake by blaring horns."

"I know the pain," said Doyle. "I'm always on the edge of a nap."

"And is there something you're not telling me, about this journey?"

"Maybe you could watch Bill, if you're not able to go. If he dies while I'm gone, the grave's already dug. Just shove him in and shovel it over."

"Stop it, Doyle. You can get so dark. Are you OK?"

He couldn't remember the last time someone had asked if he was OK. It seemed an ordinary kindness, a standard curiosity. But here he was at ninety, and he couldn't remember anyone asking, or even if it had occurred to him to ask himself, pray tell, to assess his wellness in relative terms. So for Johanna to ask him endeared her further to him. They'd been intimate, had some regular if low-intensity sex, been neighbors forever and friends for life. He wanted to tell her everything because she really had asked him, beyond the standard courtesy, if everything with him was OK.

"I'm hoping to enact a surpassing gesture," he told her. "Something worthy, memorable."

Johanna's eyes narrowed; she stopped shuffling the cards. She put out a hand and took Doyle's hand. She put her other hand on top and looked him in the eyes.

"What are you saying, Doyle? What do you mean? Surpassing gesture?"

She sounded worried now, suspicious, overtly concerned.

He wondered if he could tell her everything. They were still playing rummy at the kitchen table. The ball had fallen on the TV in the living room. There were fireworks over the lake out front. He hedged his bets with some half-truth.

"They're doing *Romeo and Juliet* at the Tulsa Opera on Friday the thirteenth of January. I've never seen it. Would you like to go?"

"I never knew you were an opera buff, Doyle. Seems like a long way to go. Can't you get it on YouTube?"

"The soprano is said to be one of the best. And it's sort of a homecoming for her. She grew up there. Could be a very special performance."

"I never knew of anything very special in Tulsa, besides the Prayer Tower and Oral Roberts University. My poor husband used to be crazy for those TV preachers. Faith healers, scam artists, prosperity apostles, it didn't matter, he watched them all. The more he watched them, the darker he got."

"A guy I knew in the Corps grew up with Oral Roberts. Claimed he could heal the sick and raise the dead. Just like Jesus. Was your man a true believer, Johanna?"

Johanna never followed a conversation far in the direction of her dead man. "I loved him and couldn't fix him," is the most she would say, and let the talk fall off the cliff it always seemed perched upon with her. And if it took Doyle twice as many years to come to the place poor Carl must have come to, he knew there was no turning back once there. Possibly that's what made Johanna wary—his calm, his ease with the eventual outcome of it all. Of course she could never tell if it was just the long years he'd spent embalming bodies or something newly fatalistic, some fresh sense of life's meaninglessness that made him eager to finish it.

"I cannot see myself at ninety-one," he'd often tell her. "Nineteen I remember, like yesterday. But ninety-one? I just can't see it."

Doyle owned five books that he read from those nights when he woke up in the dark time, too tired to get up and make the coffee, too brain-awake to sleep. An anthology of poems Sally had bought him at the Salvation Army—*Modern American and British Poets* from Emily Dickinson to James Merrill in the first instance and Thomas Hardy to Sidney Keyes in the latter— the collected works of Michel de Montaigne, a 1948 translation of his essays and letters and travel journals that he'd bought for no reason he could remember at a library sale at the community college where he once taught embalming for a semester, and a Holy Bible that he got to join the Bible study some of the old guys had at the funeral home years before. He also owned *The Big Book of Alcoholics Anonymous* and its companion, *Twelve Steps and Twelve Traditions.* This handful he kept in a wooden box on his bedside table and would grab one at random when he woke up at night and read himself back into dozing. If one didn't work, he would try another, then another. He never had to sample more than four, his seven hours of steady repose interrupted by poems he now knew by heart, stories about drunks from decades ago, Old and New Testament chapters and verses, and the rambling essays by a man with a more comprehensive library, a curiosity about the human condition, command of more languages but who, not unlike Doyle, had come to trust the voice he talked to himself in.

"Each man bears the entire form of man's estate," he would remind himself, quoting from page 611 of the Montaigne, from his essay "Of Repentance." Everyone's the same as every other, is how Doyle thought of it. But different. Such mysteries, contemplated in the dark hours and still mornings of his advancing years, were reliable sleep aids. He needed his sleep.

When they were young and studying English in school together, Sally thought, mistakenly, that he might be a literary man. He was not. He read from the five books he'd acquired over and over and thought they supplied everything he would ever need in the way of wisdom and literature. It never made him want to write poems or to preach or construct his own fictions. He was delighted to be scripturally literate and to memorize a poem now and then and to know how to quote from the familiar texts of the great French essayists but otherwise thought of himself as more a man of action than of words. "Nothing pays off like restraint of tongue and pen," he reminded himself from *The Big Book* or the *Twelve and Twelve*, page ninety-one. It had for him. He'd spent the first months of his widowhood angry at Sally for every cigarette she'd smoked, for the cancer that took her, for the loneliness that beset him, the rage at the desolation of these so-called golden years, during which all of their patience and hard work was supposed to pay off in long years of easygoing, deeply contented companionship. He'd imagined himself doing nothing of substance with the woman he'd loved since they were both ten and his father moved the family from Wyandotte to Detroit to take a better job at the Main Post Office and Doyle started the fifth grade and Sally was there, the redheaded girl of his dreams. Sally, who saw him off to war and wrote him daily while he was gone and pledged herself to him, albeit by proxy, now more than seventy years ago. The woman who bore his children and his night terrors and his drunken tirades, who loved him unstintingly and left him alone when cancer took first her lung and then her life at the edge of those golden years he'd been counting on. Doyle found himself angry at the God he no longer believed in, at the fates and the doctors and finally at Sally, the girl of his dreams who'd left him to these long years of anguish and desolation. He could remember the first winter after her going—she died in the last week of October and was buried on All Hallows' Eve—how utterly vanquished he felt: "Two evils, monstrous either one apart, / Possessed me, and were long and loath at going: / A cry of Absence, Absence in the heart, / And in the wood the furious winter blowing." "It is a spiritual axiom that whenever we are disturbed, no matter what the cause, there is something wrong with us." Page ninety-one.

Still, he had spells of real rage, episodes of righteous anger at whatever cruel twist of fate left him lonely at sixty-five. Even now he could remember the rheumy-eyed evenings in late summer, watching the old guy going by his place in the twelve-foot aluminum in what Doyle reckoned was fifteen feet of water trolling a daredevil or plastic worm with maybe a heavy duty leader in case he picked up a marauding pike, and the chugging of the old nine-horse Evinrude outboard that no doubt belonged to a long dead uncle and in the front of the boat his pooch and missus, who were willing, in all weathers, to go along for the ride. That's the guy Doyle most envied, and he knew it was crazy enough to be mad at a dead woman, his lifelong beloved, who never chose the cancer that would kill her in the end.

Pity poor Johanna, he thought to himself, whose Carl, crazy with religious disappointments and fervor—that he never got the Abundant Life that head case in Oklahoma was always preaching about—put the barrel of his forty-four between his teeth and squeezed the trigger of it with his thumb, leaving his head split like a pumpkin with one side of his face looking one way and the other the other for his Johanna to find one Thursday when she came home from the Methodist church choir rehearsal. That was something to be right and truly mad at. But Johanna, from what she was willing to say about it, just figured whatever pain he'd been in, it was over. Almost a relief for her, Doyle reckoned, not to be walking on those eggshells anymore, an awful riddance but better than living with that constant fear. She didn't know it was Doyle who was called in to do the prep on poor Carl that time. The local guy had never had a head case so bad, so he called in Doyle to "get him where we can at least show him, just for the family, maybe, and maybe not, but just in case."

Doyle remembered thinking how ridiculous poor Carl looked—one eye looking one way, the other the other, as if he could see things on every side, the past and the future but not the moment at hand. "The moment at hand is a gift, that's why they call it the present!" Doyle remembered the change-able sign at the Strait Gate House of Prayer reading one week years ago. Poor Carl could look at the past and future but was blind to the moment right in front of him. Of course, by the time Doyle got to him he could see nothing at all. Sutures and wax, cotton and wound filler, and all night at it; when Doyle left the funeral home in town around daylight, he went and got breakfast at Christopher's and never said a word about it, not to Sally, who was still alive then, and never in his years with Johanna, coming and going as they had, pleasuring each other, sharing meals, chitchat, the occasional movie or family event, he never said a word about it. Only once, when she was trying to figure out the connection between Carl's religious fanaticism and his depression did Doyle tell her, "Of course, Jesus was a sort of suicide by cop," as if it might be a kind of comfort. Johanna's eyes squinted, and she winced a little as if to let on that she didn't get it.

"I mean, raising Lazarus from the dead, in front of all those people. And that bit with the ass and palms. He just kept pushing the buttons because he knew the whole plot."

"So, is Judas absolved?" she pressed.

"Only a pawn in the game," Doyle said. "Like Dylan sang."

Chapter Seven

CHINA MARINE

Late November 2010

Sometimes his mind seemed a million miles away,
as though lost in some sort of melancholy reverie.
—With the Old Breed by E. B. Sledge

In the dream, Corporal Shields is writing home.

My Darling Sally,

Sorry to be so long between letters, but I had some trouble. Hope you can read the scribble. They've got me propped up and patched up and doped up. Just my luck to wait till it's all over to get wounded. It's nothing really, a scratch is all. And I know you'll say I've got some explaining to do.

It is Peiping and late November of '45, those good duty months after the bombs and the Japanese have surrendered. Doyle has only just lately come to believe that they have surrendered, though it is months since his mother sent the *Detroit News* with the giant headline JAPS QUIT, and it is three months since the ink has dried on the facts of the matter, signed by those top-hatted enemies on the *USS Missouri* in Tokyo Bay.

And he and the elements of the First Marines, in for "the duration plus six months" have been taking the surrenders of half a million of them here in China since they landed here.

Could have been a whole lot worse if he'd got a nerve or a blood vessel. As it is—a few stitches, a little tender. Nothing really. It was Wayne Primo Ally, the poor devil, gone totally Asiatic since we got here. The crazy sonofabitch. After everything we've been through. We're pals since the Cape and Pavuvu.

There'd been a kind of stupor at the news when they first heard it in August. And more or less general disbelief; perched on the cliff's edge on the northwest end of Okinawa, listening for weeks to the fleets of bombers—B-29s and their Corsair escorts—passing high overhead en route to targets on the Japanese mainland, that low rumbling drone bringing Doyle and his comrades out of their tents to look heavenward for some sight of the planes preparing the way, firebombing them every night, softening them up for the eventual invasion, scheduled for November from what Doyle had heard in hushed scuttlebutt from the other G-2s in Headquarters Company. He'd be back with his rifle team in the K-3-5, no more typing intelligence dispatches. Every last one of them on deck for the push. That was the invasion they would all finally die in, or maybe if his luck held, some kind of wound that would get him back on a Liberty ship and on his way home. Unlikely that: his number was more than up. It seemed like the only way out of the war for infantry marines—a goner, or sufficiently damaged that no patchwork would get you back in the lines. Malaria, jungle rot, hookworm, and dengue fever, the cold sweats and shakes and shits: these might get you out of a battle—they got him out of Peleliu—but they wouldn't get you home from the war, which for Doyle and most of his pals seemed endless now and certain to be fatal. The weeks of relative midsummer ease, reading books and basking in the Okinawan summer—"same latitude as Ohio" one of officers said—killing snakes and clearing yucca groves for the officers' quarters, swimming and watching movies, all of it was a way of lulling them into languor before the final attack on Japan in which they would all die, and after the tally of deaths was sufficient to appease whatever god was in charge of these things, then and only then would it be over.

He had come to believe that combat was the way creation culled men full of desire and lust from the heard of humanity to keep the order of things. The men he had known who died beside him at Walt's Ridge, and the ones who never returned from that hellhole, Peleliu, and the ones he'd helped to bury on Okinawa, all fodder for God's insatiable appetite for humankind. Had it not been for Sr. Rose DeLourdes teaching him to type in the tenth grade at St. Francis DeSales, had it not been for the bad dose of malaria and the time he spent in Headquarters Company typing dispatches for the intelligence officers, surely he would have gotten it on Peleliu. Few infantry marines survived two, let alone three, major combats.

Doyle had survived the worst of it on Cape Gloucester and the cleanup of Okinawa, mostly snipers and head cases. But the assault on Japan would surely be his number up.

Word got around the camp on Okinawa, first about the bomb and then about another, three times more powerful than the first, and then Truman's announcement that the Japanese were finished by the middle of the month. Something about the Potsdam business. Though they could all see those "surrender planes"—two Betty bombers painted white with green crosses—landing on Ie Shima from their tent camp on the cliff's edge of Okinawa, Doyle had kept on as if nothing had happened because how could all of their sacrifices never be enough and a pair of bombs, however massive, be so swiftly convincing, so quickly sufficient to the task? And what about all of the dead and buried? From his company and all the rest? Twelve thousand on Okinawa alone. Or the damaged and still

214 • NO PRISONERS

standing? Another forty thousand of those. Ought they return to planning their lives now, as if they had lives to return to suddenly? Or should they sit, as they had through most of August and September, solemn and dumbstruck and disbelieving?

The Motobu Peninsula wasn't Paris, after all, and Okinawa still smelled like war and corpses, plenty of maggoty corpses. No, it hardly seemed like the straight dope. The images from *Life* and *Time* notwithstanding—of streets in London and Paris, New York and Detroit, of hugging and kissing and happy people holding papers with headlines declaring PEACE! and WAR OVER! and JAPS SURRENDER!—for Doyle and his fellow marines, there had been nothing like celebrations. They all remained wary, solemn, oddly ill at ease, still on the lookout for the enemy, those who would never surrender.

But here in the November of his dream, it seems very possible now, very real. The war is over. He's in North China. He's engaged to be married to the redheaded girl of his dreams, who has written him daily since the November morning, three years ago, back in Detroit, when her mother kissed him and her father shook his hand and she went with him and his folks to Michigan Central Station and stood waving her hankie, weeping and smiling and waving goodbye. And him waving from the window of the train to Chicago, glad to be getting away from it all. Glad to be off on his great adventure, going west with the United States Marines. Semper fucking fi: always faithful. From the halls of Montezuma to the shores of Tripoli.

I'm so very sorry to be worrying you. Don't worry, kid, it's nothing really, like I said, little more than a scratch.

He liked calling her kid because it made him think of himself on the tarmac in Casablanca and the drizzle and the fog and "here's looking at you, kid" and the general heroics of the times.

It all happened so fast! I'll be home just like we planned. Maybe sooner with this nickel-ante wound. I'm really sorry. I have 76 points. This might get me to 80. They say we need eighty to get outta here. It was 85 before, but they might have dropped it like the bombs.

Though technically speaking it isn't a combat wound and wouldn't earn him a Purple Heart and even if it had been one of the Commies taking a potshot at him doing guard duty like those poor sonsofbitches ambushed last week at the rail station, and not one of his own guys sticking him with his Ka-Bar knife, crazy with drink, after making a pass at the Chinese waitress, all the same Doyle was on duty when he was wounded and his platoon leader said it would be worth some points. So no Purple Heart and no commendation because the war is over; all the same it might mean he will jump the line and get home, if not for Christmas, then maybe New Year's? Maybe for the Epiphany? Sr. Rose DeLourdes's favorite feast. Back to Detroit and to Sally Duffy and to his father and mother and little sister. Back to the life that went on hold in his senior year at St. Francis DeSales when Pearl Harbor was attacked and everything, everything changed forever.

In the dream he wants his true love to know that it's OK because he's probably going to live forever now. And though they haven't seen each other since the twenty-first of November of '42—is it three years gone now?—he is alive and well. He is coming home to marry her and will not be getting killed. He's going to live forever. He's had the feeling for a couple of months now. Since sometime in September, after months of assuming that his number was up and his luck would run out and he'd be, like so many of his buddies, killed in action. After months of killing the enemy on Cape Gloucester, and land crabs and rats

216 • NO PRISONERS

on Pavuvu, and more enemies on Okinawa, and killing time just waiting for the final, fatal amphibious attack; after months of C-rations and K-rations and bugbites and neck boils and jungle-rot feet and even a swipe by a typhoon that swept their tents and that part of the fleet, after everything, he had come to believe that he might have a life now because whatever those bombs did to the soldiers, they relieved him and his buddies of the obligation to invade Japan, slaughter their way to Tokyo and fight to the death with every man, woman, and child left in that godforsaken nation. Operation Coronet, General Douglas MacArthur's ultimate strategy, was a happy casualty of Hiroshima and Nagasaki.

He would come, in the fullness of time, to understand and even try on for size the revised history of things that would, decades later, regard Truman's decision to use the bomb on a civilian population as a war crime and unnecessary, but he would always regard it as the thing that saved him.

Instead of certain carnage, certain death, his outfit—first in, last out—shoves off from Okinawa on 29 September, on the *USS Monrovia*, the flagship leading a convoy of eight troop carriers, sails through the East China and Yellow Seas past Japan, past Shanghai and Korea, into the Gulf of Chihli and Bohai Bay, dropping anchor at the mouth of the Hai River on the fourth of October, 1945, among sampans greeting the returning "malines," where they offload for the train to Tientsin, maybe thirty-five miles inland, then three hundred miles north to Peiping, where they are greeted like heroes by schoolchildren waving American flags.

Outside the railway station it is crowded with rickshaws and Model T taxis and the towering Chien Men Gate and hordes of Chinese all glad to see them. Like nothing so much as landing in Melbourne midway through '43 with what was left of the

Old Breed from Guadalcanal they picked up in Brisbane and all those Aussie gals, Maddy among them, done up to look like movie stars waving from the docksides full of welcome.

For a moment in the dream, Doyle's ears fill with the shouts of "Ding hao!" as the convoy of trucks speeds them through the city streets full of cheering people the roundabout way to the Legation Quarter. For the first time in months he is happy to be alive—a China Marine on city duty, assigned to barracks with beds and a roof, if not April in Paris, then autumn in the Orient, if not exactly a returning hero, a survivor, nonetheless, of the infantryman's war with the Japanese in the South Pacific.

Please tell my folks I'm swell. Won't even leave a scar. My mother will imagine the worst. But it really is nothing, nothing. An early ticket home. I really can't wait to see you my darling, please, please say you'll wait, just a little bit more. We've made it this far my darling. Please hold on.

His outfit has been mopping up amid the military and political stew that is China at the war's end—civil war between the Communists and Nationalists and Japanese to disarm and repatriate. And because there are no MP details, L Company—war weary, battle hardened, badly damaged—has been assigned the duty to police their fellow marines and keep them out of conflict with the local police force with their pissant attitudes and Shansi Mauser pistols.

In the dream it's a bar fight with two head cases from his own outfit, juiced up and Asiatic, that finally wounds him. The place was full of head cases, all of them too long holding their breath in the dark, guarding against enemy infiltrators, too long listening to shells overhead, too long wondering if they'd ever get home. Too long sleeping in the mud and jungles. Too long certain they'd all be dead. Too long away from home. And

218 • NO PRISONERS

finally, when the Third Battalion, Fifth Marine Regiment of the First Marine Division, instead of dying on Okinawa, or on Peleliu, or in the monsoon swamped jungles of New Britain, or for a couple of the oldest of them, on Guadalcanal, when against all odds they rolled into the ancient city with people waving flags and girls offering themselves and booze and food and roofs over their heads, why wouldn't it make them all a little crazy?

And wasn't it crazy luck after all? Him getting wounded so ridiculously, in a bar fight with one of his own outfit? Who, he often asked himself, is in charge of this shit?

His father had given Sally the little diamond ring that cost him a hundred and twenty-five dollars out of his pay packet, and she'd said yes to his proposal, accomplished by mail and by his father's proxy, and their date had been set for that coming June, and here he'd gotten himself wounded stupidly by some shitfaced header in a bar fight over the proper treatment of a Chinese waitress.

So sorry to worry you, honey. It all happened so fast, I hardly felt a thing until I woke up here and the nurse was changing the dressing. That hurt like crazy. At least she speaks English.

He hung another moment between waking and the dream of his sweetheart, whom he could see holding the thin vellum of his correspondence, in the front room of the brick house on Ilene Street on the northwest side of Detroit, four blocks from his own house on Montevista, aware that her family and his family would have been panicked by first reports of his wounding. The war was officially over after all.

And now he can see her as he first saw her ever, in the fifth grade of St. Francis DeSales on his first day of school in Sr. Rose DeLourdes's class. They are ten years old, and her hair is a shade of red he had never seen in Wyandotte, where he was born, where his father was the sheriff for a couple years, chasing bootleggers on the Detroit River bringing booze in from Canada. That's when they moved to the brick house on Montevista and his father got a job with the post office in Detroit and they moved to the big city.

And suddenly he is holding her. They are dancing to "Far Away Places" at Immaculata's senior prom, and his face is buried deep in her red hair, the aroma of which he can never get enough of. And he knows he loves her. And he wants to hold her forever and never quit dancing with her. And now it is the Walled Lake Pavilion, and she is whispering, whispering, "Let's go out to Middle Straits Lake."

For a moment the image of a girl in a nurse's uniform in the big city being kissed by a sailor flashes into the dream, and Doyle is panicked at the prospect of some rear-echelon swabbie moving in on Sally because boys in his outfit have been getting those letters for years from girls who said they would wait forever and didn't wait more than the first dogface that asked them out. And even if Sally isn't exactly a nurse, she's working in the admissions office at Grace Hospital on Outer Drive and wears a kind of nurse's uniform and works on weekends as a nurse's aide. Doyle was sure that the sailor was just taking advantage, having never been overseas himself, having missed by an accident of history and birth any real action, still here he was kissing every girl he could after Truman made his announcement that mid-August. The way the girl clutched her handbag between them and, with the other hand, her skirt, and bent under the press of the sailor's embrace of her, the bend of her back, the hinge of her right leg and the press of her right toe into the pavement in Eisenstaedt's famous photo from *Life* magazine always seemed to Doyle like the embodiment of

220 • NO PRISONERS

what it was to have the threat of death lifted from himself and Sally in that second autumn of their engagement, his third year away from home, both of them twenty-one years old and alive.

Leave it to the gyrenes to overdo it, the sonsofbitches. Sorry, Sally. Will you forgive me? I never saw it coming, really. I never had a chance. We'd been drinking together, and, even if we disagreed on most things, I never thought he had it in him. Thank God he missed his mark. At least with me. Not so lucky with himself, I'm afraid. But that's another thing.

And somehow the sailor's embrace gives way to his own and he is back in the ballroom at the Eastwood Gardens "where Gratiot meets Eight Mile" in Detroit and Glenn Miller and his orchestra are playing "Tangerine" or "String of Pearls" and he is pressing her to himself, her beautiful breasts against his chest, and holding her so tightly and their legs are moving in perfect unison and he buries his face in her thick red hair and breathes deeply because he loves the smell of it. Beyond the powder and perfume she wears, the deep, sexy aroma of her hair. And he always has, since the first time he ever got that close to her on Halloween in 1937, when the two of them were thirteen, his lucky number, thirteen. Born on the thirteenth, wore number thirteen on his jersey at school, thirteen when he first kissed Sally.

The pain in his left shoulder was real and he was awake with the wound and it was sixty years and another century since, and the Asian woman checking his vitals looked more Vietnamese than Chinese and spoke with the accent of the American Midwest. "Did you have a little nap, Mr. Doyle? Can you slip this under your tongue?" and he was a long way from Peiping and Sally was gone and had been for going twenty-five years and he hated having to wake from these dreams, few as they've gotten to be over the years, in which his sense of her was real and close and all things were possible and he could remember the names of the guys in his outfit and the smell of the battle on Walt's Ridge and the bodies rotting on Okinawa, and even Maddy in Melbourne when he was only a boy.

Here in the clear blue cloudless autumn afternoon, which he could see out the window of the ICU, those sweethearts in *Life* magazine and the ones on the tarmac in *Casablanca* and his own sweetheart, Sally, were all casualties of the war that time had waged on Doyle. He was eighty-five and still holding on, and now that he'd survived this attack, he reckoned he'd be making the one hundred. A letter from the president, a discount on the funeral, a cake at coffee with the old farts, anything at all but a new lease on life. Greatest Generation indeed, he thought. Not good for much of anything now.

His Sally was dead, not getting his letters. It wasn't a stab wound but a cheap shot. Bert—that nutter with his nine millimeter—and all over a photoshopped image of two gay swabbies. And Bert was a goner now.

As it had been for some time now, the impulse to weep was one he no longer could resist. He could feel the tears forming in his eyes already and the heavy sighing that always signaled sadness and gratitude—acute, generalized, ever present—the brimming cup of which was about to runneth over.

The dead were everywhere. His cloud of witnesses was bursting at the seams. The great subtraction, which is what his Sally used to say an Irish poet might have called it, had carried on unabated for decades now, a litany of loss that quickened with his advancing years and made him sometimes think he'd be the last man standing, insofar as his crowd was concerned. His cloud of witnesses inhabited a region of being between the here and now

222 • NO PRISONERS

and the long gone and entirely forgotten. The sense that his heart was known to them and that he was being watched over by them had become increasingly real to him; now and then he got, in dreams or some peripheral vision, a glimpse of their being and being there for him. Sally, dead for years now and sorely missed, their sad and long-suffering daughter, Fiona, more recently installed, his older brother, Eamon, his younger, Leo; Sally's sister, Trisha, and Trisha's husband, Lou, dead in the same week when the flu worked through his memory care unit and her assisted living rooms—Doyle had outlived them all and thought of them now as occupying heaven's mezzanine, the sweet by-and-by and ever-after's ample entresol, that middle ground between their earthen being and eternity, where they might seem to have a foot in the animate reality they'd shared with Doyle and the still heaving, hustling humanity, and a foot in another one more distant, less accessible, entirely blissful, entirely gone, but not quite yet forgotten. A new heaven and a new earth, when the former things had passed away, was how the litter of several scriptural texts that came to mind informed his meditations.

For now, and maybe for the rest of his own personal allotment of known time, he saw them looking over the rail of a pleasant but not yet perpetually distant upper room, a space from which they could share some portion of his own humble, gravity-bound existence and yet remain untethered from that earthbound groundedness, if not yet to the great beyond, a beyond he could get an occasional inkling of, like a whiff of coming rain, the sound the lake makes icing over, or a spark of sparkling light before the dark returns.

"Say not the struggle nought availeth" was the first line of a poem Sally could recite and did whenever he got himself a little confused with the intersecting lines of his thoughts and what he called his brainbox fairly hummed with a kind of overheating.

For its part, the lake was taking its good old time icing over this winter, which signaled to Doyle either the coming end of days or possibly another in the perpetual cycle of changeable weather that Michigan had always been famous for. But then he remembered it was only May 25, according to the wristwatch one of the boys had given him that seemed to be cognizant of the time, the day and date, the weather and temperature, when his dry cleaning would be returned. "If you don't like the weather," an old bromide held, "wait around a few minutes," meaning it would change, as, indeed, in Doyle's long experience, everything always did. And the living and the dead were likewise always caught somewhere between their beginnings and their ends, their setting forth and settling in, their birth and death, and the places the dead would occupy being *redivivus* in the memories of their survivors, the yet still walking talking dead who were not entirely forsaken, forgotten—bound by month's minds and anniversaries to the lives of the living. And here he remembered to give thanks for those years of vocabulary calendars that Sally gave him at Christmas, by which he had wrestled words like *redivivus* into his ordinary talk, and the thick and unabridged, not to mention new and universal, Webster's dictionary she'd bought him at the Salvation Army in Cheboygan years ago and that he now kept on the black wooden lectern she bought at the same place and found that the lexicon and lectern seemed to be made for each other, how it made him feel a sort of secular archpriest to stand and turn its feathery pages in fingerfuls or fistfuls until he came upon a new word for the day, like *redivivus* for the way the ghosts of the long gone seemed to appear in the persons of the here among us, putting us in mind of how we bury our dead and then become them. Who would become Doyle, he thought, once Doyle was no longer? He wanted to nominate Patty, in whom he had confided more of himself than he should have over the years, his hopes, his fears, his hobbled heart and shaken faiths and lost and lapsed loves. Sometimes when she spoke she reminded Doyle of himself, and it made him smile to think she must've admired some things he said in their longstanding colloquy. He loved her so. He could only hope.

So that if he did not entirely believe in an afterlife, heaven, hell, perdition, or reward, he believed, if sometimes half-heartedly, in an afterdeath, a goneness hobbled by memory and desire, a holding on to one's beloveds before surrendering them entirely to the abyss and letting go.

Whenever he pictured this halfway-home-ness, he saw the upper gallery and its habitants, the colored balcony of the courthouse in *To Kill a Mockingbird* with the kindly churchman, bespectacled and watching over them all, and Gregory Peck, down on the main floor in his summer suit, gathering the papers of his losing cause after they took Tom Robinson away and Scout and Jem have dozed off upstairs with the Black half-citizens of Maycomb.

"The spiritual life is not a theory," Doyle could quote at will from page eighty-three of his paperback copy of *The Big Book.* "We have to live it." Then he would read the promises: "If we are painstaking about this phase of our development." He was living it now, Doyle told himself, happily haunted by the ghosts of his long life; the dead and gone were more real to him than the here and now—an old man, alone on a lake with a dog, stringing soup bones on a rope as if it mattered at all.

It remained a part of his Sunday morning routine and rubric. He slept in until 7 a.m., accomplished the abridged duties of his toilet, the standing general laving, the brushing of teeth, the dressing from the clothes tossed over chair and stationary bike, the putting of his personalia in his pockets, key fob, handkerchief, money roll and notebook, token and rosary, pen clipped to his shirt pocket or the neck of his T-shirt. Then down to let the dog out and make the first of two cups of coffee, meds, apple-cider gummy supplement, take the blood pressure and blood oxygen, turn on the morning news, make the oats, and watch *Meet the Press*. Then make for town and the party store, where Sheila, the now-middle-aged woman with the tattooed breasts who called him honey, would ask if he needed a bag for the Good & Plenty and Baby Ruth bars he added to his *Sunday Times* and the local weekly.

He had picked Sheila up once, it must have been twenty-some years ago, walking into town from the trailer park she stayed in to make her afternoon shift at the party store. She was hitching a lift half-heartedly, throwing a thumb out when an infrequent car going her way passed in the road. Sally had only been gone a couple of months, and Doyle pulled over before he could think it through. There was a damp snow falling, and though he was usually wary of picking up hitchhikers, the weather made him sympathetic to the cause. Her boyfriend had taken the car to go hunting or fishing somewhere, and the walk would do her good; nonetheless, she was glad for the ride and was hopeful for a lift when her shift was over at 11 p.m. Doyle said he'd be asleep by then but gave her his number if she found herself in a jam. She could call, and he'd come and get her. She had never called, not then, not in any of the many years since. Once or twice, while admiring the tattoos on her breasts and trying to make some sense of their meaning while she was ringing up his purchases, he'd thought he might ask her out to dinner, maybe a pizza or some fish and chips, but he never could work up the courage to overcome the twenty-five- or thirty-some-year age difference between them. He always left the pennies in the penny jar, took up his packet of incidentals, and walked out, resolving to try her next time. Alas, he never did. And now, sitting in the wide-armed Adirondack chair on the broad porch, looking out on the lake, Doyle wondered what he'd done with the day that was in it. It was late in the afternoon now, a decision about dinner would have to be made, and what about the typing he'd resolved to do in furtherance of the story he'd promised Sally to tell, of their life and times, their story, for all that it might tell the grandchildren and great-grandchildren and future generations about faith and hope and love, by which they'd lived their story out, how they'd met in the fifth grade at St. Francis DeSales and off he'd gone to the Second World War and she kept her promises to stay home and wait for his safe return, even when he ended up stabbed to near death in that bar fight in China, still she'd waited and then he came home and they were married and lived more or less happily ever after for forty-three years until she got the cancer and he remained, widowed and heartsore for another twenty-five years now by dint of a triple bypass and later a pig valve and now through the kindnesses of a woman forty years his junior who came by a few days every week and brought him groceries and meds and tidied the house and made him his 4 p.m. cup of coffee before making a dinner that, more often than not, she shared with him and cleaned up the kitchen before going home. Not to mention his unlikely consortium with a more age-appropriate, though still much younger, comely woman of his dreams who traveled with him and slept with him and shared herself entirely with him and knew his heart and disclosed hers to him without reservation or hesitation.

Second only to his regular reimagining of Johanna's first coming to him and the way she seemed purposeful in wanting to be with him, how she came willingly to bed with him, eager to engage in their having their ways with one another, second only to replaying these scenes in his mind was Doyle's replaying in his acoustic memory the tune of the "Kontakion for the Departed," a version of which he had heard at funerals over his years of mortuary work and it invariably made him think of his own obsequies—a calendar word for funeral ceremonies—and how that portion of the ancient hymn that sings, "Yet even at the grave we make our song: Alleluia, Alleluia, Alleluia" would set exactly the tone that Doyle thought ought to be set, in review of his life and his many blessings, which, whenever he did the math, so outnumbered the sadnesses, even allowing for Sally and, God bless her, Fiona, that nearing the end he would have to say that all things considered he'd had more good days than bad and was a lucky guy, any way he figured it, and whoever God was had been good to him. As often happened now, he found himself rheumy eyed and at his ease.

He could remember coming out on the porch with his second cup of coffee that morning to admire the day that was in it and likely gather his thoughts to get some more written of the memoir he'd promised Sally to finish, and he saw on the table beside his chair the single-shot BB pistol he used against the squirrels that were ever pillaging the sunflower feeders he kept out for the goldfinches and chickadees, house finches and nuthatches. Had he fallen asleep, and wasn't it about time to trade out the seed feeders for the sugar water he put out for the hummingbirds? Surely they'd made it this far north by now, their furious wings blurring with hunger and the thrum of their steady feeding. Had he shot a squirrel, or shot at one? Had the murderous impulse taken over at last? Had he simply settled into a late spring nap, what with the sunshine and the windlessness and the warm temps and the deepening sense that Sally had been right those nights when he'd wake up with

dreams of the Cape and Walt's Ridge or, later in his life's adventures, drinking dreams, though he'd been sober, or dreams
of his dead daughter taking her leap from the Golden Gate
Bridge in California, how the speed of her descent after letting
go kept increasing faster and faster until she made it to thirty-
two feet per second per second, which Doyle had never understood since hearing it years ago in Brother Murphy's physics
class, the acceleration making him dizzier and dizzier until he
achieved a kind of plummeting calm and in the dream he had
seemed to slip the grips of gravity and time and he wondered if
his poor sad long-lost granddaughter had achieved such calm,
such timelessness, and if that was the siren song that beckoned
her to place her faith and her footfall into the air. The fright
of that mystery would always wake Doyle, which always woke
Sally, who always woke up saying "there, there, darling, everything is going to be all right" because she knew that Doyle was
beset by guilt or fear or the press of not knowing what was or
wasn't next for him to do.

"Now," Patty said, "here's your coffee." She put the cup
down on the arm of the Adirondack chair.

"I thought you'd be staying home for the holiday," he
said, still groggy from his dozing off and waking up, and sur-
prised to see her.

"What holiday?" she asked him.

"Decoration Day, there should be a parade. All the veterans stuffed into the old uniforms, remembering the poor
devils who never made it home, from Korea and Nam, Iraq
and Afghanistan."

"What about old marines, like yourself, Doyle? You know
I love men in uniforms. I know yours still fits. C'mon, get ready,
I can drive you into town, they'll put you on a float or in a con-
vertible. C'mon, you said it yourself, the last good war."

China Marine • 229

"Consider, too, our talents for procrastination," Doyle read from his dog-eared copy of the *Twelve by Twelve*, "which is really sloth in five syllables."

He liked the sound of that, the matter-of-factness, the unabashed sleight of language in its declaration. It was not so much the sloth, the indolence, he thought, as the putting off until tomorrow the task that had better be done today. From the Latin for *tomorrow*, wherefore *crastinus*, thus, belonging to tomorrow. *Procrastinus:* a deferral, a delay.

The sentence had stuck in his head since the night before at the Topinabee meeting of the fellowship of Alcoholics Anonymous, which was a step-study group that gathered at the Berean Bible Church, a block west of the Straits Highway, Old US-27, which ran north along the west side of Mullett Lake and the east side of Burt Lake up through Cheboygan and thence northwest on US-23 along the south shore of the Straits of Mackinac to the bridge in Mackinaw City which crossed over to Michigan's Upper Peninsula.

"Never put off till tomorrow," he could remember declaring back in his drinking days, "what can be put off until the day after tomorrow!" It always got a laugh. And as he sat on the lakefront porch staring into the blue morning, sipping his first cup of coffee, Doyle thought he'd better call his sponsor, Woody, though Woody was fairly demented now and mightn't be able to keep up his end of a conversation. There was a freedom about talking with Woody, a sense of the connectedness of everything in creation, body and mind, experience and imagination, the past and the future, everything. It was great to have an AA sponsor who had no short-term memory left. You could tell him anything, and he'd forget it before the call was over; better than a priest for confessing, free of any but kindly

230 • NO PRISONERS

motives and driven by something that Doyle thought must be a sort of grace, abundant and undeserved.

And, too, it would keep him from the real day's work on the memoir he'd promised Sally. That was years ago now, that promise, years before her death and again before she died.

"I promise," he told her, the night before, before the seizures started, that final spiral of shutting down.

He had piles of false starts, portions of episodes. He'd just kept doing a day at a time. *Tomorrow's a mystery, yesterday is history, all that we have is the here and now, that's why they call it the present.* The bromides that filled his brainbox were full of echoes, the smarmy little rhymes he'd heard at tables, *fake it till you make it, let go, let God. No appointments, no disappointments. Want no vexations, brook no expectations.* Such were the rules he had tried to abide by. *Gratitude's an easy lift compared to grievance.*

Where his memoir had been stuck for as long as he could remember was on the overwhelming question of the meaning of life in general, his life in particular. What had Doyle been brought into being for? There must be something besides the daily round of little victories and inconsequential failures. He'd read books on the subject, men in concentration camps who took some comfort from singing Verdi's *Requiem.* Had he seen a movie about that? What did it mean? Did it give them purpose? Was their moment with the "Libera Me," that prayer for deliverance, why they had been born, and having raised their pitiful song to the vacant heavens, was there nothing next but the transport to the gassing camps in the east, in Poland, Auschwitz?

And here he was, grown old long past his life's expectancies, and still not much of a clue as to what it was he was doing here. The great moments of his life seemed, in retrospect, quite unremarkable, even meaningless, random, open to endless but ultimately boring interpretations, none of them convincing, each more fatuous than the other. What reason for a memoir when whatever happened was of little consequence, neither the saving of souls nor the changing of history, just the wringing life dry of its joy and juices, the passage of time accelerating like the turning of a toilet paper roll as it works inexorably toward its running out. The way it unwinds faster at the end, as one of his fellow alchies pointed out.

Was he, Doyle asked himself, a human being with a spiritual aspect or aptitude, or was he, as he had come to think in the years since Sally had died, a spiritual being with a temporary humanity? A humanity that had outlived its purpose and its time, but with which he still struggled to align his being. What he had come to think of as his cloud of witnesses, the dead before him in history and in his own time, who occupied now a sort of mezzanine of being between himself, here, earthbound, flesh bound, bound by his appetites and inklings and desires, his humanity, his soul, his spirit, his being beyond all contemplation and imagination.

He'd given that book to Fiona when she turned twelve. Sally was still alive then, and he'd asked what she thought he should give their bookish daughter. Sally had her original copy from 1960. They gave it to their daughter, who became, ever after, an activist for civil rights and women's rights and the rights of gay, lesbian, BTQ, and other nonconforming people. She had helped to organize the MLK Day events, parades, and seminars in the lily-white suburb where she'd grown up, and she dated men of color in her twenties: Henry, who went off to join the army in Georgia, and Yuri, a Costa Rican man she brought home from her travels there—they'd settled into a bungalow and seemed truly happy until her lifelong struggle with bipolar disorder sabotaged their courtship.

Her breakup with him was the beginning of a year of conflicts, each ending in some form of drama and retreat, the last of which resulted in her rejection of what she called her "family of origin," an estrangement that lasted fifteen years and ended badly. Doyle never thought of it without wishing he could have spared his sons the heartbreak and desolation.

"You did everything that could be done," Doyle told his heartbroken self. "You tried everything; you were an exemplary father."

To which he replied that the father of a dead daughter is at some level unsuccessful as a dad. Just as he always planned on predeceasing Sally, he'd always taken for granted that his sons and daughter would outlive him by years. And there were not a few mornings, in the weeks that turned into months that turned into years of mourning, often long before daybreak, when Doyle awakened, held his shaking shoulders, and let himself weep. There was no comfort, nothing to be said, only to sit with the hollowed man he was, the damaged goods he had become, to sit in silence before a mystery too deep to fathom.

He hadn't been lazy. It wasn't indolence; procrastination wasn't sloth. Rather, it was wanting to dodge or divert what it felt like when he considered taking full hold of the task at hand. If one bellied up to the bar of the job, one risked the possibility that one wouldn't be sufficient to the task. That's when he'd begin to wonder what a guy had to do to get a drink around here. Which seemed, now that he thought of it, a central question of his life and times. What's a guy got to do to get a drink around here? That's when he could say, like John Wayne or Clint Eastwood or one of those manly men in the movies, "Set 'em up. I'm here to knock 'em down." There was something he was sufficient for, he could hold his liquor, knock one back after the other, still stand upright and make sense to himself and anyone in earshot. Hadn't that been part of his story too? Hadn't he always risen to the occasion? Whatever was thrown at him, hadn't he been ready and willing and able to do his part, to pitch in, to do the next right thing? To be the man?

Still, there was a fear at the base of everything—a sense that if he started he might not finish. It might take more than he had in him. Was it a kind of performance anxiety? Procrastination? That maybe the story he'd promised Sally to tell, the story of their lives and times, mightn't be much of a story at all—just another everyday garden variety episode everyone knew the outcome of. We were born, we loved, we made babies, we had a life, we died. Nothing exceptional, nothing of note, nothing out of the ordinary. Not One of a Kind but one of a kind. Lowercase and unremarkable in all the usual ways.

It had been the same when he tried out for the team at St. Francis DeSales a lifetime ago. Would he be big enough, fast enough, fit enough, strong enough, rough and tumble enough to block the giant from Gesu or Redeemer? Would Sally feel the same about a skinny right tackle as her girlfriends felt about tight ends and halfbacks, runners and glory boys? Was it enough to show up, shut up, pitch in, do his part when no one kept track of his blocks or tackles the way they kept track of yards gained running or passing, touchdowns scored.

It was much the same in the Corps in the war. Had he the guts, the gumption, the killer instincts; did he have what it takes to kill a man? Could he save his life and the lives of his buddies? Would he make it through, measure up, be enough of a man, belly up to the existential business of life, death, daily rounds? He and Billy Swinford Smith and Donald Crescent Coe and Wayne Primo Ally and the rest—those triple-named, government-issue leathernecks, frightened boys in the dark, with their M-1s and their gung ho's and their procrastinations?

234 • NO PRISONERS

There was always that anxiety about getting the job done, looking the part, rising to the occasion.

He felt it when he came home from China and showed up at Sally's in his uniform, a dangerous man with scouts' and snipers' eyes and half a bottle of sour mash in him to see if she'd been semper fi to him those long years he'd been gone. Would he know? Could he be sure? Would it matter? And then the night of their wedding in that suite at the Botsford Inn after the reception, would he have what it would take to make her glad she'd waited for him, and wore the ring Doyle had given her by proxy. Would she be glad she'd thrown in her future with his? Was he man enough, good enough at pleasing her? Did any of it matter in the end? How accomplished he felt when she turned up pregnant. Like a real man, having shown up, shut up, and done his part, to please and impregnate the woman he loved.

What if after everything it meant nothing at all? What if there was no one keeping track of the tally of kindnesses and short-falls? No God in His heaven, or Hers? Hadn't that been the question of the ages, of his life and times—what if, what if not? I wonder if there's anything at all. I wonder if he hears us when we pray. These are the things he always thought about.

What if Sally wasn't, anymore? What if when she died she'd ceased to be, entirely, irredeemably, inarguably, could not know his heart, didn't occupy someplace like heaven's mezzanine, looking over the edge into the world's ongoing dramas and imbroglios? What if she was only moldering in the grave like every corpse, working toward its disappearance in keeping with the laws of nature and rotting, putrefaction, and decomposi-tion, returning to the earth, to earth, or ashes to ashes or dust to the dust we humus beings, we human beings, were wrought from—the handful of dirt God breathed into, inspired, put a spirit in? What if all of that was only a story we told ourselves to make the death of our beloveds bearable?

Since her death he had been searching for a cause, a purpose for living, something worthy of the gift his life with Sally had always seemed to him. She had exacted a promise from him that he would write their story down. "I won't be around to tell our grandchildren, Doyle, how we met and courted by correspondence through the horrible war and still managed to come together again and marry and build a family and keep body and soul together and love one another for the whole of our lives. We passed through our times, our little lives, together and remained true. You must write it all down so there'll be a record of us having been. It's the only inheritance that really matters, Doyle, the stories of the dead and gone that bring them back into the talk of the living."

She was such a bookish woman, Sally was. Always reading something, anything; it calmed and transported her those evenings when the rest were watching TV or playing out of doors. She would curl up in a corner of the sofa and open a book and read and read and read. And maybe that's what kept her so free of want and expectation, willing to live life on life's terms. "We play the cards we're dealt, Doyle. Everything is going to be all right."

He was glad she hadn't had to endure the worst of it.

And here it was, another Feast of the Epiphany, the feast of beholding things the way they are, Sally had always told him, the little Christmas when women used to celebrate another season of family and in-laws and elders and presents and big meals and sleepless nights behind them, when wise men looked upon the mother and child and beheld salvation wrapped in swaddling cloths. Here it was another early January, another Wednesday in ordinary time, the lake unfrozen, his heart still broken, his oats on the boil and him waiting on the toaster for something to happen. He'd have to shower up and shave before Patty showed up with the groceries from the list he'd given her.

Reports in the news of veterans' suicides, twenty-two a day, according to reports, had caught his attention. Young men and women lost to the realization that nothing mattered, not the sacrifice of their own time or the ultimate sacrifices of their fellow soldiers who'd come home in boxes festooned with flags in the belly of a transport plane. He was haunted by the story of Clay Hunt, who seemed to have his shit together but who ultimately took his own life; despairing, Doyle supposed, of finding a purpose worth living for, he simply quit.

Maybe that was what happened to his daughter, Fiona, when she leapt to her end, having quit her family of origin years before, having quit her husband of fifteen years, having escaped the horse and dog and rabbits she'd made her pets and cared for and the twenty-some acres she grazed them on and sheds and stables she had spent her days in and, sick with voices and fears and delusions, driven across the country to find the end she imagined for herself, stopping on the southbound end of the bridge, leaping the barriers to the pedestrian walkway and, having achieved the edge of the massive structure, let go of her grasp on life and time and her being in it and achieving the acceleration of gravity that bodies in free fall will achieve, to wit, thirty-two feet per second per second—per second squared— she hit the surface of San Francisco Bay with a blunt force sufficient to quench the thirst that nature has for our demises.

It was Doyle that his poor son Liam called, laden with sad facts, after the investigator called from Marin County to report the presence of a corpse, Jane Doe number 247, who had been fourteen minutes in the water before the coroner's boat retrieved her from the bay. There had been witnesses. There was videotape. No one would ever be allowed to see it. This fact had been tested in the Supreme Court of California and the Supreme Court of the United States at large. What was to be done about these truths, is what Doyle's son was so sadly asking, in that desolate voice the possessors of fact adopt to say what it was that had apparently happened. They found her few belongings in the rental car, with her name on the rental car contract in the glove box; the rest had been basic law enforcement connections—state police to state police to county police to local police to the dad whose world was about to be ruined. The dad who hadn't seen his daughter in some years by her own embargo of him and his family of blood. She had chosen as an alternative a family of choice, but had, as those with mental illness often do, rejected the chosen family eventually too. Through the years of estrangement from Fiona, Doyle had arrived at his own sad options. He could think of his beloved daughter as evil or mean-spirited, or he could think of her as mentally ill. He chose the latter because he had known the years of her goodness and kindness and joy and love. Only an affliction beyond the reach of love could explain her embargo of the family that loved her. Of course, Fiona rejected any version of that diagnosis, whether parent or sibling or medico tendered it, thereby rejecting as well any medicine or treatment or remediation based upon the prospect that there was something amiss with her.

Eventually Doyle came to believe that Fiona must have come to her own conclusions about her "conditions." Possibly the sense that it would never get better, that the sadness that informed her conduct, by which she was perpetually beset, would never be undone or countervailed, left her disconsolate beyond all reach. The darkness that came over Doyle when he thought these things sometimes took hours, sometimes days, to undo. At times it was as if his life had become a blur of several shades of gray. In the fullness of time it was arithmetic that provided solace. Doing the math of it suggested that the years of Fiona's being among them would, given even generous expectancies, outnumber the years left to him to live without her. This formula worked with Sally's death too, though it had come to him after Fiona's death. In both cases it left him more grateful than aggrieved, more thankful for the times they had than bereaved at the times he would be without them. Surely there was something in the Bible or *Big Book* that must articulate this truth, but Doyle just figured that gratitude was a lighter lift than grievance and tried to live his life accordingly.

All the stories Doyle ever knew of seemed a journey or pursuit, and he wanted to frame his story of Sally and himself as an endeavor of a higher purpose, a noble search, ending, as such things often do, in a lesson learned or moral of the story. Love conquers all, or done is better than good, or two wrongs do not make a right; he wanted their story to say their lifelong love affair and her beauty and valor were all in service of a human endeavor every generation would understand and identify with. It hardly seemed like too much to ask. He'd done his part; Sally hers.

A boy who meets a girl when they are both ten, a pair of kids who get through the changes of their bodies and minds and still find the other desirable, how, on the edge of their life together, in their senior year of high school, the world is changed by violence and war.

When in search of blessings among the agonies, Doyle counted the one that Sally had not lived to see her daughter's death by suicide, to feel the helplessness, the bit of shame, the crippling sadness of the irreversible, the shoulda, woulda, coulda, if onlies that make a mug's game of the survivors of such deaths. Sally would have been on her knees every night with novenas and rosaries for the repose of her daughter's soul and the restoration of her family's well-being.

Doyle was inconsolable, his heart was broken in the structural and functional sense of things. It no longer worked. He became a stranger to them all, left with a mystery he sat silent before, only smiling and nodding on occasion in receipt of condolence or fellow feeling. Doyle was helpless, of course, and truth be told he was heartbroken too. Her death was a sort of dry socket, the pain of which waxed and waned with intensity, but like the moon, never went away. Second only to Sally's death, Fiona's filled his pool of sorrows to overflowing. Sunsets, big music gatherings, smarmy commercials on the TV turned him rheumy eyed and breathless. He had learned to live with it. There had been, in the passing of time, no comfort, no mending, no closure, no healing.

Nor could he, now nearing the end of his days, cobble together any meaning or reason or deeper purpose for the gift of his life. Nothing seemed to amount to a difference made or disaster averted or goodness assigned to his account.

But for that map in the dead soldier's breast pocket, they might never have bothered. What were the odds? Some gyrene looking for souvenirs comes across the gassy, buggy, shot-up body of this Japanese officer, hoping for a flag or diary or letters from home with photos of his geisha or little wife and instead he finds this crude map of Borgen Bay and its environs—Silimati Point, like a nose in profile, that was the tip-off, at the northern edge of Borgen and the circle around where Target Hill would be and what they'd been calling Hill 660 and inland something called Aogiri Ridge. And the red ink notations in Japanese that translated as *defend at all costs!* The hills were plain enough to see, but they'd never heard about this other place, never known about Aogiri Ridge or the gathering of Matsuda's foot soldiers there in the dense triple canopy of cover. Put those points together, and it began to make sense—the little flags and arrows and numbers and parabolic lines, the Japanese soldiers' weapons caches and storage dumps and encampments and their retreating lines of defense so they had to hump their way south through this green inferno in the daylong, nightlong rain and the goddamn ants and mosquitoes, nevermind the snakes, for their date with destiny.

They were happily bivouacked on the beach, still plump from their Christmas dinner on Goodenough Island, still reading the mail they'd brought them there. It was good enough. They could have just stayed there on the edge of things, dodging the occasional sniper fire. Or stayed on ships in reserve, killing time, playing poker. The Seventh seemed to have things well in hand. The airstrips were taken without much trouble. What was left of the Japanese—what hadn't been killed by marines or disabled by the jungle, what with its carnivorous bugs and stinging flies and poisonous snakes and the treacheries of monsoon season with its malaria and fevers and jungle rot— were just trying to make it back the three hundred miles to Rabaul at the other end of the island, catch a transport off of this hellacious place to get back to Osaka and die in the arms of their beloveds. If the K-3-5 had left them alone, they'd all have died en route of despair and neglect and fatigue.

But they get this map to Headquarters at the CP near the airstrips, and the big brass comes over to have a look, and the map more or less indicates where the Japanese might be hiding out and biding their time in bunkers and pillboxes, and it falls to Doyle's outfit to go in hot pursuit of what Harry Rader calls their "date with destiny." All those G-2s and G-3s and even General Sheperd, poring over this dead Jap's pocket map, a half-ass likeness of Borgen Bay and the inland topographies. What was called Target Hill and Hill 660 and Hill 150, and this Aogori was near enough and might even be Hill 150, but it was up to Doyle's outfit to go out in the swamp and find the thing—Aogiri Ridge—even if it meant a "date with destiny." Fuckin Harry. He was the section leader of the weapons platoon: three squads of machine guns and a mortar section of three more squads. Thirty-six of them in all, counting Lt. McMahon and Darsey the gunny, who got two fingers shot clean off on Guadalcanal. It's them that sent the orders down to move up to positions formerly held by the Seventh. That was on the second of January. And now Doyle was really in it. He saw a sniper shot out of a tree. Fell with a thud. One shot got him dangling, then the BAR dropped him. Next day they get ambushed and Tex is killed, Carlon and Romero wounded, and they lost a machine gun in the deal. Doyle shot two soldiers with his M-1 and thought he might begin to keep a count, but he had his helmet shot out of his hand. All in an effort to get across a creek, maybe twenty or thirty feet wide and belly deep. But the Japanese had the high ground on the other side, and until the marines brought dozers and tanks in to rearrange the banks, it was hot enough. The next few days were hit-and-miss—they crossed what they were calling Suicide Creek, just hacking a way through the undergrowth of vines and roots that had overgrown the trails that retreating soldiers had made. Up and down hills, looking for this Aogiri Ridge. As the resistance intensified and the topography bent upward, they figured they were onto something. By the morning of the eighth, they could see the ridge and the bunkers they had built at the top of it, of logs and mud, and could hear the Japanese on the other side. Colonel Walt took over the battalion after MacDougal was shot. They set up a CP in a grove of banyan trees at the base of the ridge, their thick roots a sort of revetment for the radio and corpsmen and officers. Then the mortar squads, then the rifle squads working their way up the incline in the thick mud, crawling on their bellies like reptiles, all of them using their scouts' and snipers' eyes because they reckoned their opponents were everywhere in the thick growth, just over the crest of the ridge. Colonel Walt wanted the thirty-seven-millimeter cannon moved up as high as possible. The enemy kept picking off the guys trying to roll it up that muddy incline, and that kept the boys in their foxholes till Colonel Walt grabbed onto the thing itself and started pushing. That inspired a few marines, who muscled the thing up to the apex, not far from their own lines. They all dug in just before dark. It was still raining, and the ground was easy, that volcanic soil. Louis Schafer and Doyle had the machine gun on the tripod and half a dozen boxes of ammo, and across from them, the third squad was Al Henson and Billy Smith, the good old boy from Paris, Kentucky. There was maybe twenty yards between them, a good cross fire, and the riflemen and their carbines at the ready. And the cannon working its special magic with canister rounds, big shotgun shells. Doyle was dog-tired from two days of climbing in mud and waiting to be shot dead but still afraid to go to sleep because Harry Rader would have shot him for sleeping, and they could hear their opponents just over the crest of the ridge working themselves into a kind of frenzy. "Maline you die!" they kept shouting, and "Bahnzi!" And they were very close, just over the crest of the ridge no more than ten or fifteen yards away. And what Doyle kept thinking about, the thing he couldn't get out of his head so that he could make room for Sally and her white arms and red hair and the smell of her powder and the taste of her mouth, was that he might never make it home from here. That maybe this was the end of the line, after getting on the train in Detroit and going across the country to California and doing boot camp in San Diego and training at Fort Pendleton and shipping out last summer for Melbourne, Australia, to lose his virginity and learn to drink and smoke and play poker and arm wrestle and then to New Guinea and then to here, that finally he could hear the voices of the enemy, just over the crest of this miserable ridge in the middle of nowhere, where here he was, not yet twenty, about to be killed for no apparent reason. His date with destiny. What brought them here when they should have been back with their families in Japan. What brought all of the marines here from all over the United States, places Doyle had never been that were hometowns to the men he was about to die with. Tony Haas, who was digging in next to him, from Clatskanie, Oregon, and Gilbert Amdur from Conyers, Georgia, and Thurmond Hudson from DeSoto, Texas, and Billy Swinford Smith from Paris, Kentucky. He'd never been to any of those places, and they'd never been anywhere near Detroit, but here they were in the middle of some damn jungle in the middle of monsoon season in January, 1944, straddling one side of a ridge while God knew how many enemies in easy earshot straddled their part of the other side, getting ready to swarm all over them with their Banzai and bayonets and what was left of their bullets, hoping themselves to get some honorable death out of it, fearing nothing.

Doyle had half a Hershey bar his sister sent him in a packet of things that came for Christmas, and he pulled it out of his boondockers and took tiny bites of it, letting the last stage of its melting be in his mouth. It put him in mind of home, the house on Montevista near Fenkell, two blocks south of St. Francis De-Sales, where he'd played right tackle for the senior varsity. And Sally, who he'd met there in the fifth grade and knew when he first saw her that she was one of a kind. And how he always ended his letters to her, "Don't go driving that bumpy road, with anyone else but me."

The darkness on Cape Gloucester was unlike anything he'd ever encountered. It embraced them in utter blackness. And it's true that hearing gets more sensitive, though Doyle was not so sure that was all a blessing.

He'd been thinking about that night a lot. The ninth of January, 1944, deep in the interior jungle on Cape Gloucester, New Britain. Crazy how it comes and goes. Of course, there were times when he thought of nothing else, after he'd gotten home from Peiping, the long haul across the ocean, across the country, reversing his travels after three years gone, back to the curb at Montevista and the folks and his little sister waiting, though she was a teenager by the time Doyle made it home. He dreamt about that night for months, and the enemy screaming and swarming over the ridge and he and Billy Smith catching them all in a kind of cross fire, how he shot up eight boxes of ammo and would have used more if they could have got more. Five Banzai charges, in three hours of screaming and hollering, and how they kept coming over the ridge downhill in the face of Walt's thirty-seven millimeter and the light machine guns, not to mention the mortar section's constant barrage. It was like they couldn't kill them enough. They kept rising up and coming back. Burgin got one guy on the end of his M-1, just like a marshmallow on his bayonet, and kept putting rounds into him, four or five of them, as he flipped him over the back of his hole, then shot him with the .45 he aways carried. Pressed it up against his chest and just kept pulling the trigger until it was clicking empty and the soldier was unmistakably a goner. The K-3-5 couldn't really see much of anything, so they just got to where they'd aim at the voices, the screaming and panting and the rustle of feet. It helped that they announced their attack with a green flare shot up in the sky, which gave about a minute of residual light. The worst of it was between attacks. The ten or fifteen minutes it took them to regroup, work themselves up into another frenzy, send up a flare, and come on the run. It gave Doyle time to think about the odds of surviving, which were not good. And he kept worrying about the barrel of the Browning—how hot it was getting, surely it would melt away before long. He'd traded the carbine he carried because it was always jamming, traded it for an M-1, which meant he had five or six rounds before reloading. He'd have been up a creek but for the Browning and the thirty-seven millimeter Colonel Walt had manhandled up to the top, which kept spraying canister rounds on their advancing lines, and, in fairness, but for the riflemen who flanked the machine guns and the mortar squads behind, who kept lobbing their sixty-millimeter muzzle-loaded, smoothbore ordnance into the air, raining damage down on the enemies all night long. There were two short rounds, and you could hear the warnings; one was a dud and one took out part of the second squad of the machine gun section. Doyle could hear Julius Labeau screaming, "Corpsman! Corpsman!" over the mortar teams screaming, "Short round! Short round!" After a while they all sounded the same. The enemies, the injured, the feckless mortar-men—all one horrible chorus of mayhem and pain that seemed between charges to become like the droning of pipers at a Paddy's Day parade or a cop's funeral back home, and during the charges it ratcheted up to the high-pitched squeal of pig slaughter he'd heard once at Aunt Gertrude and Uncle Jeff's little farm out in Jackson. He'd never

246 • NO PRISONERS

been so frightened in his life, and the fear was like the pitch of that screaming—low and ominous between the charges, while they were changing barrels and ammo boxes and listening to the metal workings of the Japanese just over the ridge, working themselves into another frenzy, and their guys were waiting for the runners to come with more ammo or morphine or dressings or anything to put the suffering out of their misery and all of this taking place in the dark until the horrid voices of the enemy started rising into that awful incantation and Doyle was certain he could not survive it.

In the trailer for *The Road to Tokyo*, a film made for the World War II Museum in New Orleans, they mention Guadalcanal and Midway Island, Iwo Jima and bloody Tarawa, but no mention of Cape Gloucester, New Britain, where Doyle saw his first and fiercest combat, or the peninsula where he marked his twentieth birthday as the Japanese kept lobbing mortar all night or the fight at Peleliu or Okinawa or the mop-up in China after the surrender. And it made him wonder, was he part of that war at all? And what was the meaning of his killing all those men—five Banzai charges contesting Aogiri Ridge, which they'd name after Colonel Lew Walt, who saved them all that night in January and ordered them the following morning to finish the wounded off when day broke and the guns were silent and all the enemies were horizontal on their side of the ridge, dead or wounded. "We won't be taking any prisoners," he said. "Be sure they can't get up to fight again." And how Doyle and what was left of his rifle squad went among them with pistols and bayonets to finish them off. That is the small noise he still heard in his dreams, of the blade getting through their sternum and into their heart and lungs and doing irreparable damage, the slurp and gurgle that their finish made, the ease of bringing the blade back out the way it entered. Whenever he heard the word *penetration* after that it meant only one thing, which he learned that morning of the tenth of January in 1944 on the Japanese side of Walt's Ridge in Cape Gloucester, New Britain, when he learned to kill men up close, for keeps. Not the random chance, the hit-and-miss of his light machine gun and the fury of their attack and the trigger he kept pulling to be sure the belt was working its way through, spewing shells everywhere. Rather, the almost casual dispatch of wounded mammals, a moral trespass he could not reconcile with the man he always endeavored to be, who simply tried to do the next right thing.

Doyle knew just enough about something he'd heard called Just War Theory from the nuns and priests who'd made the case for Catholic men going off to fight the Japanese, as a defense of the good and punishment of evil, to protect the nation and its citizenry. It all fell near enough in Doyle's mind to an ethical enterprise, a justifiable violence. But killing the wounded and defenseless, the reparable casualties of war, seemed sinful in its bloodlust and indulgence. He'd followed orders and was forever damaged by it. He'd been taught as a boy to examine his conscience, to measure the rightness and wrongness of things, the venial and mortal nature of sins and the purgation and perdition that accrued to same. The casual destruction of the halt and lame, the wounded and yet salvageable bodies of the enemy struck Doyle as a sin outside the pounds of any cleansing, any mercy. It was a lapse beyond any redemption or reconciliation. He came home from the "good" war feeling guilty and damned. Only his life with Sally had seemed a remission of this feeling, as if he was adjacent and attached and would be forever associated with her goodness and grace and benignity. What hope he had had come from her, in whom he could see how God is love and love is God and everything might indeed be all right in the end.

This had been the morning after that haunted him. The mayhem in the dark, their endless screaming charges, came and went like any terror. But the slow, deliberate dispatch enacted on the wounded foot soldiers, the "take no prisoners" directive from Colonel Walt, the nearly casual mechanics and sporadic single shots of execution, whether it was mercy or murder, had tampered with Doyle's moral register and lodged in his daydreams and night terrors with permanence. Try as he might, he could not let go of it.

Chapter Eight

LETTING GO

His clutching of the grenade, his inability to "let go, let God," as he'd long been instructed to do, his final refusal to go out with a bang instead of a whimper whilst enacting his surpassing gesture for a cause, worthy—he thought, how could he have thought?—of the being he had come to be, all of it was beginning to cramp up his left hand as Patty turned the car sharply onto S. Lewis Avenue and made for the campus of ORU, which was the only other landmark Doyle knew, having watched the TV preacher for years on Sunday mornings, squeezing the heads of the true believers and ridding them of whatever ailed them, praise God. And while Doyle truly believed every last one of them was a huckster and charlatan, he could see the pointy top of the Prayer Tower off in the distance and thought the Christian citadel might offer some refuge or sanctuary in their time of need. He wanted a quiet place to give some thought to what might be happening next because he'd never figured on being alive for this. His hand was cramping badly, and he wondered if he could chance transferring the grenade to his limber right hand without blowing up the three of them, because Bill was still in the backseat, huffing and puffing out his indifference to everything, into whatever oblivion Oklahoma was. He looked at the look on Patty's face, that look of surprise that she'd gotten herself into this ridiculous jackpot with an old man and a dying dog in Tulsa, Oklahoma, en route to nowhere in par-fucking-ticular.

The sky remained bright blue and cloudless. Except for the grenade and the spectacle back at the opera house, Doyle could almost imagine himself out for a Sunday drive with his best gal like in the old days, making his way out to the Walled Lake Pavilion to hear Glenn Miller or Tommy Dorsey and spend the evening dancing with Sally at the beginning instead of nearing the end. There were police vehicles, lights flashing but sirens silent, working north, while he and Patty worked south, not speeding but not dawdling down S. Lewis Avenue, through the historic district neighborhoods, following the route of the Arkansas River off to the west, aiming their escape, if that's what it was, for the pinnacle of the Prayer Tower, where Doyle kept thinking he might be healed. Already his temples were beginning to throb and the headache they signaled was advancing on him, as the cramp in his left hand continued to pulse with unpredictable spasms.

"Maybe you should let me out, Patty. You don't need to be part of any of this."

"You crazy old fuck, what are you going to do? Walk back to Michigan in your Walmart boxer shorts? You'll have to lose that uniform when the cops go looking for an old marine."

It was then she noticed him holding the grenade in his white-gloved left hand and slammed the brakes on in the middle of the street. He straight-armed the dashboard as they skidded to a stop. He braced for what he assumed would be the rear-end collision, but no one came.

Letting Go • 251

"What the fuck, Doyle," Patty screamed at him. "You gonna blow us both to bits?"

"I dropped the pin scrambling from the opera house. My hand is cramping, but I'm holding on."

It was then the massive bronze healing hands or praying hands or who's to say what kind of hands came into view at the entrance to Oral Roberts University on the left.

"Let me jump out there, Patty. A deal's a deal. You've got the car, the old dog. You've done your part. Just let me out, and I'll be fine."

"But Doyle . . ."

"Have no fear, Patty. Head south then west, and find your life. Make a difference if you can; you've made a difference to me."

She slowed in the circular drive around the massive hands. In the distance she could see the Prayer Tower.

"What's your plan, Doyle?"

"A bang, not a whimper, Patty. Take care of yourself, and thank you, thank you."

She was weeping as she drove away.

The old man, still in search of his surpassing gesture, stared up into the space between the healing or praying hands that looked to Doyle a lot like Oral Roberts's hands—the ones he'd squeeze the heads of the halt and lame, sickened and bewildered with, shouting, "Heal, heal!" while the poor pilgrim winced with the miracle of it all. He considered tossing the grenade into the space between the mitts. He wished he could ask Patty what she thought of the idea. But she was gone now, really gone, and glad, no doubt, to be out of his indenture. Doyle resolved always to be grateful for the good sense to hire Patty Casey.

When he got to the base of the Prayer Tower, the sweat and the chill were making him shiver, and it came into his mind

252 • NO PRISONERS

that he'd had enough, so he lay on the greensward, like a fallen marine, and tucked the grenade underneath him and slowly loosened his grip on the clip. But nothing happened—the grenade, like the man who'd brought it there, was a dud.

He could hear Bill's barking getting closer and closer.

When Hypatia got Doyle back to the lake in Northern Michigan, from the sad fiasco of Tulsa, Johanna was waiting to tuck him in and get him rested up and ready for their winterage in the Lesser Antilles. A month in the sun, she figured, might restore his taste for life and time. She had booked their tickets, sorted the rental of their villa, Elysium, which miraculously hadn't been booked by anyone else, packed a bag for the two of them, and arranged for someone to stay with the dog and keep the house in good order until they returned a month later. She did not know what the future might hold, but she wanted to be with him, whatever happened, and wanted to ease him out of whatever pain or trouble beset him now, whether the relief was temporary or permanent.

She had prepared a proper scolding for his attempt at suicide—how could he? Did she mean that little to him? What was he thinking? Had it not occurred to him to share his heart with her? But she opted to pamper him, instead, to say nothing of the gathering darkness and concentrate on whatever was left to share between them.

She had long seen her role, indeed the role of Hypatia as well, as being a kind of midwife to Doyle's journey to his end. As with nativity, mortality required careful assistance. Johanna thought of her dead father's sermons on Shiphrah and Puah, the Hebrew midwives who resisted Pharoah's instructions to drown the male children of the Hebrews at birth. Which is why Moses was found in a basket in the bulrushes in the Nile and became a prince in the pharaoh's household and eventually led the Hebrews out of bondage. Like Moses, Doyle relied on the care of good women. And like Miriam, Johanna had a sense of mission.

That he had been apparently willing to destroy himself in front of Hypatia, his employee, rather than in front of his last and current, albeit infrequent, lover was on the one hand infuriating and on the other a kind of balm and succor, that he would want to spare Johanna the grizzly witness. Maybe she was a version of Shiphrah and Hypatia, Puah, each in her own way willing to go the distance with the old, dying man, to midwife his birth into a new form of being, which required a ceasing to be in the former way. Was it possible, after all, that Doyle was right? That the spiritual life is, in fact, not a theory, but a reality we're living? What if Johanna's dead father, the old priest, gone for years now, was trying to show her the truths he alluded to whenever he promised her, "More will be revealed"?

As was her habit in the early days of their consortium, she now came to bed naked and slept adjacent to him, making herself available for whatever caresses or embraces they might have left between them. There was no agenda, no expectations, but easy access to any available intimacy. He would wake in the middle of the night and run his hands along the edges of her body to assure himself that he was not alone, then roll over on his right shoulder and return to sleep. Or he would draw her into his embrace, cup her breasts in his hands and press himself against her backside, then work his right hand down her tummy and between her hip bones and then to her pelvis and pudendum, then unashamedly touch her labia and clitoris. By this time, her soft fingers would be reaching behind her in the dark to rub and clutch and stroke such aspects of his

254 • NO PRISONERS

private parts as his rhythmic movements offered access to. In their waking moments, fully sentient, such conduct, given their advanced years, might have seemed to each of them a little ridiculous. In the moment, however, touch had its own memory, it turned out, and their intimate fondlings, buffered as they were by their aging bodies, seemed nonetheless good for them both, whether in spite of or because of their shared decrepitude.

When the time came, Hypatia drove them to Traverse City, and they began their daylong travel to the island by way of Detroit, Charlotte, and St. Thomas by plane, a car to Red Hook and a ferry to Cruz Bay, and finally a car for the last leg of the journey to Elysium, which was perched at the end of a dead-end road cut into the hillside overlooking Fish Bay.

If the frozen lake and the cold snow cover of Northern Michigan deepened Doyle's aptitude for mortality, the lush green island and its subtropical warmth freshened the muscle memory of his vitality. He stripped away his jacket and sweatshirt and came off the ferryboat from Red Hook in a black T-shirt and a pair of shorts, wearing the sandals he always wore when socks could be discarded along with heavy clothes.

He bought a pair of mangos, green bananas, and some fresh berries from a vendor in the square at Cruz Bay, picked up Puerto Rican coffee and black tea from a shop there, hired a driver to take them out to Elysium, and called to have dinner, a seafood paella, delivered from the Lime Inn with a large piece of passion fruit cheesecake to share with Johanna for dessert. She wondered if maybe the change of weather and venue was the change of heart he was sorely in need of. Whereas Hypatia had returned a broken, beaten, painful case of a man from their road trip to Oklahoma, the old man wearing the Ecuadoran panama and linen shorts on St. John had an aspect of rebirth and renewal about him. It restored Johanna's mostly shaken belief in a loving God in charge, whose runtish step-child, hope, was briefly kindled in her.

Their days were idyllic, coffee and tea on the veranda in the morning, the light breezes and the view of white boats in the bay, listening to mourning doves and roosters at their aubades, watching for goats and deer and iguanas among the overgrown houseplants that thrived among the sea grape and noni fruit trees all over the island. Late morning they would call their driver to take them to the beach, Hawksnest or Trunk Bay, Cinnamon or Francis Bay, which was their favorite for the easy access and plentiful sun and shade and sand. Two hours was pretty much their limit now, wanting to avoid too much sunlight and its heat. All the same, they both darkened in a way that looked like good health. Their driver, Manassas, was ready to take them back, stopping for something to drink at the Rum Room, where Johanna had a cocktail and Doyle had a jar of pomegranate juice. Some meals they'd dine out for, and some they'd make do with things in the pantry or fridge. They wanted for nothing, went to bed early, cuddled into close embraces in the morning, and woke to the daylight. Days went by in a comforting blur of contentment and calm, colloquy and ease. It was a shame, Doyle said, they couldn't live forever like this. "Let's give it a try," is what Johanna said.

Still, there was a valedictory air to much of what he said and did, asking waitresses to snap a photo of them holding hands in the restaurant, with their bowl of mussels or entrees or desserts. "These will be good for the funeral video," he'd say, and laugh, and Johanna would roll her eyes. Or when he instructed her to have "Like a Rolling Stone" played as the cortege made its way to the cemetery. "It has the perfect cadence for a march," he said. "Six minutes of it. Sufficient for most processionals."

That the old trade embalmer should be of a sudden concerned with the details of his own obsequies was a sign to

Johanna that the end was near and that possibly Doyle knew something about his own pending end that he hadn't shared. Of course, at ninety, the grim reaper is a constant companion, sharpening the blade of his scythe day and night, the glint of it and the light grinding sound two constant reminders that the end is nearer than one thinks. The memento mori that the church always proffered as reminders of mortality and reckoning—the cross in the sanctuary, the smudge on Ash Wednesday, the burial of hallelujahs on the Sunday before it, all designed to deepen the believer's appreciation for the promise of eternal life through resurrection—had little meaning for Doyle Shields, whose adult life had been a chorus of corpses, each in need of his expertise to make known, by their nicely folded hands and cotton-stuffed nostrils, their sewn mouths and glued eyelids, in their unshakeable stillness and unbreakable silence the truth: *as I am now, so you will be.*

When Doyle sighed and slumped a little and slid down the shower walls, coming to rest on his haunches with the warm water pelting his bald head and his reddening face, Johanna knew the beginning of the end had arrived, by the limpness of his body, the purpling flush in his face and neck, the lack of panic in his aspect. Dropped like a box of hot rocks, she imagined Doyle Shields would have said, which is what he'd told her the first man he ever shot did, years ago. That was on Walt's Ridge, Cape Gloucester, New Britain. "Got him with my M-1; he was up a tree. Scouts' and snipers' eyes." He'd just shot a squirrel off the birdfeeder with his pellet pistol, a lucky shot, he insisted, he'd meant only to scare the scavenging rodent away from the sunflower seeds, but instead got him in the head and he fell "like a box of hot rocks," seized briefly, and then went still at the base of the old maple tree. Nothing else happened,

Letting Go • 257

the sky did not fall, the lake kept lapping at the rock by the shore, the breeze kept rustling in the maple leaves.

It was how Doyle had seemed to drop, of a sudden, without warning, a bother to no one, moaning in his usual way and going suddenly silent. She'd been giving him head in thanksgiving for the head he had given her all morning, in an exchange of intimate kindnesses they'd gotten in the habit of over the years of their consortium. And though he never got really hard anymore, his flaccid penis grew heavy with his apparent gratitude, his face looked heavenward and his eyes shut tightly and he mouthed the familiar syllables of thanks, to wit, oh God, oh God, sweet Jesus, mother of mercy, oh God, oh God. Thenabouts or soon after she would sense a sort of semen-free orgasm, but instead he'd stopped and slumped, the last oh God hardly out of his mouth, and slid down the white-tiled wall of the shower they shared as if something irreversible was in process of happening. His eyes blinked open, his mouth did too, and he seemed to be watching something on a screen before him, his eyeballs tracking the action.

There is no way she could have known that what the old man was seeing or dreaming or sensing as the warm shower water splashed all over him was the warm rainforest of the South Pacific, and he was nineteen years old again, instead of nearly ninety-one, and he was peering wildly into the impenetrable dark, watching for Donald Crescent Coe from somewhere in Illinois, he couldn't remember anymore, to bring them more ammo before the enemies came over the ridge again, screaming "Bahn*zi!*" and "Maline you die!" in yet another of their fearless, suicidal rampages.

He could hear them working themselves up for the next charge, ten yards and a little hillock of land between their lines. He could hear the panic and madness in their exhortations,

258 • NO PRISONERS

and they were coming to kill him one last time—him and Don Coe and Billy Swinford Smith from Paris, Kentucky, and Wayne Primo Ally from Ishpeming, a fellow Michigander from the distant UP who carried a snapshot of his girl back home in a swimsuit looking willing and ready. She was an Ojibwe woman and very beautiful, and Doyle wished Sally would pose like that and send him a snapshot as something to live for, the prospect of getting to know her private parts, because he loved her so, with the tongues of men and of angels. And Doyle was willing and ready now for whatever might be happening next. He knew it wouldn't really matter in the long haul of things, whether he killed them or they killed him. The dead didn't mind the constant sodden pelting of water and the taste of panic in their mouths or the taste of pleasure when they didn't die, or the taste of heaven when they were with their beloveds, which Doyle knew then, as he knew here and now at the end, as a young leatherneck and an old one, the bliss he tasted was not a permanent dispensation.

And then the unanticipated gift, a moment of clarity, the warm rain pelting the old marine, a sudden spasm of beneficence and forgiveness, whether from his own inner reserve of goodness or Whomever's in Charge, either way, the sense that his account had been reconciled and that the killing, the dispatch, with his bayonet, the sinking of his Ka-Bar knife deep into the chest of the wounded Japanese foot soldier on the morning of January 10, 1944, at the direct order of Colonel Lew Walt, USMC, would no longer be held against him made Doyle Shields briefly grin in understanding because his life and his death, his own, the poor soldier's, meant nothing, changed nothing, happened without discernable impact or consequence. And no doubt Sally, no, not Sally, Johanna, would think that his grinning

Letting Go • 259

was in thanksgiving for the sweet off-season blow job she was giving him, and he was, of course, grateful beyond words, for the years of such courtesies, the litany of kindnesses they had played out between them. He hoped that she would not assign even a passing wisp of blame to herself for the end that was nigh upon him.

Whereupon, for reasons he would never live to understand, a tune came into his brainbox with some lyrics: "In the fury of the moment I can see the master's hand in every leaf that trembles, and in every grain of sand."

At the end, what demanded the last lapsing moments of Doyle's attention was the tightening gyre at the shower drain and the little maelstrom made by the warm water that he slumped into and eventually lay down in, his cheek to the floor and his gaze gone sideways as his heart began its protocol for shutting down, in bliss, but shutting down, alas, nonetheless. The constricting vortex, the tightening spiral of water put Doyle in mind of something he had heard at a meeting years ago, from some old-timer, how life was like a roll of toilet paper, to wit, the nearer to the end it got, the faster it turned. Just so, thought Doyle, just so.

Or was it only that he'd become, finally and undeniably, surplus to requirements, redundant, needless to the enactments of life and time.

As for his brainbox, awash as it was in gratitude for the surpassingly fine blow job Johanna was after bestowing, in so far as his body had achieved its glimpse of paradise, his mind, his interior life, focused on the remaining, residual vexation of his spiritual life: if God, in accordance with First John, chapter four, verse sixteen, is love, then oughtn't it follow that love is God? He could not remember whether Sr. Rose DeLourdes,

Sr. Jean Therese, or possibly Brother Finbarr Carney had first quoted the scripture to him. Nor could he remember the names of all the reverend clergy, men and women of every religious denomination who'd ridden with him in hearses, mostly to cemeteries or crematories, and to whom he'd posed his perpetual question, whether if company men, Doyle called them, who tried to tell him it was more complicated than that. It didn't matter now. They were all dead as mackerel, and Doyle knew he would soon be too, blissful with the blow job Johanna had gifted him. He could not keep from grinning, thinking how he would soon become the punch line for a joke his cronies told that always ended "but what a way to go!"

A further, and not unrelated, concern came to mind having to do with his funeral, the details of his obsequies that might amount to a final gesture to the women he counted among his intimates and the old chronies who suddenly mattered to him, mostly as bearers of his ongoing narrative—the story of his having been among them. Had he told Johanna what he wanted to be laid out in? Had he made known his preferences in music for the eventual service? Something to make a suitable soundtrack for his remembrance. Was there a place for Glenn Miller, "String of Pearls," "In the Mood," any of those big band dance hits by which he was transported to a high school auditorium dancing with Sally or weekends at the Walled Lake Pavilion and out on that bumpy road necking and petting, being in love. Maybe a string quartet? A soloist? A smallish group of songsters, choristers, a balladeer? And what about "I'll Be Seeing You"? What would his funeral be without a dose of Tommy Dorsey and the Chairman of the Board? Doyle loved that tune, its humanity and promise, its invocation of "the chestnut tree, the wishing well." He wondered—and a sort of cognitive leisure attended his ruminations, as if time wouldn't

Letting Go • 261

soon run out on him—he wondered if those who heard this tune, at ample volume, sitting in church or the funeral home, would, as he often did, return to that moment he first heard it, the summer of '44, grinning for no apparent reason, grinning with the tune he was listening to.

He could hear Johanna calling his name, as if from afar, as if to beckon him back from the brink of the distant parish he had gotten to, beyond return or retrieval, restoration or repair. He was inexorably easing into the past tense, a person of whom it would hereafter be said that he was "gone." Or, in a style he'd always admired, "the late Doyle Shields." And he could hear Sally beckoning too, from the somethingness or nothingness to which she'd gone, his late beloved, all those years ago, and to which he knew he'd be going too, and soon. He longed to hold her. And wondered if the somethingness or nothingness allowed for such endearments.

And beyond the beckoning of lovers, of women he'd loved and lived with and had tampered with in ways that had been blissfully intimate, was the image of the young navy corpsman who treated him for malaria in the South Pacific, on Pavuvu years ago. His name was Mulligan. He always turned up in moments of emergent trouble, with his box of meds and painfully uplifting good humor, which he brought to bear upon whatever contingency presented itself. Doyle wondered whether here, on the floor of the shower, watching the circling doom of the whirlpool, he might get one more Mulligan, another do-over, another shot, however brief, at life and time. Might he rise to the occasion of being again? Might he beat the rap and live through this finish? He would try to be a better man, to use the precious gift of time and being to a higher purpose. But no mulligan, he knew, was forthcoming. He'd come to his end. And this was it.

262 • NO PRISONERS

No coffin bobbed up from the whirlpool, as from the ruined Pequod at the end, no life buoy or personal flotation device. He was sinking and sinking fast, and it would soon be over, his life and times. He would not be the one left to tell the tale. For reasons he could only barely discern, this did not frighten him, rather he experienced as freedom the letting go, the surrender to happenstance, the end of days with his name on them. The finishing.

"Not my day to watch it," he could remember Sally saying at the end, as if she'd been given the morning off, as if the vigil that the living keep with life was about to be quit entirely. And now all those little saccharine sayings they put out at meetings on cardboard posters with borders on them that alchies are told to live by seemed to be making really good sense to him—easy does it, one day at a time, live and let live, think, think, think, keep it simple, stupid, let go, let God. Progress not perfection. And the promises, the ones on pages eighty-three and eighty-four of *The Big Book*, which he'd more or less memorized by frequent repetitions, suddenly seemed to have all come true, a new freedom and happiness, self-seeking had utterly slipped away, and things that used to baffle him no longer did. Doyle was quietly astonished that he was finishing a happy man, contented as a piebald ass in fresh grazing. His whole attitude and outlook upon life had changed. He beheld it all as the gift it was and remained, even the end, even the part where the pursuit of the impossible prize is beyond his reach and he dies, nonetheless, trying to get a grip on it, trying to hold on to the time that we love. Still here on the brink of it, the somethingness or nothingness, Doyle had to confess that the prospect of timelessness had an endearing aspect to it. Ceasing to be might be like being had been: a gift like grace—abundant, undeserved, withal astonishing.

Life, he had come to understand, takes no prisoners, we die like dogs, like creatures of every living breed, of nothing more special than our age and nature, and being is the briefest of reprieves. Whereas ceasing to be now seemed suddenly endless, suddenly something to harken toward and rely upon. The beckoning embrace of the infinite end was opening to him, calling wordlessly as he'd always known, always hoped, it would, with minor chords and a womblike moisture and warmth, tenderness and the quiet calm of a Vermeer painting, so he curled his curious self into its hold, then stiffened a little, and then let go.

ACKNOWLEDGMENTS

The author is grateful to the editors of *Michigan Quarterly Review* and *Bear River Review*, where portions of this text first appeared in slightly different forms. Also, to Kate Bland of Cast Iron Radio (UK) and BBC Radio 4, which broadcast portions of this fiction.

The late Richard McDonough (1937–2020), of Irvine, California, represented the author's work in words for nearly twenty-five years and settled the prospect of this book and others with the good offices of David R. Godine, as the last among his professional services to the author, who is permanently grateful for his championing of this work and his diligence in its representation.

My brothers, Colonel Daniel J. Lynch, US Army, Retired, and Patrick Lynch, have been longstanding and curious supporters of this project. The author is always in their debt.

No colloquy has been more helpful, instructive, or illuminating to the author in completion of this novel than his ongoing conversations with Suzanne Rumsey and Corrine D'Agostino with whom he has traveled and dined, consorted and consulted through the years of this manuscript's preparation. His gratitude and admiration for their contributions are perpetual. Likewise, Celia Johnson and Beth Blachman at Godine and Tanya Muzumdar have read and edited this manuscript at various stages through its preparation. The author remains permanently grateful for their careful scrutiny of this work.

The author lives and works and occupies the ancestral, traditional, and contemporary Lands of the Anishinaabeg–Three Fires Confederacy of Ojibwe, Odawa, and Potawatomi peoples, ceded in the 1831 Treaty of Washington. The good ghosts and living heirs of these First Nations people of Northern Michigan enrich the water, earth, and air with narrative, mystery, and humanity, which the author acknowledges, with gratitude, as hospitable to the work of storytelling. As a settler on these lands, he endeavors to carry on in keeping with these Indigenous traditions.

Edward J. Lynch, Jr. (1924–1992), his beloved partner, Rosemary O'Hara Lynch (1924–1989), and Heather Grace, their first granddaughter (1975–2020), are the most pronounced and pristine voices in the author's cloud of witnesses. They have proven indispensable to this work of the spirit.